In This Book You Will Find...
# THE FACE OF OUR TOWN

Elizeya Quate

KERNPUNKT PRESS

2016

/125
0th Printing: 2016

ISBN-13 978-0-9972924-0-4

KERNPUNKT Press
701 State Route 12B
Hamilton, New York 13346

www.kernpunktpress.com

To my fam.

## Full Cast in Alphabetical Order

Aziz Ahmad
Bryce Archer
Annie Bunning
Belicia Balboa
Beyond, The
Benjamin Clough
Meagan Cole
Brent Cullen
Mike Donahue
Ariadne Dubinski
Don Eber
Ted Eckell
Stacey Gold
Dion Gold
Erl Isse
Lon Itkowitz
Koumana Jayrouz
David Jenner
Buck Johnston
Sylvester Kelling
Diana Kerns
Bobby Kerns
Marina Kerns
Lloyd Kerns
Miles Kirchenbaum
Dylan Kirchenbaum
Evan Kirchenbaum
Unica Korn
Gertrude Lamont
Chad Lippet
Ai Ling
Paul Albert Magnus

Liam McNutt
Walter Moseby
Sheila Moseby
Kaylah Moyes
Angela Munn
Clarice Munn
Elwood Munn
Jody Munn
Mark Munn
Titus Nills
Sam Ng
Keenan O'Brien
Frank Oberto
Maurice Bundy
Hypatia Pommeranz
Elias Pommeranz
Lewis Purcell
Elizeya Quate
Ricardo Reyes
Candace Rittenhouse
Theodore Secret
Larissa Stein
Kendra Tatum
Cynthia Tsang
Tina Sykes Turlington
Steve Turlington
Dwayne Unger
Angie Vaugn
Brianna Vaugn
Carl Womack
Karen Yancy

Yes, yes, that was it, not running away from me, not running away from my words, oh how light and horrible, a spider's web, don't flee from my flaws, my flaws, oh how I love you, my qualities are so small, just like those of other men, my flaws, my negative side is beautiful and concave like an abyss. What I am not would leave a massive hole through the earth.... I don't nourish my errors, but may my errors nourish me.

- Clarice Lispector, *So Near to the Wild Heart*

The desire to say words overcame him and he said words without meaning, rolling them over on his tongue and saying them because they were brave words, full of meaning. "Death," he muttered, "night, the sea, fear, loveliness."

- Sherwood Anderson *Winesburg, OH*

# Not Anything. This.

Wake up and don't fall back asleep.

Wheeenh-Oooh, Wheeeenh-Oooh.

Wake up and thank the noise of a submarine in strife.

Wheeenh-Oooh, Wheeeenh-Oooh.

Flooding. Pumping. The submarine's red lights are flashing on every corridor of every level.

Wheeenh-Oooh, Wheeeenh-Oooh.

Feel the covers cling soft and gentle around your skin. *Cynthia?* Standing with her spindly fingers outstretched beneath the aubade of a sumac-snarled fence. Remember? Wings beating upon a Detroit twilight's tarnished silvers. Blackhairs. So-lostness. Stay put now. Warm bed is warm today. Flutter. Light and more light. Dreams quickmelt across the sky gone red behind your morning's greasy eyelids. *Cynthia Tsang?* Blackhairs in knots, blackhairs knotted to collapsible fishing poles, blackhairs casting for lost gods deep in the depthlessness of Erliss Pond. Shiny hook sinks down down down beneath a brown collision of cedar twigs, oval dots of shimmering duckweed. Searching. Losing. Purling. The slow fade of signals. Tiny portholes. Gemmed with bubbles. Glowing. Errrrrr. Lissssss. And then, errrrrmmmmmmmmmmmm...

Wheeenh-Oooh, Wheeeenh-Oooh.

Jesus.

Wheeenh-Oooh, Wheeeenh-Oooh.

Come on, you'll be late! Wake up!

Think to yourself: *You aren't a fucking child anymore.* Think it louder. Think it so loud that it resounds with real poignancy. *You aren't, are you? A child?* And shouldn't you have finished shedding that cocoon of little white TV-lies, that cocoon whispering: *Come on, Mike! Anything! You can be anything you want!*

Ha! Remember that? Remember when the days all felt like that?

Wheeenh-Oooh, Wheeeenh-Oooh.

*(Ungh). Okay. Up...!* Stumble forward out of your room. Jesus, how is the living room still such an intractable clusterfuck!?

*Are? You? Ready?* Asks the wild-haired man in the aluminum-framed poster. The wild-haired man is hang gliding through a motivational waterfall. His body is taut and conveys an idea of natural freedom. He's wearing sunglasses and has one of those adventurous-looking beards.

The poster hangs off-kilter above the sofa where your roommate Chad rips snores the size of Yellowstone geysers. Fucking Chad. His face quivers beneath an orange crust of last night's Chneetos. When's Chad going to get his shit together, anyway? *Fucking Chad.* Hear yourself half-mouthing it, half-saying it. Remember from some stupid Tnwitter ad that the dust of Chneetos actually has its very own trademarked name. What was it, again? Cheebles? Chust?

No, wait...

Chneetle!

That's right!

2

Chneetle is what's crusting dear, sweet Chad's unshaven babyfat; a half-grown jawbeard of neon orange flavor crystals. Let it cross your mind that the brand identity of your roommate's snackstain is surely worth more than you are. Surely worth more than everyone in your apartment complex. By orders of magnitude. Combined.

Not the recipe, not the ingredients, not the packaging or the trucks or the factory or the workers in the factory, no, merely the idea that Chneetos have dust and that dust has a name and a personality and a factual Being-in-the-World. That is what's worth more than you. Stop and really think about that for a second.

Imagine 1,000,000,000s of Chneetle-crazed Chads all across the world, groping in the dark, snacking, snoring, fulfilling what's either destiny or some half-hearted parody of destiny. Scarfing. Munching. Tilting their faces back into nightly oblivions. Oblivia? How often these days do you find yourself reaching for the plural of oblivion?

*Are?*

*You?*

*Ready?*

Strip down in front of the bathroom mirror. Examine. Suck in. Turn. Turn again. Feel disappointing. Feel like you could be doing a lot better with this whole having-a-body thing. So what's stopping you? What getting in your way? Why aren't you better than this? Feel yourself lost in the dunes of a vast orange desert of Chneetle, feet sinking into the burning drifts of fluorescent snackpowder. Chad's massive nostrils hang like twin black suns over the curvature of the

3

horizon line, thundering, thundering, thundering away. Snkkkknnnrrrrrr! Hnnnnkkkkkfffff! Snkkkkkrrrrrrr! Hnnnnnnkkkkkfffff!

Lostness. Chad's face is a lonely desert. Sink. Sink and don't feel yourself sinking. Put your hands to your face and feel the pain running through the pinched nerve in your left two fingers where they healed wrong all those years ago. After. *Cynthia?* Sssssssssk. Lips part. Pain trades places with the air. Feel the bones beneath the flesh of your left hand. Leftness. Feelingness. Painness. *Are? You? Ready?*

Stand in the shower and feel wet. Let that sublime wetness wash up and down your squishiness in the lather of professionally odorized body wash. For a moment you're far, far, far away. It didn't always feel like this, did it?

You used to daydream of standing behind a silver microphone, surrounded by a sea of important sunglasses.

You used to be able to feel the warmth of their applause.

*Anything,* said those clapping hands.

You believed them. You were them. That crowd. Those faces. You were going to feel and do things that no one had ever felt or done before. You were going to abolish reality, invent new gods, enunciate yourself as a fugitive from destiny, from even any parody of destiny! And now here you are today, Monday, having real trouble making sales numbers happen on an Internet phone line campaign. Ugh. That's right. That's what your life is now. Monday, today. Tomorrow. A whole week of fucking Mondays.

4

Come on. Don't be late! Get out the door!

Check your blazer's inner pocket as you walk. Is your white plastic Solutioneer! RepID card in there? Feel like it's at least probably in there. (Somewhere...)

Climb into your Hnonda Cnivic and hesitate before jamming your key in the ignition.

Feel around inside yourself until you feel like you're at least probably in there, too. (Somewhere...) Huh. So this is what adult life is: the onrush of blurry, colored lights edging the hollow outline of your own Being-in-the-World today, the hollow outline of what todays you or what at least synonymizes your todayingness with the jangle of car keys against the Cnivic's dash, the crinkle of receipt paper in your oversatupon wallet, the sting of a single bitten thumbnail that *when did you even bite your thumb like that, oh fuck you suck, suck hard on* and get the tartness of blood's tinny rhubarb on your tongue, real blood on a fucking Monday morning.

*Ha ha*, says the radio man, as you turn on the Cnivic. Pull out into traffic. The radio man is laughing at his own joke. Or at a normal person who called into the radio show to be humiliated, humiliated by him, the radio man, who is only playing the part of a chipper sadist for your enjoyment, for the enjoyment of you and many others out there in radioland. That's what they pay the radio man for. To laugh. To humiliate. To play the chipper sadist. For you. For all of you. Feel briefly complicit. Wonder if you should change the station. *And this program is bu-rought to you by the good folks over at*

*Booty, the drink everyone's twerkin' about! Now available in the new risqué flavor of Klappin' Kiwi. Booty. Can you even handle this booty?*

Swallow. Change nothing.

Look at your eyes looking at your eyes looking at your eyes in the reflection oblonged by the Cnivic's rearview mirror as you drive, as you slow, as you stop, as you wait. Practice smiling, because you've read somewhere that people who smile more are happier. Correlation or causation? *Be my self-fulfilling prophecy today*, you think, tilting back your head to make the rearview mirror show your chummiest crescent of bared, wily teeth. Didn't you read somewhere on the Internet that people actually take lessons from professional coaches on how to level up their smile game? That there are videos on YnouTube you can watch to learn all of the different situationally-appropriate varieties of smiling? That certain well-known individuals have even had their smiles appraised and insured against the possibility of accident?

Mentally compare your smile with the smiles of your co-workers. Rate each mouth on a 10-point scale of smiliest to least-smiley. Buck, Kaylah and Candi probably beat you out in every category. Buck Johnston, Jesus. Now there's a smile worth insuring! Think about how your own smile could probably use some serious surgical upgrades, that is, if you were really committed to getting it 100% right. Or at least a good lip-and-cheek workout, a real, good, *regular* workout. That's the ticket. Think about how you should probably budget some personal time to really kick your smile's rear into maximum gear, at least as soon as humanly possible. Right? But so when are you actually gonna go and get shit done? Today? Tomorrow? Next week? Never? *When are you going to finally have the smile that you need to succeed?*

Sit in traffic and let the congestion on the freeway up to Troy make you feel redundant. So many other faces. Smiles. Bodies. Broke-ass cars. Plumes of tailpipe haze. Tap your gas pedal, roll forward. Stop. *...So you think he's really cheating, I mean, just because he didn't want me to know that she was texting him, that doesn't really mean — Oh honey, honey please, you just stop right there ahahahahaha...* Suck on your thumbnail before glancing over at the sleek hatchback next to you where an ultrabronzed businesswoman with an obsidian ponytail is giving you side-eye, one of those askance, judgy looks that says: *Well, well, and what do we have here?* And before you can even remove your thumb to gesture the bleeding thumbnail's explanation, this businesswoman has already scooted off and away into the fast lane's brighter future. *Hahahahaha oh, please honey, please don't trust like that, honey you'll just hurt your sweet self if you go on trusting your man like that, haha didn't anyone tell you haha men are wicked, we are wicked, wicked creatures, yes we are haha* Listen to the radio man's laughter wheezing over this parade of sleep-numbed eyelids, all tapping, scooting, rolling, stopping. Look up and down the side of the freeway as the billboards echo the same face: Koumana Jayrouz, Esq. Not a day's gone by in the last year that you haven't seen her face, billboard-glossy and imperious, gazing down into the annex of your naked, trembling soul. Not one. Single day. Koumana Jayrouz, a veritable deification of personal injury law, resplendent in her frosty locks, in the undulating lusciousness of her strawberry red lips, in the steely glint in her eyes that convey a demeanor of unrelenting shrewdness along with the force of will to take your personal injury lawsuit to the fucking United States Supreme Court if that's what it takes. Koumana Jayrouz, billboard after billboard, as if the very freeway itself is whispering: *Oh just you wait, Mike Donahue, just you wait! Your time for personal injury lawyers will come soon enough!*

Look around you. Blink. So many. Others. Others just like you. Aren't they? Just like you? So how could anyone possibly need *you*, you with all these other you-like people to choose from? Gaze up and feel totally overwhelmed by the coin-sized shininess hung above the distant, crooked horizon. Does the sky really care about the passing of a single cloud? Clouds come. Clouds go. Submarine-shaped clouds. Fez-shaped clouds. Dick-shaped clouds. You-shaped clouds. Each cloud different. And yet, aren't all clouds still pretty much the same? Their reflections wash slowly across the pollen-streaked tintstrip of your Cnivic's windshield. The sky abides. Gets lighter blue and then darker blue. Fiddles around with some weather. Does other sky-things. One single cloud? The sky gives zero fucks.

Pull into the parking lot of your company's glass-covered office tower.

Pull into the flat, little combteeth of white, spray-painted parking lines. Here you are!

And today, Monday; wow, this is all just the beginning!

*Brrrrrr-iiiiiing!* The little lobby of Detroit Enterprise Solutioneering smells of slow-rot mildew beneath the reek of oversprayed Lysol. Gertrude rolls her eyes towards the plastic budclamp of her telephone's headset. Is it ironic that an office full of salespeople selling Internet phone lines still uses a landline? Is *ironic* even the right word for that? *Hello, Detroit Enterprise Solutioneering, this is Gertrude speaking. How may I direct your call?*

Watch as Gertrude rearranges her collection of tiny plastic ponies into a small but aggressive phalanx. Catch her gaze and nod hi. Watch as Gertrude nods back. Good. Nod means good, you think. If anyone knows what's what around here it's Gertrude. Doesn't she? *I'm sorry but Mr. Kelling is in a meeting right now. Can I take a message?* The little lobby in front of Gertrude's desk is tense with fresh faces. Young women in white cotton blouses, heels and trim jackets. Boys wearing their daddy's hand-me-down blazers, rubber-soled penny loafers and skinny ties. The fresh faces are all here to interview with Mr. Kelling for a tiny number of direct sales jobs. Entry-level pays commission only, no base. You don't sell, you don't make. The job requires a car. Gas is the responsibility of the entry-level Solutioneer. Most people quit after two weeks of less than five sales, or as soon as they run out of gas money. Needless to say; interviewing is constant, turnover high. In a cohort of seven, DES is lucky to keep one past the first month. Even then they won't make base until they've been promoted.

Twice.

Think about how this whole DES arrangement is basically an audacious Cnraigslist swindle. Isn't it? Or aren't all entry-level jobs basically just audacious Cnraigslist swindles? Remember what it felt like to sit in one of those armless little lobby chairs, yourself a fresh face just less than a year ago. Flop-sweating. Jiggling your knee. *Wow, has it almost been a year? Already? Jesus.* Walk past the fresh faces and sniff at their chemical-hygiene-and-pheromone mixture: body salt and aftershave, antiperspirant and acne cream, adrenaline and cortisol, the odor of oxidized pennies.

Time for panic. *Are? You? Ready?*

Enter the Staging Room and notice how the whiteboard is already filled up with last week's sales numbers. How Kevin and Angie are busy marking jagged exclamation points around the Daily Team Superstar Goals for Max-Delivering Kickassery. Nod at Kevin and notice when he doesn't nod back. Angie? She's busy giving all the exclamation point these hollow tittles, then bulls-eyeing each exclamation point's tittle one by one. Pairs of exclamation point-tittles become eyes, the exclamation point-sticks become eyebrows. Angie gives each pair of exclamation tittle-eyes-and-point-eyebrows their own crescent mouth and sawtooth smile. Glance slowly around the room. Buck's eyes are on his phone. No nod. Swallow and try not to wince from the pang of sudden vertigo as the onrushing Monday sharpens its claws on your stomach lining. Gertrude nodded. Kevin didn't. Shit. What does that mean? What does anything even mean anymore?

Lean against the office's lone bookshelf stacked with motivational tomes on time management and how to most quickly improve your sales personality. Take out your phone and thumb over to Tnwitter to discover a smattering of articles about some new suicide bomber. A lady suicide bomber. Pictures show twisted wreckage, black smoke and burnt sand. Wonder what it must feel like to have a bomb strapped to your body, to be walking into a place ready to die. Feel distinctly unready to die. Feel distinctly unready to commit a protagonizing climax of any kind. To be the subject of some mordant, heavy-handed blog post about how sick, how sad how sudden global society's doom has now become. *What would it feel like, to feel ready? To really feel ready? To die?*

Decide to fire off some tnweets in rapid succession, then tnweet: *Hi Monday, you feel like a butt* then delete and tnweet *So Monday, we meet again #fml #thatsaleslife* then delete that and tnweet *Munday Funday #yay* then delete that and with your face stiffening and the blood still singing in your bitten thumb tnweet *Gameface strong, ready for this #DES #thatsaleslife*.

Let your eyes flicker up to where Aziz is strolling into the little lobby beyond the Staging Room's glass door. Watch his head nodding at the row of fresh faces, appraising, judging, creeping. Remember from a previous conversation that Aziz is probably now

11

placing private bets about who is and who is not going to make Mr. Kelling's interview cut. The new girls are all looking at the floor now, swallowing, too scared about not getting this job to notice Aziz's sharp chin counting them off one by one.

*What'll I do?* They're thinking. *If this doesn't work out? This? Job? Today?*

They are practicing how they'll exude this sense of desperation during the interview. That's what the Cnraigslist ad said, right? That: *We Want Hungry Sales Associates? To Join? The Team?* The new boys are either blankfaced or practicing scrunchy smiles into their phone cameras. They're making sure the smiles look salesy enough. *Hungry....* they're thinking. *Make me look hungry!* When they get a good smile they Snnap it, share it. So that their Followers know that they're here, that they're nervous, that they're ready for the big day, today, their DES interview.

Watch as Aziz enters the Staging Room through the glass doors. Beelines your way. You and Aziz understand each other. He gives you a bro-ish shoulder punch.

*Hey buddy*, he nods.

*Hey buddy*, you nod back. Glance back down at your phone as Aziz starts saying something about tigers and the weather forecast for this Wednesday, thumbing over to Fnacebook where Elwood's just posted some picture of what's got to be a Phnotoshopped beaver dam made from either mannequins or crash test dummies.

*That can't be real? Can it? Is that even what beavers looks like? Couldn't they maybe be otters? Or doesn't one not build dams?*

Wince as Kevin yells *Hey!* and you reflexively yell *Hey!* back, your voice joining the chorus of the other Sales Associates as Kevin calls out and you all reply letter by letter *D! (D!) T! (T!) S! (S!) G! (G!) F! (F!) M! (M!) D! (D!) K! (K!) Daily Team Superstar Goals For Max-Delivering Kickassery!* and then all burst into a flurry of whooping, snapping, pumping applause. Circle up with the others, steeling yourself against the inevitable. Kevin circles a column of sales numbers with a blue dry erase marker. Numbers are columned by nickname, K-Rizzle, Doober, CanCan, ZeeZ, Lady-A, KayMo, B-Money.

*Your numbers are down, Doober.*

You look up, feigning stunnedness.

*Stunned*, you tell your eyes: *make me look stunned!*

Kevin/K-Rizzle is pointing at you. Finger extended. Accusing. Projecting a line from his cuticle to your forehead.

Shit. The whole stunned-looking sympathy ploy must not be working! *Ummmmmm...*

*You are not Max-Delivering, Doober. You are not Kicking Ass.* Angie calls you a dewberry, and Buck and Candi giggle. Kevin giggles. *Stop being such a dewberry, Doober.*

Even Aziz laughs a little, nervously. Feel small and hot-faced with shame, as if what makes your life livable is no longer any bigger than a quarterly sales goal. Realize that you should be more thick-skinned

13

at this point. Shouldn't you? After so much time in the field? After so much time dealing with rejection? Because that's part of the sales grind, isn't it? Dealing with rejection? So then, why? Why do you *always* feel this way? *Come on skin! Thicken up!*

But it hurts and you feel it hurting. Failure. You. Even though you do not know what a dewberry is. Or why it is funny that you have been called one.

Sit down at the long wooden conference table with the other Sales Associates and talk about the weekend in vague terms that inexactly echo the banter of the previous Monday.

And the Monday before that.

Talk about the Territory Idiots in other DES campaigns, the ones who caused that old lady down in Wyandotte to call the police for trespassing.

*What morons!*

*Right!?*

Compare Territory lead lists with Angie and Buck. Repeatedly let slip that you got shafted. Stuck with a dry well.

*It's okay, Mike*, Kaylah says. She's a quiet one, like you. Think about how her smile would probably be insured for a high six figures. Maybe not as high a six figures as Buck Johnston's perfect smile, okay sure. But hers is also better in a way. Different-better. Kaylah's smile looks kind. Forgiving. And maybe she even means it. That it's okay. That you'll survive. That you shouldn't be panicking. She's the only one at the office who calls you Mike and not by your DES Solutionickname.

*You'll get one this afternoon*, says Kaylah. *I'm sure you will. I can feel it.* Her mouthcorners lift upwards and outwards and fill your head with golden light, bells and the clamor of little angels. Catch Kaylah's eye and smile back. Nod. This is how you show her that you're grateful.

Smoke with the other Associates in the parking lot. Stare up at the tinted glass windows of the office tower, at the reflection of the passing clouds. Notice how one cloud looks like Chad snoring on the sofa. When's Chad going to get his shit together, anyway? *Fucking Chad.* Feel the blood rise to your cheeks, hating Chad, hating Chneetle, hating motivational waterfalls and the glow of tiny submarines.

Think back to the conference room where Kaylah and Angie have probably already started *Practicing the Sales Conversation* with the post-interview cull of fresh faces. Teaching the vocab. Practicing the delivery. It's all really hard the first time. They all need to learn how to sound more meaningful with fewer words. Punchier. Harder hitting. More impactful. Landing a real haymaker with the opening line. That's Rule #1 of Sales Conversation. That words are bludgeons, best used for tenderizing the Customer. The fresh faces learn to practice speaking in the second person. Because it's all about you, about the second person, about the Customer. Tell the Customer what's going on. Move from the second person to the imperative. Cut to the chase. Call the Customer to action. Frame the sale as an exclusive opportunity. That's Rule #2. Impulsing the sale. It's all about the present tense. Act now! Don't miss out!

Remember learning the word *impulsing* first from Kaylah and Mr. Kelling during your own post-interview *Practicing the Sales Conversation* nearly a year ago. Impulsing involves the Associate *harnessing* (manipulating) *the competitive instincts* (deep-seated insecurities) of the Customer within a fast-closing window of decision time. In or out? Decide now or lose your chance forever! Urgency plus scarcity equals the full-throttle impulse. The sizzle starts deep in the Customer's voicebox and before they even know what's happening: *Aaaaaaa, okay yes! I'll do it! Where do I sign!?* Walk over to where Aziz is letting his lit cigarette dangle from pursed lips as he stares down into his phone, scanning past the suicide bomber news to reconfirm his prediction of Wednesday's weather. 50% chance of rain. 50% chance of not-rain. *If no rain,* says Aziz, *then we're doing the Tiger's game. For sure. Tigers versus Nats. You down, bro? Won't be too many games with this good a head-to-head left in the season.*

Nod and hear in the back of your head the echo of Kaylah's voice. *It's okay, Mike.* Maybe she'll be free on Wednesday? For the Tiger's game? If you can just make a fucking sale. If you can just make it through all the hours until Wednesday.

Your mind is back upstairs in the conference room, remembering your first day at DES nearly a year ago. If today's *Practicing the Sales*

*Conversation* goes how yours did then Kaylah will already be launching into her lesson on FOMOing. FOMO is an acronym for: Fear Of Missing Out. Verbing makes executing the conventions of sales conversations easier, simpler, stickier. There is really nothing subtle about FOMO. You FOMO someone by telling them that their competitors have already bought Internet phone lines. That people on their block have already bought Internet phone lines. That their police department and school district and neighborhood barber have already bought Internet phone lines. You inform them that even their Stone Age fucking in-laws are technological light years ahead of them as far as Internet phone lines go. Make them feel like they, poor souls, are still clinging desperately to the last vestiges of a hopeless, Internet phoneless past.

Internet phone lines are everywhere, you tell them.

Internet phone lines are inevitable, you tell them.

Not if, but when. Why wait?

You allude to the fact that there are words for people who cling to hopeless vestiges.

You allude to the fact that there are words for people who *get left behind*.

Without knowing why, their ears prick up. They feel roused to action by primordial terror. And most people are so used to getting FOMOd by everyone and everything around them that they never even suspect that you're playing them by a script. That, really, a you-looking robot could probably FOMO them just as hard, just as well, with about just as much success.

Check your Tnwitter to see if anyone's read the only tnweet you didn't delete. Nope, no one did. Delete it. Hear yourself say to Aziz: *I'm in. If it doesn't rain. I'm 50% in. Upper 50%. Waist up.* Aziz gives you a weird look. Say nothing in response. Start walking towards your Cnivic. Look up as Candi makes eyes at Buck. *See you at lunch.* Toss your own cigarette butt at the screw tail of a broken lightbulb. Think about collapsible fishing poles knotted with black hair, about submarine signals lost beneath a purl of viscous duckweed. Erliss Pond. Years ago. What was left there, waiting, wanting only now to be remembered?

Pull up the Territory map on your phone and locate the first set of West Detroit addresses. Thumb into Fnacebook just for a second, you think, just for a second before you get on the road. Those beavers are definitely not beavers. Definitely Phnotoshopped. Otters? And those mannequins look somehow fake, too. Or isn't that the point? Aren't all mannequins fake? Is it even possible to make a fake mannequin? And beaverdam a river with them? Otterdam?

Out on Wyoming Avenue, two machinists named Don and Lon just don't trust the Internet.

*I dunno...* says Don, lifting the left handlebar of his moustache up into his nostril with a drawn-out, pensive sniff before finally letting it fall back into place. *I just dunno...*

18

Tell them: *Fellas, you gotta put it on the cloud.* Tell them about how the Internet works. *Magic!* Act nonchalant as you nod skyward, up to where a passing thunderhead suggests the shape of a monstrous, eyeless poodle. *Everything's going on the cloud, folks. Phones, credit card processing, everything. Don't you know about the cloud? Not if but when, fellas. That's what they're saying, anyway.*

*Cloud?* says Lon, following your nod, squinting up at the eyeless poodle. *For phones?*

*Sounds complicated...* says Don. *Think we'll just be stickin' with th' real phones for now.*

Tell them: *It is a real phone! Just on the Internet! An Internet phoooooone! Emphasis on phone!*

Tell them: *Why not?*

Tell them: *Save some cash! Save a bundle! Act now! Don't miss out!*

Don and Lon close the machine shop door in your face. Nearly bust up your nose. Jesus. Maybe the Territory is rotten after all. Maybe you should just trust Kaylah. That it's okay. This. Failure. That you just have to keep trying. That you'll still get one sale today.

Walk slowly back to where your Cnivic's parked beneath a row of nervous-looking mulberry trees. Glance over at your brown lunch bag lying crumpled on your passenger seat floor mat, its mayonnaisey contents scarfed down hours ago. Feel your stomach rumble uselessly. Wanting more. Wanting you to become bigger, pouchier, fleshier. Ugh. Even your own stomach is conspiring against you. Feel your throat tighten. Feel your palms go clammy. Feel your fingertips begin to tremble. Feel your bleedy thumbnail throb. Think. Throb. Suck. Think harder. Throb harder. Blood. Sucks to suck, doesn't it? Try to figure out how you screwed up, not just the last sale but the last seventeen consecutive sales before that. Close your eyes and see Angie's hollow tittle, a bulls-eye annulus, then two bulls-eyes and a maniacal sawtooth smile drawn in blue dry-erase marker on the whiteboard of your underface. Turn the Cnivic on and idle it, then pull out into the street to pause at an off-kilter stop sign. Does the inexorable off-kilterness of this stop sign perhaps portend some deeper, darker meaning? Try and fail not to read too far into what your inexorably off-kilter stoppingness might really mean. Try. Fail. Look up into the rearview mirror and see your own reflection gazing back at you. Your face. Not great. Not great, but at least not terrible. Right?

Maybe you're just not cut out for this. For anything...

Not anything. This.

Remember what it felt like to stand in front of a crowd? You were that. Once. That applause? That silver microphone? You do remember that, don't you? Abolishing reality? Inventing new gods? Enunciating yourself as a fugitive from destiny, even any parody of destiny? Feel yourself filling up with the shape of nostalgia not for what was but for what might have been, the bigger, more many-splendored sum of all your youthful ambitions. You're still young, aren't you? Young-ish? *Anything.* No, but not anything. This.

Feel that cocoon of childhood peel off in a zillion gossamer threads and blow away. Now here you are. At a crossroads. Cocoonless. Naked.

Adulthood is an unexciting kind of nudity.

Nudity is a metaphor. The crossroads are not a metaphor. *Hoooooooooonk!*

Tires screech with sudden acceleration as a red Mnazda revs around you and speeds off in chinwagging exasperation. Tilt your chin back to watch the sun twist shadows around the far-off branches of an ancient, crooked yew.

You are not succeeding.

You are not Max-Delivering.

You are not Kicking Ass.

What was it exactly you thought the cocoon promised you?

Anything? Ha!

Scan Fnacebook for the faces of your childhood. Elwood, Cynthia, Marnie. Scroll back to Like Elwood's beavers. Otters. Whatever. Push Like to Like. *Mike Donahue Likes this*, says Fnacebook. You. Like. Great. Perfect. Just fucking perfect.

# The Face of Our Town

Spectators of life, let us gaze over all walls with our eyes worn out, with our eyes already expecting never again to see anything new or beautiful... May our face consist only of a wan smile, like that of a person near to crying, their gaze held faraway like that of a person who doesn't wish to see, a person who holds disdain in every feature, a person who despises life and lives only to despise it.
- Fernando Pessoa, *The Book of Disquiet*

Most mornings that I have to go to work I wake up an extra hour early to dick around on Fnacebook for twenty or thirty minutes. Usually I don't have any plan in mind to begin with, but once I log in and get clicking, well, it's only a matter of time before my adrenaline kicks into gear and my mind flies open in twenty different directions at once.

It's kind of Zen, actually, how I Fnacebook. Like a deep, sleepyping trance.

Out of nowhere all these insignificant little curiosities begin scurrying around the space between my face and my laptop screen. Questions like: What's Mike up to these days?

Click.

Whoa, looks like he and Chad have gotten pretty outdoorsy up there in Michigan! Daaaaaamn. That hunting camo, though. Not a good look, boys. My cursor arrow hovers, wanders past their fresh kill, a buck deer splayed on the pickup truck's flatbed.

Looking, not Liking, boys.

22

I mouse over the blood-spatter, making a little invisible circle on my laptop screen. At least it's not another picture of him with his sales clique looking suave and vaguely predatory. Of course I still like Mike a lot, I mean, we grew up together and everything, but I'm not exactly wild about that sales clique of his, with their oiled hair and their black leather document carriers and their taut, angular smiles. I scroll down to look at a couple of his sales clique #squad photos, just to let them register my askance disapproval. Then I get bored, bored and feeling homesick and so I start clicking through Toulous people, people from my high school, people who once lived in my hometown and now have mostly scattered.

Like, what about Kendra?

How's Kendra holding up these days?

Click. Ugh!

And Larissa?

Click. Double-ugh!

Oh wow: so back in Velton Brent's just now commented a winkey face plus a smiley face on Stacey's bachelorette party pictures without realizing that Stacey cheated on him with one of the restaurant's wait staff on the floor of a motel bathroom at five in the morning. I mean, he has no idea!

Well, I guess I only heard about this because of Tina, Tina who was my TA at Velton State for a semester of *History 301: History of the Crossword & Other Common Puzzles* and who's also my source for the freshest in local Velton scuttlebutt. And she was there, Tina

23

was, at Stacey's bachelorette thing. She saw the whole shit show going down.

Click.

Brent, oh dear, sweet Brent! How long will you keep posting those tender emoticons beneath the Fnacebook pictures of your beloved Stacey's indiscretions?

I'll love the both of you forever, just for being you.

These are real emotions:

I love Brent.

I love Stacey.

And I love seeing them love each other. It's so, like, *human*.

I click to Love the photo. My heart-symbol pops out tomato red, flushed with the pixels of an overthinned blood supply. My own heart beats an irregular correspondence. My love loves loving my love. Fnacebook can give me quite an endorphin rush. For the rest of the workday I can feel my fingertips, like, *tingling*. After we finish doing breakfast at the café I take my extended bathroom break to jerk off and that magic tingle is still there, throbbing, right at the tips.

My co-worker Karen wakes up super-early to do some type of brand name exercise routine and I told her yesterday that I basically do the same thing, only with Fnacebook.

She gave me a look like: *Elwood, that's not the same thing at all!*

(Karen basically sucks as a human being. Not only doesn't she get my witty use of sarcasm but her arm flab is indescribably gross. She is always giving me mean looks for no reason. I don't visit her

Fnacebook profile very often. There's more than enough of her to see at Yourmug Café day after day after day.)

I know that a lot of people go on Fnacebook just to check in on family members or keep up with friends who have moved away. But that's not why I go on Fnacebook. For me, well, it's the same feeling of human warmth that other folks might get from being right in the thick of a big crowd. Like, I'm suddenly finding out about every little thing that's going on in the world. Not missing out. Never missing out. I'm plugged in. Right there, as it happens, front row seats. Right!? What Fnacebook really does is make me feel connected to other people's shittiness, allowing me to live vicariously through their most humiliating moments. I love it all. Their misfortunes and calamities. Their petty feuds and disappointments. Their confessional, tragically overshared shortcomings. And there's something about this feeling-connected-to-poorly-disguised-but-totally-genuine-unhappiness that really gets me going. Schadenfreude? Whatever that cliché about trainwrecks is. Not looking away. Never looking away. Not even fucking blinking. For me, Fnacebook is more like a whole circusworth of trainwrecks.

I can see it now! Can't you? The Circus of Fnacebook! Cirque d'FnB! Gates flung open, those welcoming fairgrounds — you enter in a daze beneath the tuneless blare of a hurdy-gurdy. That farty smell of peanuts. That muddy, stomped-over grass. You enter the big top tent and oooh and aaaah with the rest of the denimed onlookers, holding your breath as the trapeze artist flips once, then

25

twice, then too many times (oh no!) and jackknifes sideways, missing her trapeze partner's desperately wriggling fingers to begin the long, groundward plummet.

Oh no!

(Eep!)

Down she goes, arms and legs unprofessionally akimbo to land in a sickening crunch.

Around you the crowd's working up into a good, desperate frenzy.

Is she dead?

Is this possibly somehow *all part of the act?*

The remaining trapeze artist is still hanging from his knee joints, face sculpted in a bug-eyed mask of shock and horror. And there are other sounds, besides. Snoozers are being roused with unkind elbows. Children are gulping with glee, rejoicing at the pandemonium. Jibjab the Koala-Headed Man bounds out into the circus ring, his howls laced with notes of primal loss and agony.

*Miranda! Miranda, can you hear me? Miranda say something!*

Tears stream from Jibjab's pained, marsupial eyes.

And you can see this!

You can see him, Jibjab, thinking exactly this!

Because this is Fnacebook!

The great menagerie of glass heads!

Now the ringmaster's going berserk as two contortionists struggle to pry the lion whip from his fists. The crowd erupts into a nervous frenzy. Reeking of eucalyptus, the frantic Jibjab attempts CPR onto Miranda's cracked-open face with his comically large koala head. To no avail. He raises his head again to scream: *Aaaaaaaaaaaa! Why!?* Phones are out. People are dialing 9-1-1. People are taking snapshots. Blowing up their Instagrnams. Taking full-length high-resolution video files. Streaming anywhere and everywhere. #trapezefail is trending. First, #tragedy is trending, then #farce.

*Whoah*, says everyone to everyone, over their shoulders. Infants wail. They have become bored and wish desperately to go home. Home, to where the maternal glow of the TV awaits them! Come on! Are we there· yet! *Whaaaaaaaaaannnnh*! But for once, no one pays any attention to the infants because they are simply nowhere near as interesting as the primordial catastrophe of death, sudden and real and unfolding right before their very eyes. Adults crane their necks trying to see if there's blood, and how much blood there is. Maybe a lot? They are horrified, but at the same time: if it's going to be bloody it might as well be really really bloody! Because if someone's dying down there, well, why not gift a little *memento mori* for our citizen journalists' social media feeds!?

This overextended fable climaxes with two tanker trains filled with fryolator grease jumping the nearby train tracks and crashing through the canvas walls of the circus tent, flash-frying everyone to an ecstatically incendiary crisp. The crowd, phones up, proceeds to videotape their own immolation until they no longer have thumbs. Or hands. Or faces. God reaches down to dip a couple members of the crowd in ranch dressing before popping them into his massive, spittle-flecked mouth. Chewing. Swallowing. *Mmmmmmmm. Delicious!* The end.

(Moral: Someday, we will all wind up becoming the same grotesque psychological snackfoods that we have spent our lifetime's worth of clicks munching on).

I have heard certain people (Karen, Tina, even my boss Maurice) complain that they find dicking around on Fnacebook to be a waste of time. To these people I say the following: you are not using Fnacebook correctly.

You have failed to turn Fnacebook into your own personal phantasmagoric fire-orgy erupting from a circus of wrecked trains. And that, thankfully, is not my fault.

I cannot help you. Using Fnacebook is a talent. Some are born with. Some are born without.

I cannot help it if I am a motherfucking Fnacebook genius.

*

*Hey Karen. Lucky Benny told me you're going to die. And you know what? Right before you die, you know what's going to flash before your eyes? Not your life, not your apartment, not your loved ones or your treasured possessions or even your mother and father but a slow-motion, ultrahigh-resolution pan across, yup, you guessed it: this guy! Slow-motion pan across my gummy-smiling, eyebrow-raised, rosy-cheeked face. So close-up that you could play Connect*

*The Dots with my fucking pores. And then you die. Boom! So what do you think about that?*

*Eat me*, says Karen.

The mental image of me eating Karen causes me to experience an involuntary full-body shudder. Karen is definitively one of the most inedible people I know. There are many reasons that this is true. Namely, her arm flab. I peck around in my phone looking for the correct emoji to express my disgust and notice that the emoji for :grinning: is indistinguishable from the one for :grimacing:, not identical, but still indistinguishable. Huh. Maybe that's how I'm feeling right now? Neither cunning nor flummoxed, but an emoji that effaces the difference between the two. Huh. The seconds of not-eating Karen tick by.

*What*, I say finally, half-seizing the moment. *Look, Karen. Everyone dies. It's part of the circle. Parallelogram. The Great Trapezoid of Life. And who are you to call Lucky Benny a liar, anyway?*

*Let's play the Elwood-shuts-the-fuck-up game, shall we?*

I swallow, return to my lukewarm bath of cunning/flummoxed-indistinguishableness. The reason that I often invoke Lucky Benny is that he can be used as a sources-cited for any stripe of outlandish claim since, quite frankly, he always might have said basically anything. Think of anything, anything at all. There's a good chance Lucky Benny's said it. The guy's got a weird mind and no filter.

All the regulars at the Ugly Bar know that Lucky Benny's called Lucky Benny because he won the lottery in 1983. Now we're not talking about the big Pnowerball lottery or mega-millions or whatever, but Lucky Benny still wound up getting cut a $50,000 cashier's check. Which for a guy with Lucky Benny's appetites is basically more money than he could gamble, drink, smoke and fuck away in a single weekend and so might just as well have been a cashier's check for infinity dollars, at least the way he talks about it. Lucky Benny went through the full $50,000 in exactly four months and thirteen days: a whirlwind of cocaine, hookers, and hotel rooms plus an extended hot streak in Las Vegas that went suddenly very cold.

If you ask Lucky Benny he considers every dime of that money well-spent. It has, you see, provided him with fodder for the past thirty years of bar stories, and a good story, says Benny, is worth its weight in gold.

Which, as metaphors go, makes only as much sense as you really want it to.

Recently, Lucky Benny has started reading tarot cards at the Ugly. Bryce and the other bartenders don't mind. To his would-be customers Lucky Benny announces proudly that he has never learned a single thing about reading tarot cards. According to Benny, that is how you know he *ain't faking*.

The best thing is to ask Lucky Benny to predict the outcome of events that have already occurred. He prognosticates using some kind of formula that involves a high degree of randomness. You'll ask him how certain he is that Obama beat Romney or Gore beat Bush. You'll ask him if he thinks humans will ever clone an animal, or if Y2K will bring down all of global civilization.

*No way*, he'll say. *We can't even clone a damn rock!*

*Sure*, he'll say. *Too many zeroes. That's why I don't keep a calendar. That's why Lucky Benny is Y2K-proof! Ha ha!*

Lucky Benny is the second most popular tarot card reader in Velton after Madame Pommeranz who is a full-time professional fortuneteller. In addition to tarot cards, she also does palms and that New Age crap with the amethyst crystals. Okay, sure, Madame P makes her money. But on Fnacebook the Lucky Benny fanpage created by someone who is definitely not Lucky Benny has nearly 500 Likes!

Madame Pommeranz isn't even on Fnacebook!

But she's the one making a steady living off her readings.

How's that now?

Maybe some people actually think Madame Pommeranz knows the future. (Those people, by the way, are morons. If Madame Pommeranz was so hip to the future, what the hell is she doing reading tarot cards out here in the Podunk netherworld of Velton when she could be raking in buttloads at any casino? Or making real money betting the market on Wall Street? That's my take on the fiscal realities of professional fortunetelling viz. the plausibility of occult forecasting methods, anyhow).

But not so with Lucky Benny. No, what people like about Lucky Benny is his careless sense of certainty. He knows the cards don't mean what the books say. And if they do mean what the books say, well, he hasn't read about it.

Because are books for Lucky Benny?

Are they the kind of thing that you would expect a guy like Lucky Benny to fritter away his precious hours on?

Hell no!

Lucky Benny does not need books.

Lucky Benny does not give a fuck.

*Look*, says Lucky Benny, shuffling around his laminated card deck. *Who the fuck am I? Nobody. Just some chump who won the lottery in 1983. But tell you what, that's not nothing. How many people you know won the lottery? That's what I'm saying. I got that proven luck. God-proven.*

*Am I gonna promise you I'm right?*

*That I'm the be-all and/or the end-all?*

*Nope.*

*Not a chance.*

*I ain't promising shit!*

*Why would I?*

*There are no guarantees in this world. But at least here you know you got it from Lucky Benny.*

*I'm a bona fide winner. I don't have no regrets.*

\*

Recently I've started sleeping with a girl named Annie. She's kind of short and white and freckle-faced and has a small scar on her chin. Her Fnacebook profile picture is of her taking a selfie with a different Fnacebook profile picture (also of her), which itself involves a different Fnacebook profile picture (also of her), forming a kind of nested picture-within-a-picture motif. What's that called again? I used to know this... mise-en-abyme! It's the type of fact I could easily spend the rest of my life uselessly remembering without a single opportunity to deploy it during Ugly bar trivia. Which, who's that the sadder comment on: them or me? Maybe it's a sign that someday soon I'll be needing to take my trivia talents elsewhere, that I'll one day feel the urge to level up. The original photograph was of her, Annie, standing on top of a rotting log in the Clough Wilderness Area with a red sun setting behind her. By the time I met her she'd gone through enough abyme-cycles of photo nesting that the sunset had shrunk to a ruby-colored dot set like a stud-piercing into her Fnacebook picture's squarish navel. You had to squint to even see it. To see the ruby-colored sun, surrounded by eight-ish smiling, scowling, side-eyed, and expressionless Annies, all posing with the inset self-images of their not-so-distant pasts. I mean, there's something to that, right? Something kinda hot? Ish? And I'd be lying if I said I don't sometimes imagine all of the Annies nested in her profile picture crawling out of their frames and having sex with all of the Elwoods in my last eight Fnacebook profile pictures, either separately or perhaps even noodling together in some deeply uncanny, Boschian clone-orgy.

I mean, right?

Last night Annie and I went bowling with two of her guy friends, Liam and Keenan and I told her if we didn't win at bowling I would break up with her.

*Ha ha*, she said.

*You're funny*, she said.

*No I'm serious*, I said.

*I don't want to date a loser.*

*Especially because it's your guy friends*, I said.

*If it was your girlfriends, I could probably handle it but if your guy friends win then it's definitely a sign that things won't work out between us.*

*That sooner or later we'll break up.*

*Then, in a weird gesture towards their dominance at bowling tonight, you'll eventually end up dating one of them.*

*Maybe both of them.*

*One after the other. Maybe both at the same time.*

*It could happen. It could totally happen.*

*Ha ha*, said Annie. *You're such a weirdo!*

*I'm not kidding*, I said.

I was kidding.

But I do really hate losing at bowling.

Checkers, Connect Four, Candyland, Monopoly, Settlers of Catan, Taboo and Scattergories I am okay with losing. Even bar trivia (which I hate-hate-*hate* losing) I am at least so-so-okay with losing. I have lost enough these kinds of games enough times to know how to do it properly. But bowling isn't something I do every week or even every month. And the only way I can get in the mood for wearing those weird shoes and inhaling hours of stale old-people smell is to get super worked up about winning. And doubly so when our opponents happen to be these two stocky red-haired kids named Liam and Keenan who have chosen to attire themselves solely in the apparel of professional skateboarding brands.

Who does that? I mean like, what are these guys trying to prove? That they skateboard? Come on, guys. And if that weren't bad enough, both Liam and Keenan are wearing these Celtic thumb rings that they have to keep taking on and off every single time they step up to bowl. *What in the actual fuck? Is this some kind of complexly humorless joke?* Liam/Keenan's little on-again-off-again routine with the Celtic thumb rings has started driving me quietly bonkers.

Annie turns out to be a fantastic bowler. She bowls three strikes in a row and our score rockets ahead. I get so tight-assed about the Celtic thumb rings routine that I completely lose my focus and gutterball. Twice in the first half I scratch completely. Either Liam or Keenan makes a joke about my shitty bowling. Without thinking I mutter back some invective like oh yeah well at least I don't suffer from a latent predisposition towards alcoholism and large families of unwanted children. As with most cruel zingers based on offensive cultural stereotypes, it's a line that surely could have worked better with a bigger crowd. Liam/Keenan must have overheard my muttering because next thing I know I'm getting a very warm, stubby finger jabbed in my chest. Before I can determine whose finger is doing the jabbing one of the daywalkers is calling me *a cocksucker!* and *a dipshit!*

It's all happening really fast.

Then Annie gets in between us and says *hey hey come on come on, stop it, you guys.*

She ends up forcing *me* to apologize, which I do in the most sheepish, pissed-off sounding way possible. We play the rest of the game in angry silence and Annie and I lose in a landslide. I barely get in a spare and by this point Annie has also lost her thirst for victory.

On the way back to her place she tells me that Keenan's dad is a recovering alcoholic and he's very sensitive about it.

*Oh and by the way,* says Annie, *you totally suck at bowling.*

*

The town of Velton sits along a series of lazy-looking hills that sprout up unevenly on either side of the Velt River. These hills have never been in any kind of serious hurry. *What's the rush?* you can almost hear the hills saying. *Just let the Velt sort it out! Whatever it is, well, we're pretty sure it's got nothing to do with us.* No lie, these hills are pretty much my role models.

At the top of the one there's the intersection of Gottlieb and Houch Streets and the northeast corner has got this little dog park roughly the size of an Olympic swimming pool. Houch Park. It's got well-mowed Bermuda grass and a couple of standard wooden picnic tables. At the park's edge sits a massive, gnarly-rooted oak stump with the heart rotted out; a reminder of nature's hideousness. The park's only about a seven minute walk from my apartment complex down on Burlingham so when I don't have anything serious going on I'll walk up to Gottlieb and then hook a right up to Houch and sit right on the lip of the stump, look out over the wide sweep of Velton while I tap through Fnacebook on my phone.

The view is distinctly unimpressive. Total Podunk fucking netherworld. Jesus. I try to picture what a shitstorm life must have been like for people to get excited about living in a place like Velton. What a thought! Probably life back then was even more desolate, more catastrophe-riddled and way, way, way more boring than it is now. Right? Screens of playing *Oregon Trail* flicker back through my memory, plodding covered wagons and wives dead of dysentery. As a child I learned how to colonize, how to mistrust computerized Indians and slaughter pixelated buffalo. *We live in the greatest country in the world at the technological apex of human history, don't we? We have so much to be grateful for. Pfffffffffff,* I let a lungful of exasperation die between the dryness of my lips.

Now it's 5:12 PM and the early autumn sun's already fading into strokes of lucid red and gold over the hills. Slowly I move my head left to right, appreciating the smooth camera-pan offered by my twentysomething neck's well-lubricated spinal column. To my left sits the Clough Wilderness Area with Paper Creek running though it and the fake-clean smell of soap from the little soap factory saturates the lukewarm breeze with notes of artificial lavender, chamomile and honeysuckle. There's not a sound in the whole sky, nor a bird, nor a cloud. Looking straight ahead now I see the crested marquee of Bule's Theater down Colling Street from the tall steeple of Second Methodist, tapered like the cap of a very square wizard. Second Methodist sits right across Colling from the outlined signback of Yourmug where I work, and Dodd's, where I've only eaten once, a plate of flavorlessly battered fish and fried potato wedges. Panning down I rest my gaze on the frosted glass of the Magnus Building, named after Albert's grandfather and containing one of those pointless, self-fellating wine bars and Yourmug's rival coffee shop, the loathsome Stempler's Roast. Out to my sightline's right the Velt River sweeps its umber blues out past the edge of town to meet up with the train tracks at a little covered bridge, its grassy banks edged with cedar, oak and hawthorn as it zigzags towards the horizon and then slowly disappears.

For years I used to walk by that river on my way to classes at Velton State, staring down into my reflection and feeling either homesick or that feeling-a-thing-that-I-can't-quite-say-what-I'm-feeling-except-that-it-takes-me-out-of-myself-out-of-the-present-moment-because-my-shape-within-the-light-playing-across-water-is-the-light-of-far-off-places-places-that-I've-never-been-and-never-will-be-places-filled-with-all-the-faces-that-I'll-never-see, and yes, I used to walk along the river and think about the future in whorls and eddies of over-hyphenated vagueness, wondering if the water of the Velt River knew that it was going somewhere, if it knew that it was being pulled along according to particular bends and swerves in the river banks or if, from the water's perspective, its movements resembled only a hopeless and intrauterine unknowableness, a shrug, a let's-see-where-this-flowing-thing-ends-up kind of journey. Questions I meandered around: *Does the Velt's water have any notion of the Mississippi into which it will one day flow? Or what about the delta down in Louisiana, the delta where it will shed its banks and mix with a thousand plants and creatures, mix around in that warm labyrinth of bayous before finally emptying out into the sea? Do the waters dream of the bayous as they sleep, flowing throw this hilly part of Iowa? Or are they just as clueless about the shape of the future as I am?*

Strolling along I wondered whether, if you were to take a cup of water from the Velt River and put it on a space ship and lift it up above the curve of the Earth's atmosphere so that it could look down and see the path that it would take fullsweep, spring-to-Gulf, *whether the Velt would even want to go on flowing? Or would it lose its thirst for rushing, flowing, eddying and whorling, knowing exactly where it would have to end up? And what of us? Don't we, too, have banks and bayous and deltas, and don't one day we shed them, our*

*edges, our bodies and our very selves to empty out into the great
and overwhelming mouth of the Beyond?*

That's why I stopped walking by the Velt River after dropping out
of school. After Marnie graduated early. After Marnie moved away.
After Marnie and I fell slowly out of touch.

I guess that river just kept coming at me with too many weird
fucking questions.

It's already getting dark out. Rising from the stump lip I take my
phone out and take a picture of my Houch Park throne, the oak
stump, heartless and gold-smeared with evening light. Post it to
Fnacebook #thatstumplife. Nice. I wander down from my little perch
in Houch Park, turn left on Klapp and instead of making the next
right on Burlingham I keep going, heading in the direction of Delaney
Street, Moseby's Playthings and the Velton Cemetery that rises up on
a sloping hillside before the entrance to Clough Wilderness Area. The
houses down on Klapp are all that somber style of Victorian, some
with creepy little turrets and ancient cobwebbed widow's walks. I
pass by one house in particular, one that I've noticed once before
because there are crescent moons made from tinfoil hung in every
window and because the yard's overgrown with clumps of wild .
chicory and milkweed. I stop out in front and take out my phone,
check Fnacebook for no reason and then put my phone away.

What draws me towards this particular house I cannot say, but as
I approach its northeast corner by the garbage cans I can hear from
the basement level a woman's voice whispering, as if reciting the

words for a spell, over and over and over: *blackberry-blackberry-blackberry.* I stand stock still for a moment, listening, letting the hairs on the back of my neck get nice and stiff. Nothing. Wind. My mind's gone racing, wondering now if I really heard the voice at all, wondering what drew me to the corner of the tinfoil moon house in the first place, what caused me to stand and listen with such a keen and sudden breathlessness?

I turn and walk back up Klapp Street, heading towards Burlingham and my apartment complex, fishing my phone out of my pocket as I do. Checking on #thatstumplife. Somewhere out in Detroit, Mike has Liked it. *Nice,* I think softly to myself. *I'm glad he likes it. That's nice, isn't it? Isn't that kind of nice?*

*

About two in the afternoon Ricardo comes over. I'm laying on my sofa thumbing through Fnacebook with my bunny slippered feet propped up on the coffee table and I think about getting up to say hi but then I don't get up and Ricardo just comes in and sits down next to me and we say things like hi and what's up and not much and we talk about the fact that we both just found out that Tina's actually married, like full-on married, and how about that? But then it's weird because she, like, she still comes and hangs out with us at the Ugly's bar trivia even though her husband doesn't come with her. Isn't that weird? I don't know if that's weird, we both say, wondering. Her husband's named Steve, right? Why does that sound so familiar? Then I look up from my phone and notice that Ricardo's got both of

41

his ears newly pierced with a pair of the ugliest salmon-colored earrings I have ever seen.

I tell him that I think his earrings are totally ugly and he looks kind of hurt.

*These aren't the only earrings I'm ever going to own, you know,* says Ricardo. *They're just, like, placeholders. They keep the piercing open until I can get something nicer.*

I tell Ricardo that he can't just go through life sticking himself full of placeholders.

*That's no way to live, Ricardo.*

I tell Ricardo that he needs to take pride in his appearance.

*What about Belicia? What about your girl, homie? Doesn't she have some earrings you can wear?*

Ricardo's face darkens and he tells me that he and Belicia split up a couple of days ago. His voice gets quiet when he's telling me about it, like he's still feeling pretty raw.

*Well,* I tell Ricardo. *With earrings like that it's no wonder you can't hold onto a fine woman like Belicia.*

I tell Ricardo that women don't go for men who lower their standards for the convenience of a short-term piercing discount.

I tell Ricardo that he might be a loser, but he doesn't have to look like a loser, okay?

I tell Ricardo to go get us both a PBR.

Ricardo heads into the kitchen and I can hear him opening the fridge and rooting around in the bottom drawer for the beer cans.

Then I hear him closing the fridge and opening the cans of beer one at a time.

*Ssssst! .... Ssssst!*

The sound of a carbonated beverage being opened is one of the most sublime sounds in all the world. Cnoke, beer, either way. It's Pavlovian. And I find myself genuinely surprised that the *Ssssst!* is not sampled more often as a compositional element in Top 40 pop music. Right? Because many of us Top 40 pop music listeners, I feel, would really appreciate that *Ssssst!* sound, maybe somewhere in the bridge or even right before the beat drops.

Ricardo comes back in and hands me the PBR which I immediately throw back to try for a one-and-done chug.

My eyes redden.

My face reddens.

I end up spluttering nearly the whole beer down the front of my bathrobe.

Ricardo is laughing.

The truth becomes clear to me. Ricardo must have taken my bottle of Sriracha hot sauce and squirted in a hefty dose of fire before handing the beer to me. I tell Ricardo: *What the fuck, Ricardo!?*

Ricardo sips his own un-Srirachad PBR and takes his time swallowing.

*Next time don't be such an asshole*, says Ricardo. *You were totally asking for it. Now we're even.*

I tell Ricardo I hope both his ears get infected.

I tell Ricardo I hope a wolf spider lays its eggs in his ear piercings, the kind that hatch ~600 baby wolf spiders.

*Not now*, I say. *After they hatch. Then. Then we'll be even.*

*

It's morning on like a Thursday or something and I'm sitting in the back of Yourmug on my break. This feature of working in a café, where you can occasionally take breaks when the place isn't totally slammed with customers is probably the only reason I've stayed at Yourmug for the past year-and-a-half rather than taking a more lucrative service industry gig as a waiter or a bartender. Because here I am, in that blessed interval after the morning rush and before the lunch crowd and what am I doing? Yes, that's right: *I'm reading!* Not Fnacebook, but an actual book. Paper. Glue. Its pages are soft and fresh-smelling. *Ahhhhh.* I exhale a little sigh of pleasure.

The book is called *Ideas for Words* by one E. Quate. The title is a pretty apt description of exactly what's inside. I read the introduction to it online a week or so ago while I was lying in bed half-drunk from bar trivia, sleepy but with enough itchy-lidded Internet brain to not really be able to fall asleep. So, as sometimes happens, I began fingersauntering my way through Fnacebook, my eyes half-open, my jaw half-closed, my index finger haloed by the glow of all those liquid crystals in my phone screen's display. Then I saw the post on Marnie's timeline; *phryptolage (n) the slow, living process by which a single thought or memory decays over time, forming an intricate and*

44

textural code at the memory's substratum; the patternistic warping of past events. *[Section: Portmanteaus & Contractions: 3a; Mutacrypts]* It was from a Tnumblr also titled *Ideas for Words*, and she had commented *Hello? What's this?*

Click. My phone opened a new window where the book's introduction, entitled *Lingua Optima, or Why Not Make Better Words?* appeared available in full. Half-asleep I began to thumb across the opening passage:

*Welcome to Ideas for Words. This is a book full of words that do not currently exist, but perhaps ought to. Many of them are related to or described using words that currently do exist, but perhaps ought not to. Each time a new word is born, an idea is given a home. Each time a word is repeated, the idea is given an opportunity to press itself into the warm embankments of our minds, where perhaps it will mutate and/or multiply. Currently, this process of creating new homes-and-spawning-grounds for better ideas is ad hoc, disorganized and completely irresponsible. This Introduction will demonstrate why a laissez-faire approach to the future of language is both wrongheaded and dangerous, concluding with a discussion of some reasonable alternatives.*

*Much like social technology platforms, words today are evolving quite quickly and with very little thought. Each year we wind up with a new batch of awkward portmanteaux, STEM-flavored loanwords and the brand names of companies that offer us new habits of living* and doing, (e.g. new verbs) where the noun of the company's brand is effectively verbed for our use (to Fnacebook, to tnweet, etc.).

This trend of verbing nouns is hardly new and follows from the vernacular of management consulting-speak e.g. 'to task', 'to onboard', 'to calendar'. It also incorporates the lesser trend of nominalization, where a complex verb is compounded as a single noun and then re-verbed e.g. What are you putting out today? → What's your output today? → What are you outputting today? Along with the appending of definite articles to imperatives, interrogatives and adverbs (e.g. the ask, the what, the now) this spiral-shaped do-si-do of nouned verbs and verbed nouns is how we end up with sentences like: Hey so before timelining your future outbounds can you please reference corporate's internal content requirements?

Furthermore, the increasing reliance on emoticons, emoji and excessive punctuation within persistent (neverending) streams of one-to-one dialogue or many-to-many groupchat has radically transformed the evolutionary pathways of textual English slang. Whereas the most popular topic of idle chitchat was once the weather, today the most common topic of communication is the unaddressed personal update, which is typically: here's where I am/how I'm feeling/what I'm doing. No interlocutor is required in advance of posting the update and potentially anyone is invited to co-write/co-click themselves into the conversation. This trend helps explain the growing popularity of single punctuation marks (e.g. ?) as indications of basic incomprehension, especially in long email threads *where the original context for a comment may have been lost entirely. Bubbles of text in chats resemble enough the speech bubbles of last century's comics that we should hardly be surprised to see comics/graphic novels' tropes becoming ubiquitous in our own interpersonal exchanges, including the hilariously pointless hemi-grawlix (e.g. f\*\*ck instead of fuck, sh\*t instead of shit, and so on). As this trend of life taking on comic repertoires intensifies, one wonders whether the ? itself will be recognized as a word, along with the ... and the ! along with numerous other superalphanumeric symbols which have, via the mobile Internet, acquired their own independent word auras. Ball's in your court now, OED.*

*Simultaneously, the ubiquity of wirelessly inter-networked computers (predominantly in devices that are for some reason still called phones) means that we are rarely, if ever, experience conscious reality free from explicit reminders about the behaviors/expectations/judgments of numerous, multiply-significant others. Caught within a dense social fabric quilted from ill-fitting systems of metasymbolic exchange, we face and interface, mind and remind, act and transact our many selves with an oversupply of mutable others. This is how we manufacture familiarity at a distance. This is how we build our new relationships, click by precious click. Owing to their ubiquity, we may even forget what a truly staggering percentage of our daily cognition is bound up in the functioning of these metasymbolic systems and how much of our capacity to act, create and cogitate has been outsourced to algorithms or remote storage memory services. We may forget how much of our own memories reside in someone else's robot brains.*

*There's an overtold joke about two goldfish swimming along and one goldfish says something like:* Boy, the water's sure cold today! *And the other fish goes quiet for a minute, kind of looking down at the orange tips of his fins and starts to ask:* What the fuck is water? *but then thinks better of it and just nods and says:* Sure is! *The point is that we're the fish and it (the quilting of metasymbolic systems into daily cognition) is the water. The real question becomes: should the fact that our innermost habits of desire are constantly being sculpted by the eerie all-the-time persistence of remotely networked behaviors/expectations/judgements give us any · cause for trepidation?*

*More than us,* words are us. *Words set the rules on all games of power, attraction and happiness. Words are how we measure success and define failure, for ourselves, for our kinship networks and for our broader communities. Words contour the limits and enable the expansion of our collective social, political and economic imagination. We ignore their privatization, automation and disposability at our own peril. For precipitous obsolescence of words shall become ours as well.*

Ideas for Words *argues for conception of a* lingua optima — *the optimal system of wordmaking that we may one day reach via the conscious acceleration of desirable trends in linguistic evolution. While some form of* lingua ultima *is by definition inevitable, there are no guarantees that our current approach of compounding, portmanteauxing, verbing-nominalizing-and-re-verbing will get us to where we'd like to go. Without a conscious effort taken on behalf of accelerating the evolutionary success of our more desirable words towards a* lingua optima *we'll end up, almost by definition, getting stuck with one of several* lingua sub-optimas. *That's why Ideas for Words will propose a series...*

The book arrived a week later, exactly I imagined it, pressed into an orange-colored package the size of an oven mitt and sealed with shiny plastic packing tape. Small and blue and full of slender, alphabetized sections: mass nouns, pseudoverbs, onomatopoeia, expletives, portmanteaux, eclectic miscellany and, as promised, a series of somewhat snotty verbnounverb re-nominalizations. Turning over the book I noticed Quate himself peering out from a stamp-sized photograph, a small, androgynous figure wearing black, circular sunglasses. Head cocked to one side, lips pursed, smug and stern and somehow consummately dweebish. Flip. *Shhttt.*

*bribule (n)* a bribe using the implausible illusion of monetary value e.g. ineptly counterfeited bills, deeds to properties on imaginary continents, mineral rights to planets located within the Sun.

Flip, flip, flip.

*clickitch* (n) the sudden and irrepressible desire to touch-click on an unclickable object, e.g. to mistakenly attempt to use a tablecloth or a tapestry as a touchscreen.

Flip, flip, flip.

*fnordize (v)* to use of the letter 'n' to draw attention to the felt ubiquity and use of a particular brand name as both a meaningful, distinct signifier and an instrument of social control. See *fnord*; Principia Discordia, 1965.

Flip, flip, flip.

*slazzerweak (adj.)* temporarily lacking the ability to open a doorknob, pickle jar or other sealed container due to one's hands being coated with a lotion, lubricant, grease, sweat or other slippery, grip-thwarting substance. e.g. *Her hand slazzerweak from eating copious strips of bacon, Laura felt briefly infantalized by her struggle with the childproof Tylenol cap.*

*gratwit (n)* an excessive or gratuitous use of hackish wit, especially headline puns, twee meta-ness and/or postmodern devices (e.g. books-within-books, characters-within-characters) to the point that it comes off as intensely grating.

Flip, flip. Somehow reading random out-of-order entries in this little book I begin to feel that special kind of vertigo I get from looking down into my phone's Gnoogle Maps, first at a satellite of the US American Midwest, then unpinching to zoom down into Iowa, then down into Velton, then down into the part of Colling Street where Yourmug sits across from Second Methodist, then down into the little pixelfuzzed skylight above the back of Yourmug where I sit beneath my own brown-haired head dot and boom, I get it again, that self-causing recursive loop of vertigo, a feeling that only comes from looking at the back of my own head looking down at the back of my own head looking down at the back of my own head (exactly). I wonder if maybe this little blue book has a word for that, has a word specifically designed to house that special feeling of vertigo? Hopefully?

*Elwood? Hey man, break's over, okay?*

*

This week I went to Moseby's Playthings way down on Klapp Street to buy double-A batteries for my flashlight. The owners of Moseby's Playthings are a husband and wife named Walter and Sheila Moseby. You can tell right away that they are both very political. They even play the Rush Limbaugh radio show extra-loud on the toy store's sound system so that no one has to miss out on Rush's sage advice. Plus, they have a large toy gun section that I always browse because, even though I don't like guns, I secretly really like guns. My favorite gun sold in Moseby's Playthings is a gun that shoots candy. It can shoot Jnolly Ranchers or standard-issue marshmallows or even Hnershey's kisses. There's a picture on the box of a kid's birthday party where some beaming American dad is firing Hnershey's kisses into the open mouth of his son, the birthday boy. This kid on the box is wearing a pointy birthday hat and looks pretty much like a dork. His lips are smeared with chocolate from all of the Hnershey bull's-eyes that his dad has been hitting. And his eyes? That kid's eyes are peeled back wide in a look of almost religious ecstasy.

The main reason I sometimes fantasize about owning this candy gun is that I could shoot people I dislike while pretending that my real intention was to give them a gift.

This would allow me to shoot Karen without going to jail.

*It's a legit present*, I would explain. *From me to you. The gift of candy!*

*Ow*, Karen would say, rubbing the fresh bruise purpling on her arm flab.

*You're welcome!* I'd reply.

I have spoken with Mr. Moseby about the candy gun and he has informed me that the gun is being recalled by the manufacturers on the grounds that shooting plug-shaped objects into children's mouths is now regarded as a choking hazard by those fatcat regulators down in Washington.

*That's awful*, I told him.

*Yeah*, said Mr. Moseby. *Tell me about it. But I think me and Sheila are going to stand our ground on this one. Her cousin Steve's a lawyer and he said that even the candy guns should be covered under the Second Amendment.*

*Phew*, I said.

I don't really want to buy the candy gun. But I want it to stay where it is in Moseby's Playthings so that when I need to go buy batteries I can continue to fantasize about shooting Karen with it. Nothing really wrong with that, is there? Fantasizing about meaningless acts of pretend violence? I mean, really, is there anything actually wrong with that?

*

My boss at Yourmug is a guy named Maurice Bundy. Maurice is short but I guess he used to be kind of fat. Basically he had this little round potbelly. Skinny arms, skinny legs, but then a little round potbelly. On this potbelly Maurice had gotten an XL tattoo of an upside-down penguin with its orange feet tied to the strings of a rainbow-striped hot air balloon. Maurice showed it off the second or third time we met and explained that not only did the tattoo have nice symmetry, it also expressed the sentiment of a flightless bird finally becoming airborne.

*Oh,* I said, at the time.

The truth was that I didn't really care for the tattoo. It was a gaudy, clownish-looking penguin and, to my mind, represented exactly the sort of indelible mistake that ought to be harnessed for frightening America's youth. But I liked Maurice okay and I appreciated that this tattoo really mattered to him. It was one of the few things that could reliably make him happy.

Last year Maurice's doctor told him that he needed to lose some weight.

*This is life or death*, said the doctor. *Seriously Maurice, drop those pounds. Not tomorrow. Today. Get cracking.*

So Maurice went into crunch mode.

He exercised a lot.

53

He fasted during the holidays.

He bought some celebrity cleanse formula and shat out a bunch of weight.

For a while he smelled awful and then he started to smell better. His arms and legs grew nice, potato-shaped muscles. And, slowly but surely, Maurice's potbelly began to shrink.

Now, where Maurice's potbelly used to be there's just a bunch of loose skin. On Maurice's loose skin you can still make out the tattoo of the penguin and the hot air balloon.

The penguin looks miserable.

The hot air balloon looks deflated.

Its bright rainbow stripes are discolored and droopy.

Maurice still shows off the tattoo, but not as much. Even he realizes that without the potbelly, the tattoo no longer really makes sense.

Seeing that hot air balloon on Maurice's loose skin really bothers me for some reason. It reminds me of a windsock I saw once when there was no wind. It reminds me of a flaccid, iodine-colored body stocking. I have a lot of questions I would ask Maurice if he were not my boss. They relate primarily to tattoos, potbellies, decisions to lose weight, and sacrificing parts of who you are in order to live longer. Because without the potbelly, let's face it, Maurice isn't even really Maurice anymore. See what I mean? At least he's not the Maurice I met when I started working at Yourmug a year and a half ago. Not even close. It's amazing how you can take away one or two qualities from a person and they become almost completely pointless. The old Maurice is dead. His rotund charm is gone. And his clownish penguin is no longer even plausibly aloft.

Maurice has recently told me that he's considering getting the tattoo removed. The doctor told Maurice he probably bought himself another fifteen to twenty years with all the positive changes he's made in his lifestyle. Maurice sounds gloomy when he says that.

Like: *What am I going to do with all that extra time? Eat dinner salads?* I know that at some level, Maurice wishes he had his potbelly back. Really what Maurice wants is to go back in time to the era when he had three girlfriends without any of the girlfriends knowing about the other two. Those were the real heydays for Maurice Bundy. When he talks to me now that's what he really wants to tell me about.

*

Annie and I first met in the comments section of an online article about this new trend of people using their old analog camera baby snapshots as Fnacebook profile pictures. She was impressed by the manifesto-length screed that I had typed into the comments section. I had written so much because I was mixing a stiff rum-and-Booty with a moderate dose of benzodiazepines, because I had nothing better to do and because it was after four AM on a week night. My manifesto was against the creeping infantilization of Internet culture. In a sub-section labeled: *Say No To Womb Candy!* I argued that many, many, many aspects of Internet culture are poorly disguised attempts by the Global Infant Industry to recreate the atmosphere of a baby's crib beneath a truss of shiny objects spinning round and round.

*We raise our tiny fingers to wiggle-waggle upon the Sky Daddy's qwerty sparklebits, and for what?* I posed, perhaps rhetorically. *To return to a terminal state of wombish unthinking? To cloak ourselves in the ass-buttoned onesies of slavish obedience? Why else? Infantilization is the journey, creeping totalitarianism is the destination! And this, Internet, \*this\* is where we find ourselves: a netizenry of far-too-easily self-amused crib-slugs! Pathetic! Can we imagine the Founding Fathers using \*their\* baby pictures as Fnacebook profiles? Can we really imagine the Founding Fathers tickling their own feet in such a self-indulgently tacky way? What about the Emperors of Rome? Or the Vikings? Hell no! No horncapped Viking berserker would ever stoop to such a humiliation! Wake up, Internet! You are a baby no longer!*

This, as most good Internet comments-section rants are wont to do, went on for a while and got pretty nonsensical and repetitive. I declared that I, for one, do not want to see our Internet's cultural clickbait reduced to some kind of drooling stroller-parade. *Down with false innocence! Nothing is true*, I typed, feeling as if such a declaration might add a certain roguish credulity to my overall thesis.

*The baby is a lie.*

*The kitten is a lie.*

*As much as any unicorn: a lie!*

*Even Fnacebook itself is a lie!*

*A wonderful lie! That's the only reason we believe it!*

*But please, forego the baby pictures. Is that really so hard to ask?*

My eyes were half-closed. My jaw slack.

I couldn't really tell whether or not I could feel my own face.

My face couldn't feel my own face, that much I was sure of. I could sense that I was making a lot of minor-or-perhaps-not-so-minor spelling errors. Should I care? If so, how much? I stopped typing to fret over my semicolons. Then I worried that I had perhaps underused my exclamation points or my Caps Lock key. Whatever. I posted.

Annie Liked it.

She was still up. Annie? Annie who?

Four AM on a weeknight. She messaged me.

We chatted about how babies are gross. She said she thought babies always look pukey even when they aren't literally puking. I said that babies always remind me that I will probably die alone. She said that's morbid. I said I know I'm a morbid person who is constantly saying morbid things at inappropriate times. Like this one.

*Really I can't help it*, I said.

*Rrrrowr*, she said.

*That's hot*, she said. *I have a thing for morbid guys.*

I asked for her number. Texted. She came by the house later that week.

So there's a new tagger in town. I know this because whoever it is recently tagged over one of my longtime favorites in the alley behind Yourmug, which depicted a tall, blockheaded giantess crouched over a small mob of stick figures. The mob appeared distraught and wailing. *Wail all you want to,* I would think, whenever I looked at it. *Go on and wail. See what good it does you. You fools!*

That alley, which stretches halfway between Colling and the offices of The Velton Eagle on Klapp Street, is about as piece-of-shit as alleys get in a small town like Velton. There's a big gray electrical transformer mounted on a rickety platform above a few puddles of viscous, yucky-looking water. This little alley is always abundant with water. Sitting water. Standing water. Running water. Thinking water. I think strong thoughts at the water and can feel the water catching them, holding them, warping them, thinking back my thoughts at me. Reflection. Phryptolage. Among the waters there's one mega-puddle that I call Erliss Jr. after the old Erliss Pond back in Toulous. Erliss Pond was pretty near where I grew up and on weekends Mike and I used to go down to its banks and walk around and around when we couldn't find anything better to do, which was basically always.

When I stand above Erliss Jr. in the little alley behind Yourmug and The Velton Eagle I can see my body's reflection as a mute wraith, a figure faded with out-of-focus blurs and pinched Giacometti isthmus-joints. For a second the ghostface of Jibjab the Koala-

Headed Man swims back into view from another reality, and I watch as he fists eucalyptus leaves, sobbing his adorable sobs and raising his furry arms above his head in a gesture of ineffable, cosmic surrender. Suddenly I begin to moisten up a little, a spontaneous gleek of empathy. From why? From how? *Poor Miranda. Poor Jibjab.*

Then when I look again Jibjab is gone, back to someone else's puddle-underface. Erliss Jr. goes on seeping down slowly into the harborage cracks and little ant-bunkers tucked away beneath the cement. Seep. Seep. Seeeeeeeeeeeeeeeeeep. His jaw is edged in a beard of shallow gravel, traced across with wisps of a lacquerous bluegreen rot. This bluegreen must have some kind of nefarious organic chemistry afoot, as it seems to be eating away at the base wood of two nearby telephone poles.

Erliss Jr., menace to society.

Erliss Jr., public safety hazard.

In the harsh Iowan wintertimes he freezes up hard. Cracks out like a fat lip. People slip on him, twist their ankles. Erliss Jr. I look down and smile. Look at him smiling back. My water. That's nice. Isn't that nice?

*

Ricardo told me that a group of Amish people moved into the old Jenner house at the end of his block, near Burlingham intersects with Gottlieb. Mr. Jenner moved his family to Western Australia to keep him company while he becomes a wealthy copper mining magnate. For months their house has been on the market, sign out front, empty.

Then, just this week someone came by in a horse-and-buggy to drop the Amish people off. Ricardo sounded pretty excited telling me about it. I guess it's not every day you see a horse-and-buggy on your own block. Ricardo had watched as the Amish unloaded four wooden butter churns. Then, he watched as they had swept the front porch using those old-fashioned brooms that look like they're bundles of twigs tied together. How about that?

*That's interesting*, I said when Ricardo had finished. *I wonder if Albert knows about it.*

Albert Magnus is a friend of ours who makes pornography. His grandfather was an enterprising con artist and moonshiner who went around collecting royalties from well-known musicians on the utterly spurious assertion that he had invented the four-four time. Clearly, that kind of enterprising spirit runs strong in the grandson, too. To make his kind of pornography, Albert needs only three ingredients: a camera, a penis and a girl who will do more or less what Albert says.

For a camera, Albert uses his phone.

For a penis, Albert uses his own.

For a willing girl, Albert uses Crnaigslist.

He started doing this when he was in the tenth grade and has more or less kept going with it on an uninterrupted and highly lucrative basis. He's even had offers to get involved in more serious stuff. But Albert always says that he isn't interested.

*I've got something that works,* says Albert.

*Why mess with success?*

You never see Albert's face in the videos, which keeps things open for Albert to one day run for President of the United States. These Oval Office ambitions are Albert's Plan B if he can't find a way to establish the territorially autonomous Nation of Albert, which he has been drafting utopian blueprints for since age seven.

Albert's favorite place to make pornography is in the changing room of the local mall's JC Pnenny where he has been caught twice. He sometimes brags that he's one blowjob away from a JC Pnenny lifetime ban.

*What?* said Ricardo. *You mean we should tell Albert so he can start making his penis videos with the Amish girl? That's terrible!*

*Why do you think the Amish people moved into the house in the first place,* I asked Ricardo. *Maybe they wanted a taste of something new.*

*Well I don't think being in Albert's penis videos was exactly at the top of their list,* said Ricardo, looking exasperated.

Ricardo and I sat in silence for a few moments. I thought about what Ricardo had said, trying to figure out why he was wrong.

*The truth is,* I began, *that neither of us really know why the Amish people moved into the old Jenner house.*

*You're probably right. But the fact of the matter is: we just don't know. I don't know. You don't know. Neither of us know. It's an unlikely reason to move into a new neighborhood, sure. But the fact is that we have no idea what their motivations were. So let's not rule anything out, okay?*

*

Officially Velton's population is about thirty thousand people when Velton State's in session, but you'd never believe it since most of these people live in outlying subdivisions somewhere between the town proper and the Interstate. Twice a day they clog Colling and Delaney Streets with their station wagons picking up and dropping off at Colling Elementary and Velt County Day schools, but otherwise are rarely seen downtown. These are the type of people for whom the word *home* is profoundly meaningful. Ha. What losers.

Sitting on the lip of my stump in Houch Park I narrow my eyes over the Magnus Building at Burlingham and Colling, the Magnus Building with its stupid wine bar and its stupid Stempler's Roast, Stempler's Roast with its stupid-faced Dion and stupid-faced Meagan and stupid-faced Ariadne who always end up beating me and Annie and Ricardo and Belicia and Tina at the Ugly's bar trivia night even when we play with Albert on our team, Albert who has not only has memorized an encyclopedic list of all the fictional, historical and Internet-famous Alberts but has also the names of the state capitals pretty much down pat, even, like both Carolinas and the Dakotas which I, despite strenuous efforts, can absolutely never keep straight. So how is it possible that the stupid-faced Stempler's Roast crew keeps on swanning their way to eleventh hour trivia victories?

Well, ever since Bryce took over doing trivia at the Ugly things have gotten a little lopsided because Bryce basically despises Albert (something about a girl, I think I remember Ricardo telling me) and so purposefully chooses topics related to crocheting or yoga positions or Justin Bieber's hairstyle that of course the Stempler's Roast crew are going to have an absolute trivia-monopoly on, no question, especially during Final Trivia when it's basically everyone throwing out their best wager-it-all for a Hail Mary. And even when Albert doesn't play with us Bryce still ends up throwing out softballs at Stempler's Roast because, that's what he spends all of his prep time getting ready for, just in case Albert shows up. Grrrr, that shit really steams my clams. Bryce is basically the sole reason why our team's bar trivia record is so atrocious, that and because, as Tina puts it, we all absolutely refuse to stoop to the level of learning even a modicum of what's taken the Stempler's Roast crew a lifetime of self-congratulatory tweeness to master.

*Don't try to out-asshat an asshat,* as Mike would say. *No one wins. Not even the ass wins.*

\*

When the IRS came to arrest the Mosebys for a decade of poorly concealed tax evasion the armed standoff made regional headlines. Everyone and their mom was posting about it on Fnacebook. The Velton Eagle ran a series of cringeworthy headlines in the vein of *For Local Merchant's Tax Dodging, Playtime Is Over* and *Moseby's Playthings to IRS: Don't Toy With Us,* hoping that people would post links out of pure exasperation. Which, as a readership strategy, totally worked. Hell, I posted a link. #gratwit from *Ideas for Words* and tagged Marnie in it. She Liked it, off wherever she was, posted a gif of some 90s rom-com starlet rolling her eyes. Someone was on location at the Mosebys' Tudor-style house, live-streaming the standoff, posting updates from behind the police line. That morning I managed to take little five-and-ten-second breaks from my line of dark roast pour-overs to watch the real-time action on my phone. I was stoked. Even though I like Mr. and Mrs. Moseby and don't want them to get killed or go to prison. But yeah, totally stoked. This was all just way too real to miss.

Mr. Moseby claimed that he and Mrs. Moseby had a hostage. The IRS agent was a man named Lewis Purcell, an older black man with a chin beard trimmed to sharp right angles. He traveled with a maroon-colored megaphone and a Smith & Wesson 9mm side-arm. Lewis Purcell had arrived on the scene with the support of the local sheriff's office. They had the Mosebys' house pretty much surrounded.

Lewis Purcell bellowed through the megaphone that he was not born yesterday.

Lewis Purcell bellowed that he meant business.

Lewis Purcell bellowed that it would be a real shame if anyone were to trifle with him or other members of law enforcement, say, by faking a hostage crisis.

*No one's going anywhere*, he bellowed. *What, do you think you're the first tax freeloaders I'm bagging up? Is that what you think?*

Purcell smirked, turning to the deputies. Then he turned back to do some more bellowing: *What's the alleged name of this alleged hostage? Huh?*

Purcell waited. Purcell flicked the maroon-colored megaphone on and off with his thumb. The sheriff's men rested their buttoned-up navy blue guts on the white hoods of the three Crown Victorias that were pulled up into a tight semicircle in front of the Mosebys' well-mowed lawn.

Mr. Moseby yelled out: *Er, yeah. She's —*

*There is no goddamn hostage,* roared Purcell, flecks of spit jumping up from his teeth like spawning salmon up a waterfall. Purcell's eyes bugged out. You could tell he was thoroughly enjoying this.

*We already know there's no goddamn hostage! You morons! Ever heard of a little thing called thermal imaging? Oh and by the way, don't think for a second that you're gonna pull any of that self-righteous patriotic tax-dodge bullshit on me. You're on the wrong side of history.*

*Don't like paying taxes?*

*Go live in a shittier country!*

*Don't use our roads!*

*Don't use our schools!*

*Don't expect emergency professionals to come running when you have to dial 911. And never, I mean \*never\* refer to yourself as a patriot. Because you are actively undermining all of the men and women who put their lives on the line to make this country great. Who are those men and women? I am one of them. These officers are, too.*

*So:*

*do*

*not*

*fuck*

*with*

*me!*

Purcell screamed each of these last words as if they were gunshots. By the end his voice was high and ragged. When Purcell had finished the officers burst into a smattering of supportive applause. There was silence for a second, before Mr. Moseby yelled shakily back:

*So they've got you falling for that Big Government line, huh? Ha! Ha-ha! Ha-ha-ha! Don't you get it? Federal debt is the new American slavery! And you, tax man, you're just a slavemaster's pawn in the government's —*

Purcell raised the maroon-colored megaphone to drown out Mr. Moseby.

*Hey asshat,* said Purcell: *I! don't! care! Now there's an easy way. And there's a hard way. Your call, okay?*

Mr. and Mrs. Moseby haggled with Purcell for another twenty or thirty minutes, inventing variously contradictory details about the nonexistent hostage. Mr. Moseby yelled some things about Waco and Ruby Ridge. Purcell just leaned back and laughed into his maroon-colored megaphone.

One of the bigger officers was sent for coffee and he came back with an assortment of pastries. Purcell chose for himself a raspberry Danish. He loved a good Danish during standoffs. Agent Lewis Purcell wasn't in any hurry.

Mr. Moseby considered taking a shot but then didn't. He must have thought about how long he and his wife could go to prison for. Mr. Moseby had never really hurt anyone in his life. How long would they be locked up for shooting an IRS agent, anyway? Mr. Moseby thought about becoming a martyr for American liberty. But in the end he just laid down his weapons and came out. He and Sheila and no hostage.

*See,* I yelled to Karen, who was in the back of Yourmug warming up a sandwich. *No hostage, after all. Did I not totally call that?*

*You did not totally call that,* yelled Karen back at me. *At least not to me. When did you say anything about there being no hostage?*

*You're all the same,* said Purcell, as he cuffed Mr. Moseby with a little laugh of contempt. *You talk a big game. But you always come out. See, you're smart. You have way too much to lose.*

*Go to hell,* said Mr. Moseby.

Purcell shook his head.

*You know,* he said. *I'd like it if just one time you maniacs went through with it. Went all the way. I'd be here, just waiting. I'd take you out. Pow-pow! Two in the head. I wouldn't lose a night's sleep over it. Really, I wouldn't.*

*You federal scum are what's wrong with this country,* snarled Mr. Moseby, through gritted teeth. *All you goddamn takers. Have you ever owned a business? Made an honest buck in your goddamn life?*

*Really,* said Purcell, smiling. *Really, I wouldn't.*

\*

The afternoon in the windows of the Ugly Bar grew old too quickly and I'm already mostly drunk. Ricardo stands up and knocks his hands together *knick-knock* and says *Aight I'm out, homie* and I mumble something stupid back like *Fade ya later alligator* and since then I haven't even budged a millimeter or bothered to register my aloneness as much as I guess I'd never really registered Ricardo's presence, returning each line of his jokey speech with some half-handed question and swinging what's left of my voice painfully around the Ugly's noisy atmosphere, like a clown playing tennis with a broken arm.

*Chkraggh,* I clear my throat, sniff heavily, lick the last drops from the dregs of my pint glass as the Internet jukebox careens into power chords, into animal screams, into low footprints of indigo tracked across my sightline, low feels of some enigmatic exhaustion that forms my slazzerweak grip upon the moment. Today's a slow drunk because it's Tuesday, because on Tuesday I do a slow drunk until midnight when (theoretically) I will get paid. Bryce lets my tab go til midnight and at midnight I refresh the browser window on my mobile banking app and miraculously I'll have money and then I can go to the ATM and settle my tab at the Ugly. But now it's still barely nine and I have three hours here until I get paid, until I can pay and leave and sleep.

Across the room my gaze travels over to where Dion from the Stempler's Roast is shooting pool with one of the hostesses at Dodd's who I've never met but who looks a little bit like Stacey as in Brent and Stacey and for a moment I wonder if she knows, if she's Fnacebook friends with Stacey, what she thinks about the upcoming wedding situation. Or are they already married by now? I don't know, I guess. I guess I've really been losing track of time lately. My mind darkens to that dusty Claude glass of introspection as a familiar set of questions float across my insides: *Why am I here? Not just here, alone, but in Velton, alone. What am I doing with my life? Huh? Pull it together, Elwood. You need to straighten yourself out!*

I burp. Bryce brings me another beer, nodding. Knowing the drill. The thing about drinking to keep in mind, I think, is that regardless of situation it's only something I that do myself. Meaning: no one else forces me to drink. I do it. And usually I do it alone. Now maybe I feel some kind of way about that, maybe I'm bored of all the other hours in the day and so drinking's just a way to feel interesting again, or maybe what I really want is to feel like I'm full of so many invincible tomorrows that trashing one more won't matter.

69

*Shot on the house, if you're feeling so inclined. Irish. Gal at the end there changed her mind on it.*

*Ha. Sure. I'll be so inclined.*

To me a phrase like *so inclined* is a perfect example of an antimetaphor. I mean, gravity does reliable work, doesn't it? The ground inside me always feels tilted upward and/or downwards. Just pour something in and you can watch which way it rolls. Up, you hope. *Make me feel not-dead-like-I-always-feel,* you think. I think. And then I feel it rolling down. Down, down down. Shit. Drinking like this, with these questions: I always start thinking in the second person, as if I'm trying to teach myself some kind of lesson in casual, introspective agony. Drinking in the second person. *No one makes you drink like this. You can go home any time. After midnight. What you are is a slope. Any liquid knows how to follow the logic of a slope. Up or down. And like any slope, you'll soon begin to feel yourself sculpted by the flow of so much not-water running down down down.*

*Another?* Another voice. Stupid-faced Bryce. I give him a big, grimacing smile. *Sure.* I order another. Why not? What else am I even doing? Tomorrow's my day off, isn't it? But the truth is that these questions, like the fifth beer on a Tuesday at the Ugly, alone in a half-empty bar in a half-empty town, well, they are placeholders for something that I wish I had and don't, something that I've never had and maybe never will, something that another two-dollar beer is neither going to find nor replace. No one watches me or clicks on me or Likes me drinking beer and watching rom-com re-runs on the TV at the Ugly. No one. And no one makes me keep thinking about the fact that I can't stop thinking about the teeth-grinding maudlinness of my own highly uncompelling biography, Karen and Maurice, Mike and Cynthia, Tina and Ricardo and Annie. Shit. I look down into my beer and scent the tell-tale odor of eucalyptus and right there I see it, floating just beneath the bubbly yellowamberness: the unblinking eye of Jibjab staring back at me, his long koala eyelashes glistening with that torn-soul rush of loss and feeling. Lift. Drink. Glug. *Goodbye, Jibjab!* My tongue rolls a lump, like what I've swallowed is actually a koala eyeball instead of just a mouthful of beer. Inside the folds of my throat I can feel my incline, my incline rolling the marsupial cornea of beeriness down, rolling me, rolling me down inside. I am he: tears of Jibjab crying cold down the back of my throat. Shit.

I pull out my phone and think about texting Annie. I compose a couple *wharu?-* style queries and then delete all of them, sending none. I don't really want to see her when I'm like this. I hear Mike's voice saying: *It's not exactly your best self we're working with here, is it?* That voice, that voice of Mikey-Mike drifts back to me and I realize that over the years we've spent apart his voice has become my second person, that he's the voice I think *you* to myself in when I'm drinking in my second person. Shit, is that accurate? How is it that I've never noticed that all my thoughts come wrapped in the richness of the voices of my childhood friends? Another sound-only memory comes drifting back, this one of Mike reciting poetry. We're maybe in fourth or fifth grade and he used to know all these old poems, Wordsworth and Coleridge and Dickinson and Poe, and although *Annabel Lee* was always my favorite I'm remembering this other one, also by Poe, actually shit, was it called *For Annie*? It was, wasn't it? Slouching low on my bar stool I let the memory wash over me, following my incline down in the eighth notes of old Edgar Allen's meter: *And oh! of all tortures / That torture the worst / Has abated — the terrible / Torture of thirst, / For the naphthaline river / Of Passion accurst: — / I have drank of a water that quenches all thirst.*

I pull out my phone and look at #thatstumplife. Only twenty-one measly Likes! Shit. And what time is it? One thirteen AM. Shit, I could have left over an hour ago! Rising unsteadily to my feet I open my web browser app and reload my mobile banking window, type in the password, making sure that the money's actually there before I stumble over to the ATM. It is.

Yay.

Woot.

Win.

*

*Dear Buttface,*

*I know it's been awhile and I wish I'd written to you earlier but, well, I didn't write you earlier.*

*So it's been awhile.*

72

*My bad on that.*

*There's a lot I can't tell you, even though I'd like to tell you everything.*

*For example I'd like to tell you that I'm 100% alright but I'm also not alright and we know each other well enough for you to not believe me unless I told you something was wrong because there's always something wrong with me, isn't there? Which is why, even though I'm so very curious to hear from you, I cannot give you a return address.*

*On the bright side, I now feel good about life like I haven't ever felt good ever before and maybe this good feeling is why I'm writing you, finally, after all this time.*

*But enough about me! How's life in Velton, baby brother? The Fnacebooks tell me that you're seeing a person named Annee Bunanee which I assume means her real name is Annie Something? Tell her your sister says she's a total babe. I mean, if that's the kind of thing you'd think she'd like to hear. Is* babe *still a thing people say? I'm now realizing that I have no idea what the hip lingo is. Actually it's kind of liberating. No longer shall I even pretend to care!*

*What else? Well, I must tell you about the mountains. The mountains here are everywhere, mountains growing from the tops of houses, from the tops of trees, from the tops of heads and knit caps with ear flaps, mountains growing from the morning vapors that gather and then burn off under the rays of sun. There are so many ways the indescribableness of the mountains gets stuck down inside*

73

me. Sometimes when it's still dark I go walking down to the foot of the nearest mountain and touch right where the rock starts rising up. Right where the mountain begins. It's so impossibly tall. Then I taste the air and it's as sharp as a far-off whistle and I think back to Toulous and okay I do get a little homesick sometimes, especially for you and Angela, Jody, too and Dad, of course. But right now the most important feeling to me is being away and not knowing if I'll ever come back.

Here's a quick little story: near to where Ai and me are staying there's an ancient mountain that was terraced by the Indians and when the Spanish came the Indians rolled big stones down and crushed the Spanish and kept them out that way, just rolling these big stones down the mountain. Then, one day the Indians ran out of stones. The Spanish came up and killed them all. The end.

I don't know why I wanted to tell you this, but I think there's something there. Maybe I just wanted to give you some sisterly advice, something about not running out of stones in high places.

Sending my love, Ai's too,

- C ⚓ Sore

My head is pounding as I read and re-read the letter and then fold it in half on the wooden tabletop in the kitchen. Sitting there for a second I hear something snap and then the wall clock falls, *crash!* just like that. Ugh. Piece of shit. I examine the fastening on the clock's back. Just my luck. The hanger nail is broken.

*

Today Ricardo and I decide it might be a fun to make a fake Fnacebook group for Jews. A Fnacebook troll, as the kids call it these days. First, we will make the group. Then, once we get a bunch of Jews in one big Fnacebook group, then boom, we'll really have some fun with them!

For a few minutes Ricardo and I just sit on the couch and watch TV. What we are watching is a beverage ad featuring two tall, lanky NBA players, one black, one white. The beverage is some kind of fizzy energy drink that the NBA players are trying to sell us by stacking cans of it on a black woman's ass while she faces away from the camera. The energy drink is called Booty and it comes in Jigglin' Jujube, Poppin' Piña Colada and Klappin' Kiwi. Once the cans are stacked up the woman turns her head to give the camera a long-lashed glockenspiel wink before thrusting into an unbelievably massive, slow-motion twerk. This twerk ends up catapulting the three cans of Booty literally through the ad studio roof (graphics-wise we've seamlessly entered CGI fantasyland) and sends them rocketing up through Earth's stratosphere and beyond. When the Booty cans reach deep space they each acquire a flaming comet tail and beeline towards a very hip-looking personification of the Sun, who grabs ahold of all three flavors and empties their fizzy fluid into his happily goateed mouth. The hip-looking Sun proceeds to gulp down all three cans of Booty only to be suddenly overwhelmed by the intensity and extreme-ness of the flavor experience. Unable to handle *the power of so much Booty* (voice-over reverbing) the hip-looking Sun spasms

75

into supernova, destroying much of the known solar system in a hip-looking shockwave. The camera then cuts to a close-up of the black woman's face. (No explanation given as to how she may have survived the planetary destruction of Earth, but okay, whatever). As the camera pulls back we see that she is now lying undressed, her curves majestically hidden beneath a grape-hued silk coverlet. On either side of her stretches an equally semi-nude NBA player, grinning and looking happily post-coital. The woman smirks mischievously at the camera as the silvery ad text pulverizes the frame's lower half: *Can you even handle this Booty?*

*Fuck*, says Ricardo, glancing down at his hands. *These ads are getting worse and worse.*

At least by this time I've got everything rigged up for me and Ricardo to troll hard on some Fnacebook Jews. Ricardo's older brother works in a phone store and so he's brought a little plastic baggie full of borrowed SIM cards so that we'll be able to verify each fake Fnacebook account we make by phone. He's also brought over three extra blank phones just in case we need the extra firepower which, combined with our personal phones and the three browsers on our laptops will allow us to be signed in from eleven unique accounts at once. More than enough access points for today's trolly purposes. We create and name our group *The Real Jews of Fnacebook*. Simple name. Ricardo makes a profile featuring the kind of Fnacebook Jew we imagine other Fnacebook Jews wish they were friends with, or at least wish they were Fnacebook friends with.

Thad Hurwitz.

Thad is a smiley, hirsute go-getter with a knowing wink and a strong jawline. His interests include intramural lacrosse, beer pong and Israel.

We put up some pictures up that show Thad arm in arm with other Jews looking chummy and convivial. Both the pictures of Thad and his cohort are pulled from the Tumblr of a Jewish fraternity branch at a small Canadian liberal arts college. You'd have to really dig to make the connection. We give Thad a fictional fiancé named Rachel Kuenzel. Rachel's profile pics and obligatory drinking-with-friends snapshots I lift from the Instagrnam of a Serbian shoe model whose social media activity conveys a strong lack of English. Again, you'd really have to dig.

On the other two devices we link accounts for a Dan Cohen and an Eric Cafritz, who we agree will be the fictional AE Pi fraternity brothers of the fictional Thad Hurwitz. Dan and Eric seem affable and inoffensive, putzy yes-men who will Like anything that Thad posts. Thad and Rachel are the perfect young Jewish couple; affluent, hip and fun-loving, the kind of Jews who don't make a big deal about God or bacon. Our Real Jews group now has four fake members. Ricardo and I high-five. It's time to bring in the bots.

At the time of this writing (May, 2016) somewhere between 49 and 131 million Fnacebook accounts are fake, e.g. controlled by bots. If you believe estimates that year after year the number of fake Fnacebook users hovers between three and eight percent of total then the actual number is likely somewhere around 90 million. Which is kind of crazy, once you really start to really think about it. That, like, the fake population of Fnacebook surpasses the real population of many countries. France, for instance. Possibly Mexico. There are enough fake people on Fnacebooks to populate at least three African Chads. Possibly up to nine African Chads. One can only imagine what the geopolitics of Africa would look like with that many Chads. These accounts were created by so-called *click farms* in order to help social media marketing departments peddle Likes. Because Likes on Fnacebook have become a valuable metric for measuring the performance of corporate branding initiatives. Many of those Likes are done through these fake accounts via what are essentially tech-savvy marketing grifts.

Many bot accounts have profile pictures of scantily clad women. That's no accident either. And thus, it's not uncommon for these fake account to accumulate many real (mostly male) Fnacebook Friends. Because if you're some poor shmuck clicking away your life through Fnacebook and a scantily clad woman offers to be your Fnacebook Friend, well, who are you to say no? Right? Exactly. And bots love being invited to groups, because, well, they pretty much love everything.

Our Real Jews group goes from four members to 148 with bots that Ricardo and I select mostly on the basis of sexy profile pictures. Then we have Thad add some content: a *Welcome to The Real Jews of Fnacebook* group moderator post, a *7 Ways You Know*

*That You're A Real Jew* quiz (linked from one of those endlessly unoriginal list-and-quiz websites), plus a ludicrous and largely incoherent guide to Yiddish emoji. Dan Cohen and Eric Cafritz Like all of Thad's posts. They comment things like *haha* and *yassss*. They seem happy to support Thad's social media outgoingness. Rachel posts a toothsome selfie with #Proud2BeARealJew in magenta spritzed across the bottom. Dan Cohen follows with one of his own, also in magenta.

*LOL* Eric Cafritz makes fun of that one and Rachel calls him a copy-cat. The bots Like. They post some winky emoticons. Ricardo and I high-five. *This, my friend, is Fnacebook banter.* We've worked up a nice little lather. Our Real Jews group is finally ready to troll. I search Fnacebook's directory using a list of common Jewish last names pulled off Gnoogle and Ricardo and I use our fake accounts to start inviting the real Jews. In under an hour we go from 148 fake members to 310 total members. Eric Cafritz posts a Real Jew Story about a recent JnDate experience and urges others to share their own JnDate experiences. Haha, right?

Thad Likes it, Shares it. Shares his own.

Eric, Dan and twenty bots Like it. The real members start posting their own content. Loosening up. Liking. Sharing.

Our sexy bots start getting chatted up. Uncapitalized epistles of the 'ohai cool pic' or 'so where r u from' variety. Ricardo handles the nervous suitors. Keeping our bots coy, our horny interlocutors feeling uncertainly reciprocated. Spurning the creeps in exactly the way that the creeps would expect to be spurned. Keeping up appearances. Keeping the real users typing. A group of newcomers who seem possibly related (Miles, Dylan, and Evan Kirschenbaum) start posting memes that substitute the faces of rabbis with cats. They call this #RabbiMeow. Content has really started pouring in. Ricardo stands up, complaining that he's getting carpal tunnel. I tell him to stop being such a fucking baby. We re-rig his laptop's extension so that he can control twenty bot accounts simultaneously using a Master-Slave protocol. When Ricardo's Dan Cohen Likes a post, twenty other accounts Like the same post. To keep us flying under the radar, our Master-Slave protocol operates on a time-delay of seven seconds that increases by one second after each subsequent Like, a runsum of 7,8,9,10...26 that completes in five and a half minutes (330 seconds). Every runsum cycle Ricardo increases the number of slave accounts by five, creating the perception that more and more active users are signing onto the group, co-stimulating actions by the number of real invitees. It's like watching one can-can dancer pilot a marionette of twenty mannequins who are waterfalling their can-can legs one after the other after the other. It's amazing how well this actually works. And on Fnacebook, Ricardo's Phnotoshopped bots are more vivacious and titillating than any can-can dancing mannequin might be.

So far our Real Jews seem to be having a good time. By early evening Ricardo and I have polished off the better part of a twelve-pack of PBR, listened to all the newest Ghnostly and XXL Frneshmen tracks and grown our Real Jews of Fnacebook group to just over a thousand, 800 of whom are most likely real. Inside the group a community atmosphere reigns. A father posts pics of his son's pet rabbit wearing a yarmulke. Some Jewish mom-types fawn and dawwww. A twentysomething cocktail waitress shares a recipe for a version of the Cosmo martini that involves Mnanischewitz. Lots of Likes for that one. A mohel posts a link advertising his services, *All Sizes Welcome!* Snarking. I'm getting a little dizzy from all the beer so I go microwave some Krnaft Mac'n'Cheese and me and Ricardo slam it down in heaping, Sriracha-covered spoonfuls. Our lips sting and glisten spicy red. I use Thad Hurwitz's account to post a playful chain letter-style come-on: If You're Really A Real Jew Invite 5 Other Real Jews RN!!!!!! (RN stands for Right Now in Internet-ese). Membership explodes.

By eight PM EST we have crossed the 5,000 member milestone. A blog called Jew Eye For The Gentileguy posts a couple of screenshots of our Fnacebook group activity, the blogger wryly wondering aloud what, exactly, determines a *Real Jew*? Nevertheless the post gets re-blogged by J-O-O and Jewvenilia and even a blog called Jewnteenth, a site for North American black Jews who are honestly a demographic neither Ricardo nor I had even anticipated existing.

The Jewnteenthers join in droves, a few of the younger ones posting selfies hashtagged #RealestJewsofFnacebook, pics cornered in digital rhinestones and virtual Shabbat bling. A couple Jews for

Jesus try to join and I have Thad give them the boot to widespread Real Jew approval and some genuinely nasty sniping. Our Real Jews close ranks, kvetching with relief and satisfaction. The list of people waiting for admin approval to Join grows and grows. We can't keep up. A discussion begins governing group bylaws and I make Thad appoint some of the Kirchenbaums to admin positions. Membership pushes past 12,000 and requests to Join show no sign of slowing down.

Thad Hurwitz finally resigns to an admin Emeritus, lets the Kirchenbaums take the reins. Subgroups are formed. A steering committee. Several members announce plans for a Real Jews meet-up near Bayonne. Another posts about an upcoming Birthright journey to Israel, asking if anyone has a couch to crash on the night before his flight out of Newark. They most certainly do.

*Thx Real Jews!!! Real Jews 4 lyfe!!*

Ricardo begins de-activating the sexy bots one by one, leaving only the handful with 100+ in-group friends. Those can still prove useful later on. The others won't be necessary. Now we have it, thousands of Real Jews, right in front of us. A perfect troll. Over on the kitchen table I watch as the fallen wall clock hands close in on midnight.

I glance over at Ricardo and slip him a tired grin. Our fingers and thumbs are cramped and sore from all the Liking. My eyes ache. His eyes look somehow both tired and wired. Screenburnt. Glowburnt. Standing up I feel and the blood rushing to my head, to my face, to my forehead, to pool in the back of my throbbing eyes. It fuzzes out the bare walls of my living room, the TV where that same Booty commercial is on its 30th+-ish replay.

*Can you handle this Booty*, I ask.

He gives me one of those shut-the-fuck-up looks.

*Now what?* I say. *Ready to fuck with some Jews?*

Ricardo shrugs.

*I don't know, man*, he says. *What were we even going to do, anyway?*

I shrug. What were we going to do? I have literally no idea. Huh. Maybe the group itself was the troll, after all.

*

*What DC comics superhero is also a city in the nation of Turkey, that's Turkey, as in the Thanksgiving gobblers, Turkey as in why-did-Constantinople-get-the-works, and folks we are looking for the name or the superhero, just the name, nothing else, okay that's one, one or two words, yup okay we'll keep it going for ten more seconds, ten more seconds then please, please bring up your papers for our trivia's lightning round to conclude...okay, ten...nine...*

Bryce's countdown echoes in my head the next morning at Yourmug, as clear as any temple bell's ka-bong-oooooooooong. Recalling the panic of not-knowing. Of looking around and across the Ugly to where Dion's smug, plumcheeked little grin was nodding along to the shimmer of Ariadne's tinsely-blonde bangs nodding along right back. Of the shadows cast by soiled neon on the woodgrain of our little table. Of Bryce's irritating-voiced countdown running out the time. *Turkey? Superhero?* I lean forward against the counter behind Yourmug's iPnad cash register with my arms folded across my chest, feeling my pulse at the inner crook of my left arm and watching out the window as the street performs a vibrant thesaurus entry on the word walking; striding, moseying, sidling, jaunting, sauntering, even slightly skipping, buoyant movements of bodies young and old, lawyers and shopkeepers and joggers and dogwalkers, beverage delivery personnel handcarting boxes the long way around to the loading docks of Dodd's or the Ugly, students in giddy twos and threes tromping up the hill towards the Magnus Building or crossing down to the corner of Colling and Delaney where there's now this little shopping pavilion squeezed in next to Bule's Theater or else walkrunning down towards the cluster of classroom buildings that form the sole quad of Velton State, glancing down at their phones, thumbing furiously at one another's faces through their screens. Why the fuck had I said *Catwoman?*

*Catwoman*, I blurted out, caught in the heat of the moment, the rush of bar trivia filling my veins and because no one had anything better, well, down it went, Annie nodding seriously as if saying: *okay, that's not what I would have said, Elwood, but I trust you, don't we all trust you?* even as my head was already shaking, shaking no, shaking no that absolutely cannot be the name of a city in Turkey, no city in Turkey would be named Catwoman, thus very obviously satisfying only half of the trivia clue's requirement and being, well, I guess not necessarily worse than nothing but certainly not much better and, couldn't we please think of something just a little bit more plausible? Especially given that a superheroes question ought to be an easy win for us, a gift from Bryce versus the loathsome Stempler's Roast crew during this, the crucial midway *lightning round* of bar trivia but no, Annie didn't stop writing, didn't stop folding even as Ricardo muttered *Catwoman? Really?*

Shit. That was the moment I knew that there was no hope of winning, either the question or the round, and that not only had we lost but that I alone would bear the blame. I poked at a round knot in the heavily varnished wood of the bar table. I wanted the knot to open, to show me a drop-down menu, to allow me to navigate inside the table's secrets or at least to show me some folder icon names. Clickitch. Huh. I always get it during bar trivia, when we aren't allowed to have our phones out because Gnoogle/Wnikipedia, of course, are strictly verboten. Come to think of it, bar trivia might be the longest I'm away from my phone all week. Shit. Is that right? That can't be right. That's totally right. Well, except for sleeping. No, even including sleeping, that's totally right.

*

Up at the stump's edge of Houch Park I let my eyes linger on the shadows made by clouds, oval guerillas holding in their foxholes against the quickening violets of an imperial dawn. It's a little after five-thirty AM. There's a bird in the sky, maybe a red-tailed hawk. I watch it cut a loop above Clough Wilderness Area and head off to circle above the asterisk where the steeple of Second Methodist has burst the yolk of the sun, sending warm, eggy light scrambling over the streets of Velton. Sitting low I watch as the light washes over the Magnus Building and Yourmug and the alley behind the offices of The Velton Eagle. Oh dear old Yourmug, place of my weekly tirednesses, pregnant sighs, place of Karen's insufferable non-personality, burnt hands and coffee spills and my frequently incorrect change. When it comes to change of any kind, I find the guesstimation method most expedient. And this morning, well, even the dawning sky above Velton looks like a wrong guesstimation of change, the guesstimation of a large, tired person photographed so out of focus that not even their face is recognizable. Who could it be? I wonder if what the sky holds is in fact the face of all of us, the face of Velton, the face of this Podunk netherworld raised up in radiant swirls upon the distance. Wouldn't that be something? That if, at certain moments when no one happens to be looking skyward, this face reveals itself in a broad and knowing grin, grinning down over my shoulder into the lacquerous bluegreen waters of Erliss Jr., down into my little circus of trainwrecks, the world of Miranda falling and Jibjab weeping and the berserk ringmaster and the flashfried crowd videotaping their own crispification beneath the fingers of a hungry, waiting God.

The whole planet is visible now, visible from satellites stilled in deathly space, visible from cameras and street signs, from cars and hotel lobbies, from drones and the odd peeping of Doppler weather balloons. Where's left to hide our secrets, to hide the places where we keep our hoped-for worlds? Aside from my self-evident narcissism the reason I've always liked the reflections of Erliss Jr. is that I know he's hiding something, that all puddles conceal within their thin fold of microbial wateriness much more than they ever reveal. The inch below the reflection: it could still contain anything, couldn't it? For some reason I think about Mikey. *Anything?*

From the stump's lip I watch the dawn until when I glance down at my phone I realize that I'm actually late for work and have to text Karen *sry brt* before I hustle down Gottlieb towards Colling Street.

A bachelor party is waiting for us to open when I make it to open up at Yourmug. I guess it's the season for them. Karen's already there, just prepping away in the back.

The bachelor party looks like they've been up all night.

The bachelor party smells like they're very, very drunk.

They're sweaty, too.

One or two of them reeks of wet cigarettes.

Karen does a little mopping over a place where there had been a spill late yesterday. I tell her not to mop because the bachelor party could slip on it. She pretends not to hear me while furling a few strands of her reddish hair around an ear. As if to say, *did you just say something?*

I go to open the front door. This might be just about the glummest bachelor party I've ever seen.

*What's up fellas?* I say, as they slink in. *You folks look like you could really use some coffee. Come on in!*

The bachelors come in and order their coffee. One of them dejectedly prices a crumpet.

Thinks about it. Then sees no one else is getting baked goods.

Ixnay on the umpetcray. The bachelor apologizes for not ordering the crumpet, as if it's some kind of big deal to me. Him asking the price and then not ordering the crumpet after all.

*I have never cared*, I tell him truthfully.

The bachelors ignore Karen, who heads into the back to putter around. I yawn. It's still early.

I fix myself a cup of coffee. Two creams. Two sugars. I stir it with the handle of a stainless steel bottle opener. I listen to the bachelors talking.

There had been a stripper. The stripper had refused the bachelors advances. They had been told over the phone that they could pay extra for *more*.

None of them had ever had *more*, but they liked the sound of it. They had gathered several hundred dollars in the hopes of getting *more*.

They didn't know what it would be like. Maybe they would take turns?

But this stripper just plain refused.

Even after they offered outrageous sums, she refused.

Even after they tried to get her drunk, she refused.

But over the phone you said — they pleaded.

*Sorry*, said the stripper.

*Not in the mood*, said the stripper. *You must have got the wrong idea. And I never* never *do more than one at a time. Not how this works.*

*Really sorry*, the stripper had said. *Now who wants a nice striptease?*

The way the bachelors are making it sound now, the stripper was not sufficiently apologetic for refusing their advances.

*We shoulda just made her dooit*, one of the porkier bachelors keeps saying over and over. *We shoulda just made her dooit.*

Then the bachelors go outside and sit on the cement flight of steps leading up to Second Methodist across the street. I can see that they are still arguing. I can see that it's not going anywhere. Then all of a sudden I realize that the porky bachelor is Brent.

As in Brent and Stacey. Wow has he packed on the pounds! Jesus. No wonder he's still using that Fnacebook profile pic from like two years ago! I wonder why he didn't say hi to me just now? Probably he's way too out of it. I peer over across Colling Street. Boy, he really looks awful. Face like a raw steak.

For a moment this terrible gray feeling wells up in me.

I don't want to think about it. But I keep thinking about it.

I think about the picture Stacey posted on Fnacebook.

How Brent had Liked it. Winky-faced *and* smiley-faced it. How happy they had looked together. It's enough to make me go a little greasy-eyed.

Karen returns from her puttering around in the back.

*Did anyone slip*, she asks. The way she says it sounds catty, but I don't have anything readied in reply.

*No*, I say. *No one slipped.*

I sigh, heavily.

*

The main reason I liked Annie in the first place was that aside from her being clever and attractive in that bored, angsty sort of way I also thought she was genuinely desperate. That was how she seemed the first time we met, at least. Dry spelling. Cockhungry. Whatever you want to call it. If I had known she might ever break up with me I don't think I would have tried to date her in the first place. I mean okay, maybe I would have tried. But I would have also made an effort not to get, like, too emotionally involved. When it comes to other people, saying that I'm guarded would be strong bet for Gold in the Intergalactic Understatement Olympics. Most people I can't fucking stand. I don't like myself very much, either. Who would? I often cannot avoid making situations incredibly awkward.

There are hawks circling in the sky above where Houch Street turns into Highway 15, little black periods in a vagrant ellipse as the sun dims everything to viscous reds and oranges, changing all edges to slow fades, filling up the clouds with the bright smudges of their coming disappearance. Nightfall is a preview for death. *Coming to a theater near you!* I pull into the parking lot and watch as slowly the bright colors drain, one by one pulled back over the horizon and the hawks' flight is subsumed within the sky's blueblackening obscurity. I take out my phone and stare into the darkness of its screen reflecting the darkness of the sky until the parking lot's sodium lights switch on atop their metal stalks and become bright periods in the negative, a more ordered, anchored series of ellipses stretching out the silence of twilit Iowa away towards the Interstate. The sodium light ellipses fill up the parking lot with a sense of waiting, waiting, waiting, as if the parking lot itself were composing a very long text message that it was endlessly rewording, thumb hovering over the send button. Who would the parking lot even be texting, at this hour?

I search the sky above the flat, guttered rooftops of the big box for any sign of the moon, wanting to see if perhaps the moon is waiting to receive a text message from a parking lot, if perhaps its cratered moonface has tilted downwards into a celestial phone screen of its own. But the moon is nowhere to be found and as the twilight blackens towards the chill cracklings of a late autumn night I flick the heater on, gazing down into my phone's dark screen where a warped blur of my face's reflection stares back at me, waiting, wanting, wondering what precisely we are doing here, what precisely we might be waiting for.

\*

Dear Buttface,

Hey so it's me again. I know you can't exactly write me back without a return address and I still, argh, I still can't give you one but for the first time in what feels like years I find myself with extra time on my hands and my thoughts, loopy as they've always been, well, they've been thinking about you and hoping you're well and thinking about home, too, even though I haven't written home yet, nor will I. But if you end up calling Mom at least tell her hi for me, will you?

I guess I'll tell you about the potatoes. Here they have more different colors of potatoes than anywhere I've seen, red and yellow and purple and even black potatoes that taste kind of inky and as if someone stuffed all the words from an old book right inside of the potato skin. Imagine that! And Ai and me, we're always drinking this special tea with leaves, drinking it to get a little buzz and because it keeps us from getting too sick, haha. Turns out the mountains aren't all fun and games!

But still I love how people are here. They just act freer, I don't know what it is. Maybe it's as if their consciousness has just been given more room to grow, to expand, to get out of their little shells.

I hope you escape baby bro, I hope you escape before shit and fan are united in sublime collision and the Empire goes from slow decline into total freefall. Any day now! Well, I mean, I hope you've at least planned out your escape route and packed your bag and that you and Annee Bunanee and anyone else you'd like to see alive again are 100% ready to amscray to the border on the drop of a dime. How's that going, btw? Ms. Bunnanee? Getting serious?

Sorry I keep asking questions as if you could answer me, as if you could just type your answers in the margins but I can't help but wanting to pry-pry-pry. OK, well I guess until next time?

Lovethings, etc.,

- C ⚓ Sore

\*

When I wake up in the morning my phone's dead and when I charge it for a few minutes and turn it on I hear all the pent-up Fnacebook notifications popping like metal popcorn, lying absolutely still and then listening to the silence and behind the silence all the creaks and groans of the apartment complex's laborious central heating system. I think about a question from Tuesday's bar trivia that I'd actually totally nailed. *Name an English word where the plural form requires the placement of the 's' in the word's center rather than at the end.* Center, rather than at the end. Henh. I'd gotten Annie to write down *passersby* (even though Belicia had said *spoonsful*) and then when the loathsome Stempler's Roast crew wrote *forksful* I managed to get Bryce to disqualify them because, even though Belicia's *spoonsful* would have actually have technically qualified, well, exactly zero sources on a Gnoogle check supported the inclusion of the Stempler's Roast *forksful* and even stupid-faced Bryce can't argue with Gnoogle. So we pulled out a rare trivia win and I spent the rest of the evening feeling overwhelmingly pleased with myself. Now in the grayness of early hours I lay absolutely still, wondering if you'd put the plural at my center what I'd be like, life as an Elswood, I supposed, huh. Bright metal Fnacebook popcorn, popping like what I imagined the hatching of spiders' eggs sounded with the aid of some surreal amplification. Pop. Pop. Pop.

When I close my eyes I begin to experience the lucid fantasy of dwelling within the circular second dimension of a gold coin, a coin that used to belong to my Mom and which depicted the three-bodied Roman goddess Trivia, the goddess of crossroads. When I was younger it was enough to just look at that coin for me to stop breathing, and I was totally forbidden to touch it. In my fantasy I watch as Mike holds the coin and places it under the rigidity of my corpse's tongue, ignoring muffled protests from the bas-relief goddess that there are still so many more questions left to ask, so many more scores to settle on the basis of pointless facts. What would it feel like to be the goddess of trivia? To be standing forever at a crossroads? And what would it feel like to be dead?

Indulgently, I begin to picture the scene of my own funeral, a scene where I would execute one last troll, posthumously, imploring via my last will and testament that a final round of bar trivia be played between pre-designated teams of my friends and relatives using questions that I'd have written in advance. Ricardo with aunts v. Albert with uncles, Tina with my sister Clarice and on and on. If we were still together I'd ask Annie to MC, to read out the prompts while Carl, the master baker of Venus Treats, would wheel in a

94

spread of his classic dick-shaped frostycakes, laying them out one by one down the bar of the Ugly.

For questions I'd have written all these prompts concerning meaningless little scenarios that have happened over the course of my life, questions that literally zero people would be able to guess. Annie would begin reading, question after question to my friends and relatives huddled over their scratch paper with eraserless golf pencils, glancing up in morbid fascination at the shadow of my discoball-shaped urn suspended ominously from the Ugly's ceiling. Carl would prod them to eat and they would eat, forking up cake slices of frosting-smothered shaft and circumcised dickhead as slowly the trivia questions would build to the big reveal, culminating in the inevitable: *What's giant and dick-shaped and laced with the cremation ashes of Elwood Munn?* And then, at that exact moment I'd get Annie or whoever's MCing to push play on a track on the Ugly's sound system where I'd have pre-recorded about a minute of my own raucous, wheezing laughter. That'd really make all those sad-feeling twerps feel punked! And grossed out! The ultimate victory, of course, would involve initiating one of those chain reactions of projectile vomiting, but honestly even a single spontaneous regurgitation would count as a win. Because right? People who don't arrange for their own funerals to contain large-scale practical jokes are, in my humble opinion, doing it completely wrong. *What's the point in even having a funeral in the first place? So that people can leave tearful messages on the broken, fleshy voicemailbox of your meaningless remains? Feh! That sauce is ultraweak!* Closing my eyes I snuggle into the covers and decide to count to a number between forty and four hundred before waking up and showering and dragging my ass down the hill to open at Yourmug. Forty and four hundred. *Let them eat cake, that's what I say. Let them all eat from the ashy slices of my death's dick-shaped cake!*

\*

It's nearly the end of a cold, howling autumn day and I lie back with my red padded hunting jacket spreading open upon the stiff grass of Houch Park, letting my neck rest upon my oak stump's lip and the crown of my head tips backward into the rotted-out heart. With my chin tilted back like that I reach down with my left hand and fish a black Shnarpie marker out of my pants pocket, the marker that I typically only reserve for defacing the letter *u* with my unauthorized umlauts. Using the selfie view of my phone screen, I start drawing on the taut underside of my chin a large-lidded eye with five curling eyelashes, a black pupil, a rayed iris. I tilt my head all the way back into the rotted-out heart of my stump until it can't go any further, until I can no longer see what I look like and from that position I take a selfie. Readjust. Tilt way far back. Take another. Readjust. Inspect the photograph. The eye still looks kind of squashed onto my Adam's apple but overall comes out pretty good. My underchin. Ringed around a two-dimensional cyclops, my stump's broken rings look like a set of Renaissance painting haloes. Angelic. Perfect.

Totally perfect. I post it to my Fnacebook profile. Annie Likes it. Mike Likes it. Belicia Likes it. Good, I think. I Comment *Greetings from #thatstumplife*. Annie Likes my Comment. Mike Likes it. Nice, I think. That's nice, isn't it?

*

Ricardo's going to come over around four PM today to watch the NBA game on TV. I decide not to ask whether he and Belicia are still together. He's been kind of touchy about that lately. I text and ask him to pick up some French fries from this place that sells only French fries and ham-and-cheese sandwiches.

*Sandwich?* Ricardo texts back.

*No,* I text, *just the fries. Large, pls. :D Thx.*

In the middle of the table there's the wall clock with a broken hanger nail. The clock still works fine. I realize that I should have fixed it a while ago. It's just in the old days I would have just gone down to Moseby's Playthings but ever since the IRS hostage crisis they've been closed down. So there it is, the wall clock, just lying face up on my kitchen table.

Ricardo comes in with the large French fries. I give him a PBR. He asks me if I've heard from Albert. Ricardo has been trying desperately to get in touch with Albert to buy some cocaine. Ricardo's cocaine interest is a relatively new development. Albert is the only person we know who can even get cocaine. The problem is that Albert himself has been harder to get ahold of lately. I think Ricardo believes that possessing cocaine will make sex more fun on nights when he tries to fuck strangers. Ricardo has a stranger who likes cocaine. They fuck in the pre-World War II section of Velton's little cemetery further down on Houch Street towards the highway. I tell Ricardo that I have not heard anything from Albert. He curses a little.

Ricardo takes the fries out of the bag. They're thick and soggy and shine with hot grease. I go to the fridge and get a big bottle of ketchup. Part of the reason that I love getting take-out French fries is that although I love French fries and I especially love French fries with ketchup, I cannot fucking deal with those tiny-ass ketchup packets that most fast food restaurants offer.

Ricardo yawns and stretches up his arms. Ricardo takes the bottle of ketchup and flips off the top to squirt a big red glop of it right onto the face of my wall clock, the one sitting on my table next to the folded up letter from my sister. It lands on the jagged-looking 3, which is nearest to him. Ricardo dips and eats a French fry and looks out my kitchen window where some swallows are busy quibbling. Then he squirts another big red glop down on the woozy-looking 7, for me to dip.

Each ketchup glop is fat and shiny. Mine slides halfway off the edge of the wall clock and onto the table. We both eat the French fries using the wall clock as a plate. It helps us pass the time until the NBA game gets started. When we're done with the French fries the clock face is covered in a thin skin of half-dried ketchup.

The clock keeps ticking.

It looks like a TV homicide corpse.

I stare at it, listening to the sound of the *tick, dlick, dlinck*.

This ketchup-smeared clock makes it look like time itself has tried to fake its own death. It lies still. Moving. Playing possum. Betrayed by the movement of its hands.

*

The next night is really dark. New moon, thunderheads, power outages, whatever. The sky is utterly gleamless. When I step inside my apartment with the lights off the darkness reminds me of something Mike used to say about going to see this cave back in Kentucky, where one chamber you walked into was so big, *so big,* he'd say, *that you could grab the Empire State building by its needle and swing it around your head like a lasso and still not hit anything, wouldn't even come close.*

*What does space mean underground,* Mike used to ask, one night when we were traipsing around Erliss Pond, around and around and making a track by the little stands of bulrushes and fluffy-headed sorghum, one night when we kept walking and walking because I guess we'd forgotten how to stop. God, we must have walked marathons around that pond when we were younger, and Mike would repeat *underground,* as if trying the word out, *underground: because we know 10,000's a cruising altitude for airplanes or even 4,670's an elevation for mountains, I mean, we know what space means for up, ish, at least and we know floor space, square footage and all that, maybe we even know stories, like three stories, five stories above the ground, but can you even imagine what stories are like underground? Five stories down? Shee-it, man. I couldn't fuckin' tell ya. And when I heard this guy saying that you could swing the Empire State building over your head I couldn't even half-fathom what kind of space that would mean, couldn't even picture myself in it even when I was there, standing in the place. But all of a sudden, I mean, it was crazy I felt like I'd shrunk, not that the space was big but that it was small and I was much smaller, like the whole cave was about the size of a snow globe and here I was stepping out on its little round fakes now-covered floor. Tell you what, I even started trembling thinking how anyone might just reach down and grab ahold of the cave and give it a real hard shake-shake-shake. That's what it felt like, anyway. Caves, man. Well, what d'you think about that?*

I fish my phone out of my pocket and thumb around on Fnacebook for a sec trying to see if there are any actual pictures of Mike inside of this cave but then I get distracted by this photo album of him and Cynthia from back in the day, where, for whatever reason they'd both been wearing eyepatches on opposite eyes. I begin to feel my own eyes beginning to blossom little annular circlepains and reach over to flick on the kitchen lights, pocketing my phone, swallowing, inhaling a big chestful of night air. On impulse I reach down under the sink for my little Tnupperwear container, peeling off the lid and sticking my hand in to feel around in the contents. Finally

I take out a single, smooth river stone. I place it on my tongue, tasting its coolness before I swallow. *Yes*, I think. *Yes.*

*

Annie and I don't go bowling again.

When she tells me we're breaking up I ask why.

It seems like a fair question. But she groans like it's the dumbest question in the world. I ask her again. Annie says she's breaking up with me was because I can never pass up an opportunity to be obnoxious.

*I can't stand it,* she says. *You're always so awful to people. And take a good look at yourself for once, why don't you? You're a fucking alcoholic! And you're going nowhere!*

Later in the week I find out that she had started seeing Keenan even before we were broken up. Next Monday night I drunk-dial her to see what she has to say about that.

*Well,* she says, *I was helping Keenan get through a really rough time.*

*He really needed someone,* she says.

*What about me?* I say. *What about who I needed?*

*What about you?* says Annie. *Look, you're a complete narcissist! You don't need me. You don't need anyone. You have never needed anyone.*

Then she hangs up. We haven't spoken since.

About a month ago I find out from Ricardo that she and Keenan have moved in together.

*She's going to have his kid,* says Ricardo.

His kid?

What!?

But she hates babies!

That was the whole premise of our thing. Relationship. Whatever it was. *Wow,* I tell Ricardo, thinking back to that night at the bowling alley.

I guess I really wasn't kidding.

*

It doesn't take long before Ricardo gets sick of talking to me about Annie. He says he's probably got to get going soon. Okay, so I guess I might have gotten a little maudlin towards the end. Especially given that *she's having his kid.* I mean, *what the fuck, right?* Ricardo keeps texting someone who could either be Belicia or his cocaine/cemetery stranger. When his phone makes the getting-a-text buzz he kind of smiles to himself. I wonder if they're sexting. Ricardo squirms like he's got a hard-on. I complain some more and Ricardo nods yunh-hunh. Then he gets another text and his eyes light up.

I could get more sympathy from a goddamn metronome, I think.

Finally I say this out loud, *I could get more sympathy from a goddamn metronome.*

He responds, *Yeah man, sounds tough. I feel for you.*

Ricardo's not even listening!

I shake my head and decide not to make a big thing out of it. What would it get me anyway? You can't get through to someone whose phone is getting blown up with gigapixel body parts from a sultry fuckbuddy. I ask Ricardo if he has plans later and he says something cagey. Something-something-Albert. His nose twitches.

I decide to go ask Lucky Benny if I should have dated Annie in the first place. But Lucky Benny isn't there and Bryce says no one's seen him around for a few days. I get beer-drunk sitting by myself and watch some highlights from last week's NBA games. Big men in suits sit around a table and talk about basketball in matter-of-fact voices and smile sternly at one another as they discuss what it's gonna take, who's gonna have to step up their game, how people are going to really guard him but how he'll probably be able to pull it off if he keeps his head in the game. That same Booty energy drink spot plays again and again during the commercial breaks. *Can you even handle this Booty?* The question explodes into silvery particulates as the TV returns to basketball.

I spend what feels like hours staring at Fnacebook on my phone. Looking at people's photo albums. Looking at newlyweds and newly Fnacebook Official relationships. Looking at a fresh batch of charmless selfies from people I went to high school with. Looking at Annie. Looking at the pictures of us together. Looking at the new pictures of her and Keenan. Together. Her barely tumescent womb-area. Not clicking. Not Liking. Not looking away.

Finally Bryce cuts me off. Which is remarkable, because usually the Ugly never cuts anyone off. Not even Bryce. I mean, never. Ever.

*Look man*, says Bryce. *You just drank eleven beers in under an hour. At least have a glass of water or something?*

*Huh*, I think, burping. That didn't feel like eleven. Beers. Or an hour. Golly, Fnacebook really makes time fly! There's a guy in a knit cap sitting a few bar stools away from me, looking around nervously. We make eye contact.

*Hey man,* he says. *Are you here for the Real Jews meet-up*?

*What!?* I think. I make a back-and-forth hand gesture that under normal circumstances would mean something like: *please, no speak your language.*

The guy nods, flustered, apologizing. Wait, is that Dion? From the Stempler's Roast crew? For some reason I didn't recognize him. Maybe a new haircut or something? And but wait, *Dion's Jewish!?* I don't know why that shocks me, but it does. I don't know why I didn't recognize him, except oh wait, it was the knit cap, right, that's why I didn't recognize him. Fucking Dion, fucking stupid-faced Dion. Ha. Fiddling with the buttons on my padded red hunting jacket I wander outside into the night, walking down the emptiness of Klapp Street past drifts of fallen leaves until I get to the tiny Velton Spins, an ancient 24-hour laundromat which at this late hour is predictably deserted. I don't have any washable clothes with me but I have a few quarters twisting around inside my backpocket lining. I buy 11 minutes on a dryer and just sit on it, letting the vibrations jiggle the loose meat of my back up and down. Ugh. I feel like such shit. Then the dryer vibrations get suddenly way too intense. Different spin cycle or something. I manage to stagger all the way to the laundromat's unisex bathroom before vomiting a big splattery blob-shape out onto the checkered linoleum. It takes forever to clean up and in the process I run the laundromat's unisex bathroom completely out of toilet paper. At least the hand soap dispenser is this adorable little cartoon bear. I thank the universe for that bear. Its molded plastic smile gives my insides a strange surge of gentle strength.

Outside the air is chill but it still doesn't feel like November. I try to practice a shiver before remembering that shivers are something I can only do involuntarily. Stepping down into the laundromat's parking lot I happen to notice a pair of wadded up cotton panties half-submerged in a shallow puddle. The pattern on the panties is a green paisley. And the puddle itself has filled up molten silver, drunk with vagrant moonlight. Beneath the paisley it suggests a kind of farcical enchantment, a spell of make-me-into-a-moon gone wrong, a spell of make-me-into-a-puddle gone right. I imagine Annie as a nude witch, nude but for this pair of green paisley panties, incanting such a feat of lunar alchemy. *What a world*, I muse, *filled up with all its pointless, stupid mysteries.*

Up above the lazy hills I can see the sky open up wide into a brilliant smattering of costume jewelry stars. I imagine the sky as a giant ass studded with rhinestone piercings. God's ass. Night is what we call it when God sits down. On the toilet. Takes a shit. The shit that is named my life right now. If we all start off as unique little spectators in Jibjab's circus of trainwrecks before getting flash-fried, dipped in ranch and masticated to snackmush on the tongue of a hungry God, then doesn't this alimentary journey eventually terminate with our turdification, our transformation into holy shit? I think about phryptolage from *Ideas for Words* and wonder what kind of facile code I'm decaying into, what puzzle my little grains of self will leave scattered across the greasy touchscreen of the universe. Welling up with weltschmertz and self-pity I imagine who will click upon the link to my Fnacebook profile once I am dead. Will Annie? Will Ricardo? Will Marnie? Again I imagine my funeral, those gargantuan dick-shaped frostycakes, jelly-filled balls furred with edible pubic hair. Not so funny now, is it?

*Sigh.*

I feel suddenly terrible, my strength and false bravado of the previous moment fleeing like doomed vermin from a leaky submarine. Why did I do think these things? What wrongness makes me feel this way? I think of Fnacebook again, of my wall full of empty jibes, my hundred little trolls and all the posts I never Liked. And what would Karen write on my wall, if, I mean, if I were to actually fizzle out tomorrow? Probably nothing. Either nothing or something insincere, right? God, why am I always such a caustic fucking jackass to her? Like, what part of my self-loathing projects so strongly onto Karen's utterly inoffensive presence? And what makes

106

another person's inoffensiveness so intolerable to me, anyway? Can't I just live my life? I mean, what's wrong with me, really? Am I jealous of her? Of Albert? Of Annie? Of Keenan? Is that it? Don't I just wish I was a normal fucking person sometimes? Too many questions. Their curvaceous punctuation swirls around my chin and when I open my mouth all the breaths rush in at once.

I walk down Klapp past the Moseby's and past the intersection with Delaney until Klapp Street runs out of houses, down past the Velton Cemetery where I pause for a moment by the pre-World War II section to check for sex noises before turning into the Clough Wilderness Area, stopping as the sound of leaves rustles all around me in the sharp night air. I spit and my spit reeks of acid juices. I let the starlight fall on my cheeks. I try not to think about anything in particular. My mouth tastes terrible. I imagine my mouth bacteria petitioning for a better mouth. *Maybe something flavorful*, reads the petition. *We wouldn't say no to a Gnatorade. Or what about a Booty? Peep one of those Poppin' Piñas? It'll pep you right up!*

*No,* I think back at my mouth-bacteria. *I definitely cannot handle this Booty.* All at once I reach a clearing where two white-tailed deer are just now approaching one another. Their gazes are awkward. It looks like the beginning of a deer blind date.

*Hey,* I imagine the first deer saying. *Is this grass great or what?*

*Sure,* replies the other deer cautiously. *This grass is okay. I mean no, it's great. You're right. It's great!*

107

*Yeah!* says the first deer, going in for the nuzzle. *I mean, I could eat this grass all day!*

*Right? Breakfast, lunch, and dinner!*

*How about that?*

*Grass!*

The other deer plainly does not know how to handle this unwanted affection. Should she just let him do it? Or pull away and risk making him feel slighted? It would ruin the conversation. About how great the grass was. That he was having. With her. That she was half-heartedly trying to sound eager about.

*On second thought*, she thinks, *is this even a relationship worth saving?*

*After all, it's only been one date.*

*¼ date.*

*I'll just take another bite of grass.*

*Let his nuzzle miss me.*

*Let him save face by pretending to sniff the air.*

But no he's really going in for it, cervine lips in a fuzzy pucker, eyes sweetly closed.

I accidentally kick a rock and the two white-tailed deer freeze and then bolt in opposite directions.

*Phew.* Thinks the girl deer.

*Fuck.* Thinks the boy deer.

First date ruined by clumsy human interloper! That's what boy deer will tell his co-workers tomorrow around the deer watercooler.

*It was going so great*, he'll say.

*I was \*this\* close.* He'll shake his wettish black nose from side to side, holding up a cloven forehoof to indicate the degree of closeness. Make whatever sound deer make when expressing exasperation.

*Damn*, the other boy deer will commiserate. *Well, at least she owes you for next time. Amiright?*

Then they'll all guffaw stupidly.

*Don't worry*, I think, attempting telepathy with the two fleeing deer simultaneously. *I just did you both a really big favor.*

*

A few weeks later the first snow of winter starts adding crunchy sound effects to my footsteps, crunch-crunch-crunch to the point that I'm already completely over it, over the novelty of frozen white-and-gray slipperiness. I'm also completely over having a stuffy nose and seeing the loathsome Stempler's Roast crew traipsing around in their matching earmuffs and I'm more than over mopping up the filth from Yourmug's flooring about once every two hours which is how much you need to mop it in order to keep the floor presentable, according to Maurice. Who even heard of a presentable floor?

Trudging around my apartment I can no longer stand to look at the fake-dead-looking wall clock anymore and so, after washing the dried ketchup off its face, I head a ways down Klapp to Moseby's Playthings to see if they'll sell me a hanger nail. The big window is shuttered and outside a handwritten sign reads: THE OWNERS REGRET

To Inform You That They Have Become Political Prisoners of Federal Tyranny. Closed Until Further Notice.

Passive aggressive *Going Out Of Business* signs have always struck kind of a wrong chord with me, but in this case I guess the Mosebys actually are in prison. Huh. I stand around on the frosty grass for a while before heading back to my car. I drive out beyond Highway 15, out to where Velton keeps its big box stores, its parking lot skies filled with migrating ellipses. The batteries will probably be cheaper, but so what? My candy gun is gone. And what about the Mosebys? They won't last a week behind bars. Come to think of it, they probably already bled out from their shanking wounds months ago. Poor Mosebys. Sitting in the parking lot of one of those big box stores I fish out my phone to type a good-bye/RIP-style note to Moseby's Playthings and post it on my Fnacebook page. Instantly I get a smattering of Likes and some smh-style comments. Smh means *shake my head* in Internet-ese. It is used to indicate exasperated judgment upon a slow and enduring sadness. Same as it ever was, they say, *smh*.

Their Likes cheer me up some. Then Maurice Likes it and I think again about his deflated penguin balloonist. My body shudders. I wonder if Karen will see my post. If she sees it she probably won't Like it, because, well, we are still mortal enemies. But perhaps even Karen will agree with my sentiment of opposing Lewis Purcell's Police State injustice against the Mosebys.

Karen has been warming up to me since I finally broke down and told her about the whole Annie and Keenan thing. Every once in a while she even puts down her book and we talk about life, about the things we'd like to do and the people we'd like to be. For the record, Karen still sucks as a person. That said, it's nice that she laughs a little when I yell: *Fuck my life!* and make the exploding sound with my fingers pointed like a handgun at my skull while the other hand makes a gesture of exploding brains out my skull's other side. I know she doesn't find it funny but she laughs anyway. That's a sign that someone is being nice, I've learned. Perhaps the candy that I will still eventually shoot her with will be something softer than a Hnershey's kiss.

Maybe it will be a marshmallow, I think.

Not an ironic marshmallow, but a true marshmallow. A marshmallow of friendship. That marshmallow could be the start of a whole new chapter in my life.

A healthier chapter. A more mature-ish chapter.

Once the Mosebys get out of prison I'll have to remember to head down Klapp Street and really buy that candy gun.

# Mescaline

Black sun opens the sky with a greasy can-opener. Twist. Twist. Twist.

Krrrr-ck. *Detroit... It's soo uh-lec—tric* Speakers frizzle-frazzle. Bloop. Stahmp.

It's Memorial Day weekend in Detroit and Cynthia and I have driven up from Toulous for the electronic music festival. Right now we've been up all night and yeah, feeling so electric and she's looking, no, actually she's pointing out this thing to me with her finger, her finger that is so fucking long it looks like it might contain a third joint past the knuckle and my eyes follow her ultralong finger's gesture towards, well, *what is that, what is she pointing at?* I guess you'd call it a person, well, not a person but the fuzzy outline of the place where a person ought to be standing, making the shape of a vivid keyhole. I conjure the image of a large mothwinged key swooping down to enter this shape, to slide open the greased lock of our Being-in-the-World, disclosing to us and everyone assembled here the true music of existence: *Detroit... It's soo uh-lec—tric.*

*Hey Mike, look!* The keyhole-shape is triple-outlined, shivering outlines, shedding outlines, shedding them way too fast! It's shrinking! Maybe the keyhole shape is actually just one of those snakes, the kinds that have to get outside of their own skin in order to grow? Don't all snakes do that? Or just some? *Cynth? What do you think? What is that shape? Some kind of crazy lightshow trick?* Broad-shouldered, melon-headed, fez-clad. Definitely not a snake.

*Must be some kind of interdimensional doorway. Henh.* Beneath the blackness of the sun this outline-shedding keyhole shape disappears in a sudden burst of golden light and reappears as a floating-headed Spanish exclamation point i so that I nod because okay, yes, now I can at least feel certain about its intended grammatical purpose, even if it is going around shedding outlines willy-nilly. *Hey Cynth, look now. See it? See what it's doing now?* But Cynthia's lost all interest in the mutant punctuation mark and is now looking over at a patch of grass, lower lip extended in concentration, her brow deeply absorbed. Stupidly I keep on blabbering about Spanish exclamation marks, moving my mouth and forcing the vowels out one by one, hoping that she'll look back up and see the i before it disappears or changes into something else. *Oh, okay yes, that's, wow, it's really getting excited about itself! I wonder what part of Spain it's from! Maybe it crawled out from one of the sentences in, like, some really massive printing of Cervantes to come hear some of Detroit's electronic music? Cynth! Look quick or you'll miss it!*

Cynthia points at the patch of dry, springy grass with one of her ultralong fingers that, wow, that finger's got to be at least eleven or twelve miles long by now, huh? She's pointing over at this cleft tucked between two tufts of grass where a tiny orange jewel seems to be glowing, growing, gushing; opening itself up to us. *What is that? Klurgh.* I feel my tongue begin to water and overflow into my cheekpouches, tasting of butteriness and burnt toast and the bitter tang of distant cacti. She's saying something about hazards, about exits, about *oh shit oh shit oh shit.* I take out my phone and snap a picture of Cynthia's shoelaces, tnweeting it out #footnoted. I show Cynthia. She looks up, distracted and rolls her eyes, like great, good job, dumbass. *How's that tnweeting supposed to help us? Huh?* I shrug and snap a picture of my own feet, repeating the hashtag. Cynthia shakes her head and I watch her Chinese hair shimmer with indecisive sunlight. She's scratching her nose. She's staring at her ultralong fingers to see if something's clinging to one of their miniscule, distant tips. I try to mentally snap a picture of her fingers and then draw a cat's cradle geometry between her fingertips using a length of invisible scarlet twine. Two predictably lopsided pentagons ensue across my underface.

*Do you think we should get some water? Or, like, tell someone about it?*

*About the keyhole? Cervantes? Who'd believe us?*

*Mike! I'm serious! This isn't a joke.*

*You think I'm joking!? If someone came up to me with some cockamamie line about a giant keyhole turning into a Spanish exclamation mark I'd think they'd gone batshit.*

*Grrrrrrrrrrr. Mike! What the fuck are you talking about? Don't you see what's happening over there?*

She's got a nice growl, Cynthia does. Every time we start fighting about something enough for her to growl hard like that, well, I get a nice little shiver going up and down my spine. Maybe that's why we fight so much? Because I get low-key turned on by the throatmusic of her anger? Or, alternatively, because I always seem to miss the important parts of what she's saying? Like if what she were trying to communicate was equivalent with a kind of pastry then she'd think it was a Danish and I'd think it was a donut and every time she'd be like: *Why is there a big hole in this?* And I'd be like: *I thought the hole was supposed to be there? Because it's a donut?* And she'd be like: *No Mike, it was supposed to be a fucking Danish. What I said to you was a Danish. You just didn't hear me when I said the important part.*

Cynthia's looking at me, lips pursed, clearly waiting for me to respond. Shit.

*What? No, sorry I don't get it. What's happening?*

*Grrrrrrrrrrrrr.*

I watch as Cynthia lopes over to the spot in the dry, spriggy grass she had been pointing start stomping on the orange jewel, jumping up and down with both feet a few times. She turns back around and glares right at me. *Ulp....What's going on?* Then she walks back over to where I'm standing. How much time has passed? I look back at the spot. The orange jewel is gone. Gone-ish. Cynthia growls again. Rrrowr, I'm thinking. So hot, that growl. And what's more, Cynthia's wearing her longsleeved shirt with a frustrated-

115

looking zebra cartooned on it, the one that when she growls it kind of looks like the zebra's growling, too. I imagine Cynthia's zebra sitting down at the counter of some rundown diner on the Ohio turnpike, wondering how long it ought to take someone to make a goddamn black-and-white milkshake, anyway? Looking at its little zebra wristwatch. Drumming its nonexistent fingers on the diner's counter. Curling down the corners of its horsey mouth. Glowering. For some reason, a zebra becoming incensed over a delayed black-and-white milkshake order sounds like the punchline to some joke that I must have heard a lot as a kid. Too bad I can't remember the joke. What's black and white and red all over? Why was that even supposed to be funny again? Something about newspapers? Or maybe that wasn't even the joke at all. Not the one with the zebras.

Up all night, all night, head skipping like a record. *Detroit... It's soo uh-lec—tric.* The place we're at is called The Old Miami, a veteran's bar in down in Cass Corridor. There's a stage set up on the lawn out back and two big blocks of speakers on either side blasting DJ music. It's not even seven AM and the area by the stage is already pretty packed, people dancing and flailing and noodling around. The air is filled with people-smells and marijuana smoke and nag champa and cigarette smoke and patchouli and the sweet smells of dew on morning grass, thick moisture and humidity. Rancidnesses, mintinesses, tanginesses, greasinesses, muskinesses, cloyingnesses. And breath. The air is dense with a hundred shades of unsterilized human breath. Gnat breath. Dog breath, too. Clothes cling to flesh, flesh clings to bodies, bodies sway and dip and rub up on the bass beat.

*Hey Cynthia, can I ask you about the exclamation mark again?*
*Sure, Mike. Go ahead. Isn't it an exclamation point, though?*
*Mark, point. What's the difference?*
*Hehe, that sounds like someone's name. Mark Pointe.*
*Hehe, you're right.*
*Do you still see it somewhere? The shape? Lurking?*
*No, no. It went away. Back to Cervantes or whatever.*
*Back to where?*

Up all night and Detroit's dawn feels indecisive until noon, as if someone's fast-forwarding the sun and then stopping it and rewinding it and then stopping it and then fast-forwarding it again:

sun-comes-up, sun-goes-down, sun-comes-up, sun-goes-down, sun-grins-rubbing-its-glowing-curves-against-the-craggy-Detroit-skyline, sun-just-trying-to-feel-something-deep-down-in-its-heart-okay, sun-just-trying-to-get-there-to-please-just-get-there, sun-just-trying-to-burst. Flicking my eyelids down to gaze at Cynthia's triple-knotted shoelaces I let my mind autoload the textscroll of mid-level fights that are waiting for both of us back in Toulous and I feel such an immense sense of gratitude that, for once, they aren't really getting under our skin. That we've managed to somehow stop talking about all the things that never fail to talk us both into salty moods and tiny acts of passive rage. That we've somehow finally managed to just stop talking.

Detroit feels like an escape.

Where are we? Who are we? We could be anyone at all, couldn't we!? With and without ourselves, here on the back lawn of The Old Miami. *Who knows,* I whisper, too quietly for Cynthia to hear. *Maybe we could even move up here...Start over... Build out our own Spanish exclamation mark...* Because isn't this who we wish we were: an Amen break of lascivious bokeh sungolds, mouthing and re-mouthing *Detroit...Detroit WhumpaWhumpaWhonWhon*! *Frizzle-frazzle!* Speakermesh bulges, then subside. Then **something sharp against the triple-outlined** i-shape :

*Blam-Blam*

Shots fired!

Where's it coming from!? Cynthia!? I reach my hand into her warm nest of ultralong fingers, squeeze and am squeezed, okay.

*I'm right here, Mike.*

*Okay.*

*Don't you ♥ Detroit, haha.*

Cynthia whispers, smiling. The skin of her cheeks is the color of rich clover honey and suddenly I wanna lick it, I wanna stick my tongue out and taste the honey that's been gathered by the bees of her Chinese hair, the bees that buzz beneath Cynthia's face, scurrying about and pollinating all of her flowerbuds to such a furious overblossoming. What species of flower would live beneath the amberish hemispheres of Cynthia's face? Blodeuwedd? Meadowsweet? Faceflowers?

*Hey Cynthia, do you —*

Bullets.

*Get down!*

Grinning bullets.

*Where's it coming from!?*

Swarthy bullets.

*Cynthia!?*

Fez-clad bullets. (They sound strangely edible).

*Shhhhh, Mike! It's just the music, dude. Mike! Don't freak out, okay?*

What!? Oh. Oh. Okay. Music. Bullets inside of a music? For a moment I don't understand. Ultralong fingers stroke the side of my hand with comforting pressure; hereness, lastingness, stayingness. *Okay. Okay, I'm alright. Thanks Cynth!* I settle, listening in again to the aggressive percussion choices of Curmudgeon playing with The Whomsoever Twins, gnawing at myself, watching the bright panic-points fade from the spun-aroundness of my vision. Draped over the sumac-snarled fence a large vinyl banner queries in lavender-and-silver *Booty ~ Can you even handle this booty?* with an accompanying image of a sunglasses-wearing sun imp/exploding into a shimmering supernova. Two boots tromp into my sightline and I take out my phone and take a picture, tnweet it using the same hashtag. Henh. *Mike!? Why do you keep doing that?* I listen to the sproinging, whizzing galloping bullets. Bullet horses. Bullet trains. Faster and faster! I let Curmudgeon stake his musical train tracks tie by tie across the vast plains of my undulating innerness, feeling suddenly all melty-headed and out of breath. Look at us, standing on

120

this grass, nodding and staring and moving our heads around. For why? There's a tiny moon at the edge of the sky and it looks like a little sugar cracker and I reach up just a little bit with my fingers to pluck it out but my fingers aren't long enough so I can't get ahold of it. Whom do I know with ultralong fingers? *Hmmmmm... let me think...*

*Boom! Boom!*

Canons! The artillery is coming! Two men in military fatigues drop to the ground beneath a sign tacked to the sumac-snarled fence: MEN AT WORK. They lie still for barely a moment and then help each other up, dusting off, looking sheepish and then not-sheepish, feeling united by their impulse to once again survive. It is Memorial Day, after all. When I point out the two men to Cynthia we can't make up our minds if the spectacle viz. the MEN AT WORK sign is ironic or if it's entirely unironic, or perhaps, somehow, both. Metairony is when something done ironically becomes indistinguishable from the same thing done unironically because the character of its very Being-in-the-World depends upon the absolute erasure of the distinction between irony and non-irony. I think about how this erasure is also the unchanging condition of our relationship, Cynthia's and mine: that we both really mean it and don't really mean it at all because, well, it's not that we're afraid to mean it to one another but that we're afraid to not be sanguine and jaded about the idea of relationships in general because doesn't nothing last forever and isn't forever just plain terrifying because wow, soooo much time and who wants to practice forevering at our age when there's still so much entertaining insanity that we might potentially have left to miss out on? Because seriously, once we stack the equation like that we both begin to maybe feel trapped or saddled or stuck to each other just by being in the same room let alone the same cramped little studio apartment and we begin to blame each other every time we wonder wistfully at the other lives we might be leading, thinking, well, don't we have our whole lives to be dead and boring, to line our photo albums with more standard models of monogamous companionship and/or the wry melodramas of other people's erotic misadventures? Right?

So then why, if Cynthia and I both know that we both don't yet know, then why can't we just have our 19-year-old togetherness without constantly overthinking it, and/or why can't we just crawl out of our skins and become gold-limned i-shapes escaping over the marginalia of orbitally spinning, exoplanetary Cervantes tomes to move our denim hips beneath the quickness of Detroit's octopoodle clouds? Right? Doesn't that all sound kind of really nice?

Well, it sounds nice to me, anyway.

Tonight we'll be driving back to Kentucky but for now we're free, still clutching at the edge of freedom's glittering mane. *Dee-troit! Piao! Piao! Piao!* In a patch of nearby mud I see two different-sized footprints form a V at their toes. I take my phone out and take a picture of it. #footnoted? This time Cynthia smiles. *Mike. Dude. You're so lame sometimes.* We kiss, two wires touching, electricity runs between us. Soft circuits. Crackle. The blue air is crisp enough to crunch. I put my arm around Cynthia, pull her kind of half into my armpit.

*Schizoselfie?*

*Le-sigh. If you insist. Okay.*

A schizoselfie means we put our faces right next to one another and kind of squish them together and then tighten the frame of the selfie so that it's only half of each of our faces, one eye mine, one eye hers. I grin. She scowls. Our schizoselfie comes out looking pleasingly deranged. As the digital camera on my phone simulates the sound of a real camera's shutter snapping I wonder what it would be like if our skulls were permeable membranes and, then, by squeezing our heads together like this mine and Cynthia's brains could form a continuous circuit of brainwaves, thinking the same thought, feeling the same feeling, dreaming the same dream. Direct connection, with no words left to get in the way. Would I even want that? Would she? Would we give it a try, just to see what it felt like? Or would the mere suggestion of that kind of radical intimacy totally terrify both us to the point that even suggesting it would seem hopelessly naive and clingy? Because Cynthia would opine, and perhaps correctly, that after experiencing an as-it-happens stream of Cynthia-and-Mike's thoughts we'd literally never be able to look at each other again without bursting into uncontrollable fits of maniacal knowing-all-too-well laughter? *Oh ho,* our eyes would say, *I know exactly what's going on in there, you sick, sad thing, you.*

I could imagine a Cynthia-shaped avatar of Cynthia's mind wandering through the tapered passages of my own mind's mazework. Wrinkling her nose. *What the fuck is that smell?* Elbowing her way through the narrownesses. Finding the ballroom with the giant, levitating fez. *What could he possibly be keeping this around for?* Shaking her head at all the off-kilter brand signage and motivational clichés, all the tnweets and Snaps and Instagrnams and Fnacebook posts. *He's a hoarder. I knew it. He's got a whole decade of pointless Internet garbage stashed away up here. Jesus. If only there was a way to just light the whole place on fire and start over fresh...* Striding past the cage containing the disembodied mouth that spends all day mumbling the chorus-and-only-the-chorus to catchy radio songs, mumbling so persistently that, deep in my head, no catchy song ever really ends. *Well, okay I guess I probably have this thing, too. But God, so fucking annoying!* Pulling a book out of a bookshelf and then saying *Hey, what!? What's this?* As the bookshelf swivels her around into a terrifyingly vast archive of kitschy, overdramatized porn.

*Hey Mike?*

Oh no! Now the real Cynthia knows! *Aaaaaaaa.*

*Hey, no shhhhh. Mike? It's just me again. Seriously. Calm down. Please. Please just calm down. Okay?*

*Oh phew. Hey Cynthia, sorry I just really spaced out for a minute there. Got a bit stuck inside my own head.*

*Well, the new set's coming on.*

*Who's playing?*

*Discount Sheeple. DJ Said No One Ever. Someone else, too.*

*God, these DJ names are getting worse and worse.*

*When's Feelz Goodman playing? Do you know?*

*No, I don't.*

*Hey, I'm going to the bathroom, okay? Okay?*

There's a lot of distance around here. It's so loud I can't listen to any one single thing. It's so loud I can only hear what I'm here to hear. Right here. I can only understand what is 1" away from my eardrums. And even that... *Cynthia?*

No answer. What's that smell? It smells like armpits. It smells like smoke but a new kind of smoke. It smells like hair that's gotten way way way too hot. Melty hair. Frizzled hair. Omelet-viscous hair. I look down into the leaky shadow of a massive bulb-bellied man with a bucket on his head who's wearing one of those Curmudgeon shirts with a pair of massive erect-nippled breasts Phnotoshopped onto a Hitler-mustached cat. *Sniff-sniff.* Yeah okay, something is definitely burning. At the edge of the spriggy patch of dry grass I see that the little orange jewel has reemerged.

*Cynthia?* The ground is covered with foreign-sounding shadows, leaking, leaking, leaking out new kinds of smoke. I feel the tension of *whereamiwhatamidoingwhatwillhappennext* rising against the skin of my shirtbuttoned chest. Maybe if I unbutton then my heart's ventricles will finally liberate, escaping from all that boring inside-of-myselfedness for good... *Look over there!* I watch a duo of indigo bodystocking-clad women vomiting pink cocktails. Their sunburnt faces sneer happily. I realize they are vomiting onto an orange jewel, hoping to make the jewel go away. They're succeeding, ish. They laugh and high-five using indigo-shellacked fingers. Their skin is bronze. Their hair is gold. Their moonboots are silver. *Haha,* they laugh, high-fiving again. *Got it!* One woman slaps the other woman's indigo-clad butt, eyes bright and beady. Once the orange jewel looks sufficiently extinct I watch as birds land on the pink vomitgrass to get drunk from the worms.

*Kill!* says the music. *Kill! Kill! Kill!*

*He's really killing it,* says Cynthia. She rolls her eyes.

*Cynthia!? Where did you come from?* There is something really orange and jewely happening over by the i-shape. Wait, the i-shape is back, too!? Attempting to ratchet down my feeling of abject overwhelmedness I try and fail to recite the only Coleridge poem I have ever known.

Where did Alph the sacred river run again?

Through caverns measureless to Munn?

Measureless to whom?

To Munn, to Elwood Munn, my erstwhile grade school buddy who in the geoscience class of Ms. Unica Korn conspiratorially swallowed the small rocks when no one was looking and then swore me to lifelong secrecy with an oath he wrote in Latin. As if. Who would I even tell?

*You'll see*, said Elwood, a secretive grin tugging down the corners of his mouth. *I'll end up needing these.*

*When I grow up.*

*When I become a sacred river. I will need something for all the waters to come and walk upon. To skip and waltz and gallop upon. These rocks.*

*You'll wish you had yours, Mikey. My partner in all labs.*

Little egg-and-bean shaped stones he swallowed, one at a time. I watched him. He made me ask Ms. Korn for more stones.

*Measureless*, I think. There is a fearsome heat packing itself about us.

*Mike! I said: we need to get out of here! Mike, can you hear me? You need to unfreeze your shit right fucking now!*

Panickers are panicking. Calmer- downers are busy trying to calm down the panickers. It's only 50% not-working. I am totally motionless. I am back inside the levitating fez ballroom of my mind, standing off to one side, just watching it spin and spin and spin. When I notice my own shadow start leaking smoke onto the grass I bend down to clean it up but Cynthia doesn't think that's such a good idea so she tries to yank me up by my elbow which, okay so my elbows are actually pretty ticklish and then each time she does it I start laughing and she gets so infuriated that she starts growling *Grrrrrrrrrrr* (mmmmm-magic!) but then stops growling and starts coughing coughing coughing and keeps on coughing because now the air is thick with this new and unpleasing kind of smoke. Well, I'd cough too, to but to cough you need to breathe and now that I have such a clean shadow I won't need to breathe anymore! That's what I'm telling myself, anyway. My head swivels around to watch as the light of afternoon's gold bokeh starts to dim behind plumes of ash. Orange jewels are everywhere. Some of them are being worn by people. I see the bulb-bellied man with the Curmudgeon shirt smacking his hands against an orange jewel that's bedazzling his Hitler-cat's wide-set cleavage. Wait, that's not a jewel at all! It's... what's the word for it?

*Mike, shit you're on fire!*

The rusty nose of a rectilinear dragon appears over the sumac-snarled fence by the edge of the lawn. Its lips are the red of fresh blood and fire engines. *Wait a minute...* Water fills the air.

*Cynthia? What's going on? Cynthia!?*

Some people want to grow up to be scientists. Like limnologists, the type of scientists that study rivers. Elwood Munn wanted to grow up to be a sacred river. Those are the type of childhood ambitions that I still have honest envy for. Good old Elwood. Whatever happened to him? Last thing I recall is Fnacebook saying he was still living in that little town off in Iowa, what was it called? Melton? Shelton? And his sister Clarice, I remember her. She always had such a murderous look about her. Is she even on Fnacebook? I should really check up. Last we all hung out I think Marnie said something about Clarice running off overseas with a Japanese guy from New York. But I should really get the full story from Elwood himself. And now I'm wondering whether Clarice ever shared her brother's aspirations of becoming a body of water. Maybe a brackish delta. An estuary. *Measureless...*

Smoke is everywhere.

Shit, what's happening? I can't even see. *Cynthia!* Her honeycomb is threatened and I can hear the bees coming out, full-force, swarming.

*Bzzzzzzzz!*

*Wsssshhhhhhh!*

*Yowwwwwww!* There are barks, yips, grunts. There's the wailing of clown-shaped people running, tripping, clown-shaped people who have dropped small personal items of great significance on the smoke-covered grass and have bent to recover them. The other clown-shaped people trip over the bender-downers and go tumbling. *Owwwww!* There are knees scraping, ligaments tearing. Bones are snapping. One body falls and then another body trips over them. Then another body over them, and so on. Soon a small cairn of squirming bodies has formed, sticky with mucus and unwanted proximity. The bodies become a superorganism, crushed to pitiful inertia by its own disorganized weight.

*Hey! Where is Cynthia?*

I have not moved one inch this entire time. The i-shape appears, now directly in front of me. Maybe it's a floodlight on a tall stand? Maybe it's one of those new outdoor peoplewarmers?

*Where the fuck is Cynthia!?*

People are yelling: *Am I on fire!?*

*Am I!?*

And being answered in earnest: *I don't know!*

*I!*

*don't!*

*know!*

The i-shape starts running. I follow. Speed up. Now I am running. My face feels like it's coming apart at the glueseams. Smoke is pouring from the corners of my eyes. I start to unbutton my heart, hoping that will liberate its ventricles.

*Cynthia!?*

The i-shape seems to know what it's doing. Thank God. It's running in slow-motion. I run in slow-motion. We circumnavigate a squirming super-organism. This mostly works. By now the fire has worked its way up the edgegrass and somewhere inside of me. I can feel some part of me alive and burning.

I vomit smoke and vivid colors back up into the air.

I vomit a sunset, an entire sunset beginning to end.

I vomit a sacred river named Elwood Munn.

*Hey Mikey,* he says. *What are you doing here? I thought this was supposed to be a Spanish-language version of Don Quixote!?*

*Shut up Elwood,* I yell back. *Can't you see that this whole fucking place is on fire?*

*Okie-dokie,* says Elwood, and closes the book cover.

I feel him falling all over me. Water. A sacred river. It is *Measureless...*

Then all is wet and quiet.

My shirt is soaked.

My pants are soaked.

The water came from somewhere above the sumac-snarled fence. The dense air above the grass begins to clear. At no point during this extravagance has the DJ music stopped playing. With just a touch of metairony, The Whomsoever Twins have begun sampling:

*The roof... The roof... The roof is on fire!*

Is Cynthia okay? Am I okay? If both of us are okay and we survive and end up spending the rest of our lives together then maybe *The Roof Is On Fire* will end up becoming, like, *our song*. Me and Cynthia's. I could totally imagine us flailing around romantically to *The Roof Is On Fire* at our wedding while a reluctant groomsman sets a nearby, gas-doused roof on fire to re-create the original effect. I see someone looking at me, like: *Why is this guy smiling?* I stop smiling. I try to breathe and cannot breathe. I see the firefighters. Cynthia sees the firefighters. *Cynthia!? There you are! Are you okay!?*

*Mike!?* We hold each other for a long moment, her pressing me tight against the frustrated-looking zebra and I finally sweep away the bees from her face and taste the sweetness of her honey on every part of my tongue at once and feel her doing the same thing

131

back. Then we step apart. Look at each other. Sheepishly. Why sheepish? I can hear my lips moving and then Cynthia asks:

*What's measureless?*

*The sacred river, I think. Does that make sense?*

*Not really. Mike, did you get burned at all?*

*What, you mean by the fire?*

*No. Burned by the sacred fucking river. Yes, the fire. God Mike, you really spaced out for a sec there.*

The firefighters strip off their DFD shirts. Red suspenders stay on. Slabs of perfect muscle. Abs that could grate the stoniest of parmesans. Just looking at their neck veins makes me wince. The firefighters smile and wade in among the dazedness, in among the throngs of this really freaked-out, coughing crowd. It turns out that Detroit's firefighters like electronic music on Memorial Day, too.

# The Lone Inhabitant of Gratiot's
# South Leg Traffic-Control Island

*A traffic-control island is a defined area between traffic lanes for control of vehicle movements or for ... refuge.*
– Manual on Uniform Traffic Control Devices, Part V, *Islands* Section 4A-1 *The Functions of Islands*, 1961

The Inhabitant's body lies face down on a triangle of Detroit.

From 1,000' up the triangle looks like a shovel turned over. We can barely see the Inhabitant's body lying face down. From up here the tops of whole skyscrapers look like hand-drawn boxes.

Rectangles.

Circles.

Granite grays.

Titanium whites.

Tarseam blacks.

The bright dots are actually the tips of tall radio antennae.

The crescents are tilted satellite dishes.

Embedded squares are electrical transformers, water tanks, fenced-in patios for ritzy apartment dwellers to frolic upon.

Up here there is a lot of signal activity. 01000100 01100101 01110100 01110010 01101111 01101001 01110100ness buzzes and crackles in between the waves of chilly air.

The triangle is a traffic island nestled at the intersection of three large two-way streets.

Gratiot and Broadway and Randolph. Downtown. You can see the old Wurlitzer building and a haberdashery built one hundred and ten years ago.

The triangle is specked with tawny surface rock. Its beveled edges are pleated with curb cement the color of oatmeal.

Upon the triangle the grass lies in scraggly just-thawed sheaves. Like someone took the triangle out of the family freezer to de-frost the grass right before dinnertime.

In Detroit Opening Day has just begun.

Our triangle can smell fresh baseball in the air.

For the moment all is airy; stirring and earliness.

The gutters wave their plastic straws.

The gutters wave their hotdog wrappers.

The gutters wave their whorls of cigarette filters and bent bottle caps.

Even the gutters are eager for fresh baseball.

From 1" up a globe thistle shrugs its purple firework of a blossom.

It bobs its plosion of fuzzy color side-to-side when the wind picks up.

*How long shall I dawdle here?* Asks the stillness to the Inhabitant's body.

*Forever?*

The wind rifles through the grass, stirring every stalk and stem to show the shape of the Inhabitant's body not moving.

This gesture tells you what isn't there.

We are less than a hair's breadth away and even we can feel the Inhabitant's not-movingness.

Face down.

White skin gone cracked and red from winter exposure.

Capillaries frozen and then de-frosted.

Streaks of grime thick as tree rings from the years of winter.

Steam rises in large white columns up from the grates on Woodward Avenue beneath the chassis of happy station wagons.

Windows smudged with the eager breath-fog and the finger drawings of backseat siblings.

Windows smudged with the handprints of last night's make-out session between teenaged lovers sneaking out after curfew.

Windows smudged with dust, with messages written in dust by fingers.

*Let's go Tigers!*

Around us the emptiness itself begins to scurry.

The Detroit air is made of wavy silver.

The Detroit air is made of tiny cardboard evergreens that dangle from the frontage traffic's rearview mirrors.

The Detroit air is made of eagerness and fresh baseball.

*Tigers. Tigers.* You can hear the air itself whispering. *Tigers.*

*Shhhh!* It's coming. It will be here soon.

\*

Once there was a family. Of a kind. Minus a father. Minus a house. Then minus a home. It was a family that was built of minuses.

It grew strong from the first minus and then weakened as they multiplied.

Fathers became dim shapes in the distance. Silences on the phone across 3,000 miles. It was a portrait of hyphens. It was a portrait of senseless characters, the way you can draw someone's face using an old qwerty keyboard.

For a few years, this was home ______.

For a few years, this was father:

For a few years, this was life.

It stuck there. One after-image after another scraped away by pain.

Slowly it left.

Slowly the characters slipped away. One by one, to dust.

It became another minus. Home. Father. Then life itself.

Life: the big minus.

Things after things. The shape someone leaves in a bed and stays left there long after they have gone.

After-images.

After-things.

The Inhabitant was a body that shed its steps as it walked. To shed its own reflection. It learned how to fall down. It learned how to reek. Then it learned how not to have a nose. How not to smell. How not to see itself. Until one day it found our triangle.

The Inhabitant needed shelter.

Our triangle only knows how to give shelter to those who need it most.

Our triangle has figured out something that none of us humans have.

*

The Inhabitant can feel that pent-up energy just waiting to get out.

The Inhabitant can feel that baseball.

Another day.

Years have passed unnoticed. Laundered years. Years scrubbed together by the skies of soapy rain.

Between the just-thawed sheaves of grass the body doesn't move a single muscle.

The wind is filled with the truth of children's laughter.

The Inhabitant reaches out and clutches at this truth.

It forms an opening, a small hole opening out towards the Beyond.

Can you see it?

It is only just 1" underground.

From down beneath the triangle the Inhabitant can look out through this tiny hole and into [...] and into [...] and into [...]

The Inhabitant discovers us.

Now we can be made useful, he thinks.

He widens the interval with a small, triangle-shaped piece of us. It begins to grow. Soon it will form a passageway.

The Inhabitant digs at the edges of the hole.

We feel happy to be useful.

The Inhabitant notices that we have become triangular from our eagerness.

The Inhabitant sharpens us.

The Inhabitant is also eager.

The Inhabitant uses our shape to cut his way out of the world.

When some progress has been made in the cutting, the Inhabitant rests.

*Phew...* he thinks.

He sets down the black garbage bag in which he stores what remains of his heart.

It leaks with dirty blood onto the curbside, onto the pavement.

*

People cover the street. They are happy. They are proud Michiganders. People are covered with this radiance, shirts of blue and green.

Lake and forest.

Sapphire and emerald.

The great people of Michigan. They can feel how great they are. They feel this greatness in the wind and the water and the streaming sun that cups their cheeks up high to kiss them.

People are stretching their arms and lifting up children over their shoulders. People are eager. People are thanking the sky. People are thanking baseball.

People are thanking the city of Detroit.

They are grilling bratwurst.

They are spitting out the shells of sunflower seeds.

The sun reposes up on its sofa of baby blue, baseball glove in hand. Punching at the oiled leather. Ready for the opening game.

People are hugging.

People are greeting the children of friendly families.

People are lighting cigarettes and slapping backs.

People are high-fiving. People are pouring beer, drinking beer, spilling beer.

People have beer foam all over their upper lips. Look, there's Mike and Aziz! They are standing just beneath the shade of a sportsbar's awning, both wearing sunglasses, both staring down into their phone screens. Beer can in one hand, phone in the other. They are looking up. They are cheersing. They are grinning and chugging. They are getting beer foam all over their upper lips.

Everywhere there are white children. The children have brought their own baseball gloves to catch fly balls. The children are trying to sound out names like *Peralta* and *Verlander*. The children are being told to please stay out of the street. One child points at the Inhabitant. *Is he dead, Mommie?*

Mommie jerks her away by the other arm. *Don't point, Brianna. It's not polite to point.*

The parking lots across the street from the triangle are crowded with jerseys.

There are plastic Bnudweiser awnings.

There are big coolers of potato salad.

There is a one-armed man selling corn dogs.

There is a one-eyed man eating a corn dog.

Every banner and bicep bellows out the big Detroit

.

The Inhabitant can feel the tremors of joy through the fibers of his beard.

140

The Inhabitant can feel the start of baseball through our triangle and it nourishes him.

He is almost there, almost through to the Beyond.

*What would you like*? asks the Beyond.

*Take me there*, says the Inhabitant.

*Okay*, says the Beyond. *That's fine by me.*

It lifts the mind's eye of the Inhabitant up into golden lips of the sun.

Then it sets him down.

Inside.

The crowd is carrying the Inhabitant with their voices. He is among them. They want the Inhabitant to be happy with the sound of their love.

Their love for the world.

Their love for baseball.

Their love for the Detroit Tigers.

No one else notices the Inhabitant's unmoving body.

No one smells the urine tang of his denim jacket.

No one recoils at the layered grime of his pits and his hands and his underclothes.

The Inhabitant understands that his body might not be welcome.

On Opening Day of baseball season, the Beyond permits the Inhabitant to leave his body behind.

The Beyond takes him and for a day it makes him as new.

\*

The Inhabitant leaves our triangle. His milkiness floats into a body of years past. The Beyond sets him down with a pat on the shoulder.

*Enjoy*, says the Beyond.

*Thanks!* says the Inhabitant. *And thanks to you all, too!*

*No problem*, we say back. *It was the least we could do.*

He is smiling. The whole of the Inhabitant's body feels like one big smile.

*This body feels so right,* he thinks.

The Inhabitant enters the crowded hallways of Cnomerica Park. It still has that new stadium smell the way new cars have a new car smell. It feels clean. He sighs with pleasure.

The Inhabitant takes his seat just ten rows back from first base and gazes down towards home plate.

His view is unobstructed.

His freshly washed hair gets blown by a creamy breeze of feelgood cheering.

The air around him is covered in thousands of Michigan smiles. The Inhabitant leans forward. He is peering around at the crowd. In his hand he discovers a plastic mug of rich, foamy beer. This plastic mug will never run empty. It will always have what he needs. In his other hand he discovers a thick Polish sausage piled high with relish and ketchup. It is a sausage that will never run out of bites. The air about his head is filled with the aromas of spicy meat and grease, the smells of the crowd.

The smells of happiness.

The body travels on. It pushes him. It pushes his head down into the dirt and lets the slim white rhizomes of grass burrow through the fissures of his skull.

The triangle does its work.

It keeps the signal going strong. The Beyond beams down the most powerful of world-altering rays. Letting things be otherwise. Letting things be different.

*Yes*, thinks the Inhabitant. *Yes!*

Here the sky screams out with a perfect ballgame's blueness.

Here the combed stadium grass is the green of new life.

Here the people are finally ready.

The loudspeakers spring to life with that rumbling chorus:

*Puh-lay ball!*

Verlander reaches down from the pitcher's mound to rub a little dirt between his thumb and forefinger. He wolfstares the batter before throwing a blistering fastball.

*Strike one!*

The crowd goes wild. The Inhabitant goes wild. It's perfect!

The Inhabitant takes another bite of his perfect Polish sausage.

The Inhabitant takes another gulp of his perfect foamy beer.

*Strike two!*

(The crowd holds its breath and no one moves a muscle).

*Strike three!*

The ball thwacks hard into the catcher's mitt. The catcher stands, arms stretched up to the sky. The whole stadium bursts into a swelling fury of applause.

The whole stadium chants *Let's go Tigers!* (clap, clap)

Now the Tigers are at bat. Prince Fielder steps up to the plate. He loads the count before knocking another home run clean out of the park. The crowd is deafening. The crowd is high-fiving. The Inhabitant is slapping palms right and left.

The Inhabitant is pumping his arm in the air.

The Inhabitant is embracing and being embraced.

The Inhabitant has briefly forgotten everything except for how happy he is.

In every section people are smiling.

People are cheering.

People are hugging.

People are feeling good about this day. This Tigers team. This baseball game. They are in the presence of their heroes. Their heroes are winning.

*Please go*, says the Inhabitant, turning back to look at us.

*There is nothing left to know.*

## Part V.  ISLANDS

### A.  GENERAL

#### 5A-1  Scope of Island Standards

A traffic-control island is a defined area between traffic lanes for control of vehicle movements or for pedestrian refuge. Within an inter-

# Night Interval

The next night the darkness is the darkness of being stuck deep inside of a bottle of black liquid, ink or wine or deepsea water so that looking outside the windows I can't even tell if we're still tethered to the Earth. Well, I don't have anything particular lined up but for some reason I don't really feel like making plans or even heading down to the Ugly to see what old kung-fu movie they might have playing on TV. So I just sit on the sofa and watch my new roommate TN get ready to chaperone some kind of event at the school where he teaches. As he plucks at the starched collar of his buttondown and pulls tight his little striped bowtie I say nothing and then finally he claps his hands together and declares *Well that just about does it!* And I nod and tell him that I'll probably just watch the game or something.

*What game?*

I shrug. Game. No game. Whatever.

*Ha. Okay, Elwood. See you later then.*

For a little while after he leaves I try jerking off but I'm clearly not getting anywhere so I open my computer and poke around Rneddit until I find this picture of otters building what's pretty clearly a Phnotoshopped dam made from human mannequins, some with heads, others without and even though I don't understand the purpose of this photo I feel a sudden and immediate sense of affinity to its existence and so I take the link and copy-paste it to Fnacebook and then wait, refreshing and refreshing my browser window, just waiting for someone to Like it. But after about five minutes basically no one has Liked it and so I begin to feel strangely forlorn and distant from myself. My mouse arrow moves over the little Like button. I Like it, my own link, then quickly unlike it. Close my browser window. Hope that nobody noticed.

So then I open an email, just to have a blank space to type some things. Maybe I'll write another Comments Section rant, perhaps as a sequel to my screed against Fnacebook baby pictures? The cursor blinks, blinks, blinks. I begin typing:

*I believe in the power of the individual.*

*I believe in the power of money, guns and sex, which seems to be how the world is being run these days. Very well. Maybe it has always been this way?*

*I believe in places and the names of places, which is the only way that I even know the world exists.*

*I believe that somehow, somewhere, I am being watched and that the data of my image is being stored on a distant server farm where it is no doubt destined to outlive me.*

*I believe that to win it you have to be in it to win it, looking out for number one, and that's me, Elwood Munn.*

Then I delete it, all of it and start over, writing:

*I believe in the power of the greater good, the greatness of the US Americas and the intelligence of rational collectives.*

*I believe in the Internet, where basically everything worthwhile is free and shared and can be used without any depletion.*

*I believe that the Internet is a beautiful, shimmering cornucopia, and that all the world's peoples must join together in learning to harvest its magic, led by the obvious awesomeness of the US Americas where we decide all important things both for and by the people.*

*I believe in the power of all humanity, the power of democracy, the power of ideas.*

Then I delete that, too. The truth is, I don't believe in any of it: not myself, nor humanity, not the Internet, nor ideas. What was it that Mikey used to say, back when we were kids? I can't even remember that. I delete everything and watch the cursor. I type nothing. Blink. Blink. I wait.

Wnikipedia. Gnoogle Images. Tonight I'm a spectator of words. Tonight I decide to take myself to the museum section of the Internet, to look at something better than the backshadow shapes of my own failed recollections. Blink. The blink of the cursor and the blink of my eyes. Click. My eyes begin to itch.

The little gray clock at the bottom left of my screen shows three minutes past three AM and I'm still clicking, refreshing, letting the meat of my fingertips slap against the molded plastic of my lockless keys, thinking, feeling, clicking through photographs of newly famous or soon-to-be famous paintings. Warmed by the glow of the phone on the cheeks of the woman in Mark Stock's *Impulse 2* (2011).

147

Saddened and then coyly enamored by the iPhnone's radial dingbat frozen beneath the grotesque half-concealedness of the face in Jeanette Hayes' *Is My iPhone Locked* (2013). Thickening up with melancholy gazing into the expressionlessness of Edward Hopper's hunched figures depicted in Nastya Ptichek's Fnacebook and Twnitter remixes, Hopper's figures inscrutable beneath little hearts or upturned thumbs, perhaps wondering what the world really thinks about them, or if the world thinks anything at all.

What's melancholy about social media is, after all, the melancholy common to all symbols; that they reduce us, and in their reduction we feel that we've been wronged. What I'd really love is an antisocial media website or phone app, a company that's willing to level with us, the users, by advertising a superior disaffection, alienation and aloneness. For what must be the zillionth time this week I click open my Bookmarks icon for the writing of Alan Sondheim, scanning down to a passage:

```
bluntness, dulled texts in cyberspace
muted, almost inaudible

imagine the letters smaller, maybe, blurred

i want to drink to take the edge off things
i want to write to take the edge off things
look, i'm murmuring to you. closer, you hear :

everything

it's as if something came into the light
it's as if the sound of a tiny bell came into the light
knowing where everything is
```

Shit, wait, what time is it again? After three thirty AM! Jesus, and I'm on for morning shift at Yourmug. Shit. Well, I should probably get to sleep, although at this point if I wait I could just shower and head in without going to sleep, slam some Eyeopeners and power through the morning rush til noon when I'd be able to nip away for a quick nap. But how? How has this even happened!? I could have sworn that it had only been like thirty minutes since TN left, maybe an hour tops and not six or seven fucking hours. But then I blink, feeling the itchiness of my eyeballs. Blink. Click. Wait.

Finally I stand up from the couch and stretch, letting the blood rush screeching into my head, flooding my vision with a clamor of fuzzy green triangles. Without much enthusiasm I decide to sleep for the next 1.5 hours and tromp over to the entrance to my room, looking back to see if I ought to clear anything away and notice that there's still a teacup sitting out on top of the coffee table. Sighing, I go back to take it into the kitchen and try throwing away the teabag without turning the lights on. But just at that moment the string of the teabag becomes so wrapped around the handle of the spoon that I can't manage to pick it off with my fingernails and I finally lose my patience and rip at the tea-flavored tangle of string with my teeth, in the process managing to let go of the spoon, which drops, teabaglessly, into the trash can. So then I'm just standing there at the edge of the tiny, darkened kitchen, wet teabag dangling from my teeth by its string, feeling like a complete and total dumbass. I give up. Turning on the kitchen light I fish the spoon out of the trashcan and rub both it and the empty mug under a jet of scalding water. Work up a pretty good lather of lemon-scented dish soap. Feel the skin melt and numb on my fingers and the pads of my palm as I look up to check the hands on the ketchup-stained wallclock, shaking and shaking my head.

Where does time even go when it escapes from us like this? And our faces, when we can't see them stilled in saintly grinning pixels, what about them? Do they still become us, even when nobody's looking? What do we do with our faces? More importantly, what exactly are they doing with us? My thoughts thus tangled-up I place the mug upside-down on the little drying rack next to the sink and then turn to cross the narrow kitchen in a single stride, flicking the light switch off as I go. Then I cross the TV room in three strides to enter my own room and flop my back down on the bed. Three rooms, five strides, not bad, I think, not bad at all. I lie there, fully-clothed on top of my gray comforter and stare at the crack in the ceiling which has always reminded me of the crack on this one door down on Klapp Street, a door painted the same deep reddish hue as the planet Mars, a door belonging to a dilapidated clapboard Victorian with the windows blotted out by heavy drapes and hung with crescent tinfoil moons on every window. What's there, I wonder, listening closely, *blackberry-blackberry-blackberry....*

Awakening suddenly to the sound of raindrops I wrap my shoulders in the gray comforter and roll over to the side of the bed near where the window's splashed and slicked with tiny words,

150

wondering if that's what was happening in my nightmare; a world made of pure text, with no colors, shapes or smells, just words, words falling from the sky, words running down the Velt River, words of Jibjab the Koala-Headed Man filling up the lacquerous bluegreen puddlebeard of Erliss Jr., words glistening with the black pupils of Marnie Kerns' wetbright eyes. Shit. I wonder if maybe I've somehow acquired a bewitched effigy's relationship with my Fnacebook profile, where some nerve twinges every time a cursor mouses over the photograph my face, causing me to awaken in that classic grimace of frozen, seizured surprise. Somehow I can feel the uncertainty of a person deciding whether or not to click, whether or not to Like. Blink. Blink. Eye. Cursor. And haven't I had this dream before, this dream where I am dead, where my body has disappeared and all that's left is my Fnacebook profile, gazing out at the world from my underchin's expression of cycloptic, stump-haloed horror?

As happens in such nightmares the universe is flattened and projected onto the grainy resolution of an outdated point-and-click arrow, an arrow which is frantically mousing around the browser window for an ex, for some way to just close the browser and get out, even if it means killing everyone in the process. No! Now I'm trying to *Quit*, to *Escape*, to *Shut Down*, to *Restart*, but because of the salt-and-peppery pixeled hourglass I cannot click on anything and I am still trapped, still stuck here, lying fully-clothed on top of my bed, buffering, buffering, buffering, listening to the words of rain drumming their parasyllables of indifferent abyssfulness against the surface of my window.

Reaching over to my bedside table I grab at my copy of *Ideas for Words* to see if there's an entry for the feeling of being trapped body-and-soul inside a broken browser window. Half-hoping that if we have indeed invented new technologies for dreaming that at least our propensity for neologizing might begin to offer some sense of a user's manual. Flip. Flip. The paper feels soft and solid beneath the sleepfadedness of my fingers' touch. But I can't, I can't see, the page doesn't glow, I have no lamp, I cannot read a thing that doesn't glow. Shit. My fingers itch. I click on the cover of *Ideas for Words* with my thumb, half-hoping that it will transform magically into a touchscreen. The act makes me wonder if God ever experiences a similar frustration, clicking over the dim icon of my half-sleeping form and waiting for me to load, waiting for his own ancient hourglass to run out of salt-and-peppery pixels, waiting, buffering, waiting, just waiting for me to light and glow.

Finally I get up and flick on the light switch and get back in bed and under the covers and start to actually flip, to actually read. It turns out that *Ideas for Words* has a whole section detailing different affects of digital frustration and regret; *delestration* (n) a rush of frustrated regret over deleting an incorrect file, or deleting a file by accident, *effwidget* (v) to frantically fidget one's cursor around the edges of a window in order to burn off frustration energy after having mistakenly clicked on a bad link, *frerooned* (adj) feeling lost

152

and trapped within an unfamiliar section of the Internet and *screenalgia* (n) nostalgia for a particular type of screensaver, particularly one depicting kitsch palm trees with a tropical sunset. Huh. For me I think the most frequent kind of remorse is not-remembering, clicking-*and-then*-not-remembering, rather than not-clicking or not-seeing. How many memories in my brain begin with a click and go nowhere, leading backwards to languish upon the 404 Error pages of my very soul?

As I listen to the rain I think about God again, God sitting in front of His own computer in his underwear at three thirty AM, God clicking on me, waiting for me to load, waiting for me to buffer sufficiently to maybe *finally* do something cool. It feels good to think about being clicked on, about the cursor arrow of an exotic, interdimensional intelligence moving across time and space as easily as my two-dimensional arrow moves across the computer screen. Closing my eyes I can feel this cursor moving through the rainy sky above me, swiping back and forth with an impatient effwidgeting, knowing that time's almost run out, that a countdown's end is drawing near.

# Wrong Bones

We barely talk. It's OK if we barely talk if we are happy. I know that's what God wants – for us to be happy.

And we are, I think.

*

We eat Lucky Charms right from the box. No bowls. Pour the milk down the plastic liner and dig in. Clarice eats first and then I eat. There's only one spoon. And I think usually she's hungrier than I am. So it makes sense that way, for her to eat and then for me to eat. She really wolfs down those Lucky Charms and then burps and then looks up and me and says: *What!?*

*Nothing,* I always say and she says back that that's what I always am: nothing. So it is. Clarice can be mean sometimes but even her meanness makes me swell because she is her with the sharp princess-face and I am me with the wrong-boned me-face so the fact that she is even directing words towards me is by itself full of God's blessing. So it is. One year ago I would not have imagined. This. Her. Saying that I am always nothing with a sneer that looks sculpted from my favorite of all tomato-based condiments. One year ago I would have already forgotten what it was to be touched. To forget such a thing as simple and basic as the feeling of skin: this is a lengthy process. And what it feels like isn't nothing. It crackles. It singes. It burns. The forgetting does. It comes thick and stale, layering year over year in the ovals primary colors unmixed beneath

154

my squeezed-shut eyelids. This act of slow forgetting creases around the bones beneath my skin with unspeakable intensity. Never have I been able to sit or stand without feeling the feeling of my bones feeling my skin, feeling identical with my skeleton much more than my face, much more than the flesh of my body or this brain that is supposed to do so many thinkings that it does not do. The forgettingness jars badly at even the mere suggestion: gesture, stroke, touch. Skin is a key, turning, turning in my lock. Touching. There's the real miracle, my skeleton believes. Thank you God, for giving me this feeling to be alive on the inside of!

Clarice puts her hands over my mask when she's on top of me. I spread my arms out on either side and turn my palms toward the ceiling and she puts her hands over my mask. I feel them traveling over me, over the distance above my bones, above the places where the seams of skin are creped together: wrists, armpits, collar bone. My skin is rough like tree bark in places but Clarice doesn't seem to mind. She covers over my eyes with her pale crab-like hands so that I do not see her, so that I do not look at her. She lies on top of me and spreads her hips apart and says: *Stop thinking about it, stop thinking about it, stop thinking about it, stop thinking about it* over and over again and I do not know if she's talking to herself or to me or to the ghost of Ai who is sometimes very palpable in the smoke around Clarice's mustard-colored hair. Afterwards I feel a thousand blissful nothings and wonder if this is what happiness is supposed to feel like? When people say the word *happiness* is this what they

155

mean, this feeling that sits inside of me like a traveler upon the lip of a hilltop stump at the end of a long day? My afterthoughts are touching only at the tips inside of a maple-colored cistern at the bottom of my skull. There are dead leaves wilted to lacy skeletons and I spin, drain, drip them off one by one underground, my maple-colored afterthoughts.

I clack the halves of my beak together: clack-a-lack

*Eeeeeeeep*, says Clarice.

*What*, I say.

*Don't do that*, she says, slurping a big spoonful of Lucky Charms. *That clack-a-lack. Don't.*

Ai doesn't need to eat anymore, not since he died last week.

Soon the three of us will begin to make God's natural acts again but I do not know if I can summon up enough emptiness for Ai yet. Because my skin was pulled over to one side from the way Clarice puts her hands over my eyes and I just need a little more time to tug it back over so that I can see again. Ouch! My beak always hurts when the skin gets pulled too far over to one side. And this plus the mask I have to wear: well, it makes my face feel like it is wearing two masks at once! Too many masks, I think God would agree.

*So many bones in people*, says Mother P, *some are bound to be wrong ones, aren't they?* When Clarice kisses the mouth on the mask I get smoke in my own beak from her breathing. Her lungs are full of white fibers and I can feel when they melt apart into my soul. When

156

I open my own beak the smoke fibers trickle out. They sting up my eyes with salty tears.

She says *Ai...*, holding this sound in her dry throatstrings until it is too stretched out of breath and falls silent.

*

For many moments afterwards on her concrete balcony we stand with our bodies nearly touching but not touching. To me these moments feel like years. Sunrise pulls the shadows of our creatureliness into confused shapes on the balcony's concrete, confused shapes which either resemble the spirits of waterfalls or do not resemble anything at all.

In my head I know that Clarice is my girlfriend, even though she makes me wear the mask. It's okay because Clarice has long US American-style hair the color of mustard. It's okay because for someone like me, anything touching is maybe okay. The deep circles under her eyes resemble stains of coffee. She wipes the coffee up with the crumpled paper towels of her cheeks. There are spots from birth upon the long sides of her face. There are lines of sadness, growing.

*

When I first met Clarice she and Ai had only just moved to Peru. That in itself was remarkable. It is not every single day that people from the US Americas move their whole lives to Peru, especially in a not-so-big city far outside of Lima.

She and Ai were the type of lovers who enjoyed yelling at one another when there is a third person who can see the yelling and feel the shame on behalf of both of them. This was my job on a number of occasions. Mother P says I have a special talent for the shame.

It's funny how clock-ticking time in Peru has a way of getting used up so fast. Strong hands squishing that tube of hour-filled toothpaste! To look at a calendar you wouldn't recognize how many days are lined up against the skinny air and the orange Creamsicle light shining on Clarice's breasts at dawn.

Did I first meet her and Ai only 1 or 2 months ago?

Something like that. Ai told me that they were hiding from the US American government. They were pretending to be involved in some kind of fake business. In fact they weren't involved in anything except for crimes-using-a-computer. This crimes-using-a-computer Ai said is a pretty new branch of crime and is viewed by many as being adventurous.

Mother P says crimes-using-a-computer is a passing fad, but Ai did not agree with such a statement. He and Clarice had papers and photographs and lots of invisible "bits" that mean $$$, so they say. That was why they got an apartment in the top of a tall building full of old retirees who don't ask them anything, not even *How are you doing, Clarice and Ai?*

I think the retirees are mostly Japanese. I have found that there are many Japanese in Peru, which at first surprised me. Ai is also Japanese but he also told me that Ai is not his real name. (I think he was lying about that and that Ai is in fact his real name. Mother P says that I do not know when people are lying except when what they are lying about is also a lie. This is another talent of God I have, for tasting always this special flavor or lying). My girlfriend and Ai couldn't do much going outside of the apartment on account of being worried about the invisible eyes of the US American government. That was why Ai got Erl to bring the groceries.

*

The part of my Clarice's apartment I most dislike is the bathroom which is too bad because I often have to pee. This has been the case for me my whole life: peeing often. Mother P used to say things about it to the other mothers, as if it were a joke. I never found this joke was funny. There is something bad in the bathroom which is always smelling horrible. It is better to not think about it too hard, and not-thinking-too-hard is another one of my special talents, says Mother P. But still, I always have to take a moment of bad remembering when I go pee.

Outside above the balcony I see one airplane cross the sky and it crosses out the crescent moon with a white line of airplane steam as if the moon were a typographical error. Daytimes run together since last week and my mind is cloudy with happy not-sleeping. The clouds here look like a brand of buttermilk ranch dressing I once enjoyed eating by itself, without dipping. There was a café back in Velton that used to have the best ranch dressing and Mother P would go and get it and bring it back to the basement so that I could get my face around it. Mother P always talked about the little man from the café, what was his name? Morris, I think, or Moe Riss, or maybe Maw Reese? I cannot remember. In my skeleton's process of forgetting the forgetting feeling of not being touched there are a great many little "bits" that the land beneath my face has thrown away.

*Eeeeeeeep*, says Clarice.

*What?* I say. I am confused.

*Stop,* says Clarice. *You're doing it again. That thing with your beak. You need to stop doing that, okay? It really freaks me out.*

*Sorry,* I say. Sometimes I do things that I do not know that I'm doing.

Peru's the place where the mountains started having kids and never stopped, just pop-pop-pop, more mountains. Like little-grassed swoops and terraces and roadways that are like brown ribbons tying up the gift of land, a gift that's the glory of God, his gift made for us all. I think about how the mountain sun above us is the palace where God's face lives, cutting the world into precious pineapple rings from the tin can of Heaven. I let my mind swim through each ring, like a winged fish doing circus tricks. So often the air on Clarice's concrete balcony allows me to become such an utter sense of freedom, wow, it's really great! Up above I watch as God's face waters up with a red shape that comes bigger and bigger, as if the red shape is approaching us with many tall-minded intentions. Where do our reflections go when we are not using them? Maybe the place above the sky above Peru, I wonder, or maybe they go live inside the reflection of the face of God.

*

Erl was my friend before, even though he stole from me once. Because it was a not-much thing he had stolen, I forgave. Sometimes having a friend like Erl is more important than having a not-much thing that remains unstolen. When Erl asked me to help him carry the groceries up that first time I did it without asking questions. He huffed and puffed because his gut is like a sack of soggy fertilizer. Even though the groceries did not weigh so much Erl still lost all of his breath. *I'm not cut out for this*, said Erl. *Pond for twenty goddamn years now look at me? Hoisting oat mush for some friggin' expat American crimeyuppies. Watershed work don't pay, kid. I mean it. Don't let 'em suck you in, kid. Don't wind up like me, okay kid?*

My girlfriend who was not my girlfriend yet and Ai were very angry at Erl for bringing me up with him. Erl said *Look this was a favor I was doing you, just as a courtesy, okay? So I don't wanna hear another smart word. You know I'm supposed to be friggin' retired, right?* Clarice and Ai tried not to look at me because of the wrong bones in my face. Clarice said *I don't know if our friend Mr. Pond can be trusted anymore, what do you think Ai?* And I saw Erl stiffen up when they called him that, when they called him Mr. Pond... like they had some XL napkin filled with Erl's badness hidden inside of a utility closet of their minds. All three of them knew which utility closet it was and what the badness was. Maybe they thought I didn't know because I didn't understand what they were saying but I did understand or at least I think I maybe did but I didn't ask them to explain because the awkwardness was already like marmalade on a cold toast and I didn't have any knife of feeling with which to spread it. They were not lying but they were lying about lying (silence) because sometimes not saying can be a lie as well. Mother P says I have this as my special talent for always tasting out this specific flavor of lying. And Clarice and Ai were steamed-broccoli mad because Erl had brought me, Elias, a stranger, up into their hiding place, even though they had his XL napkin of badness and knew which utility closet to keep it in, even though that is true he still brought me. Why? Maybe for the same reason he stole a little thing from me, a thing of not-much importance. Erl is like this, you cannot always tell things apart from each other when it comes to his acts.

Clarice spoke at Erl in loud, smashy brrrr-a-bup-a-drup words strung together all at once and I could hear that many were about me, about my wrong-boned face, about why and how and about the invisible eyes of the US American government. But Clarice didn't say any of the things about me towards the direction where my body was standing. Clarice didn't even point towards me with the I-shape of her finger. I guess it is hard for people to place their eyes upon my face and especially my beak unless they have become readied beforehand, and even then it can cause severe distress. This too is part of life, and so with the rest of life that God made for us I have to say *yes please!* to this part as well. Mother P says it is a face just like any other. I do not agree with Mother P on this, even though I agree with her on many things.

Says Mother P: *Lots of people have stupid, boring, pointless faces. Why shouldn't God have taken a nice creative risk with your?* I trust Mother P when she says such things because Mother P makes her living telling the future to people with quite grave concerns. After some minutes my girlfriend and Ai had their yells back and forth, enough to make Erl blush and mumble. I did feel the shame for all of them, and it crept between the forgettingness around my bones. *Finally, something will happen!* I thought to myself, and began to itch a little with anticipation. Then things calmed down and we all took an oily herbal treat. These herbal treats were full of relaxation and made Ai and my girlfriend become no longer suspicious of me. This was all way way way before last week, which was when Ai died. Afterwards I accepted Clarice's offer for her to be my girlfriend, which felt like Getting Saved by God all over again, even though I have to wear the mask that has Ai's face printed on top of it. *That's okay,* I think. Because at least through the mask I can feel the warm crabs of Clarice's hands making their little nests, pressing down against the places above my eyes. It is okay if I look like Ai, what are looking-like-anythings for anyway? We all look like things sometimes, with faces or with words; both are just another kind of mask and if mine looks like myself or like Ai, what would God care? God is about looking, not looking-like. The looking-like, that's what God leaves for us to frolic upon, to make into the warm wrapped-up skeleton shapes of ourselves. Doesn't he?

Mother P would not approve of all this that's happening here, I think, but she has not yet known about what is happening and anyway she lives far away back in Velton, back in the US Americas.

*

Down below the Japanese retirees' garden is dying.

The women have little white umbrellas when they garden, which I wonder: is it a superstition? Because it is never raining.

From Clarice's balcony I can see what they are doing better than they can. The situation is hopeless. Every single flower has wilted, leaving only stalks. It is too bad that they do not understand that the garden will die no matter what they do.

1 or 2 of the men have potbellies and red faces the color of a welt, the way skin turns bad after it has gotten hit with Mother P's belt.

Together the men stand around in their too-tall slacks and talk politely using their hands, or else they also try to feed the plants with cans of water.

It is no use.

The retired Japanese have already wasted so much time saving what cannot be saved. The plants have already decided to turn yellow and then gray and then be dead. When something decides to be dead like that you can't just water it back to life.

*

The smell is horrible. No one has taken the trash out since Ai died. I once said that it would be OK if I took out the trash and Clarice yelled at me and said that we couldn't take the risk. Because of the US American government. But Erl won't do it either because he's in retirement, so it just stays smelling badder and badder.

Smells aren't so important to me after I had the bad accident to my brain. But I still prefer that the trash is taken out, because what else is the proper thing to do with trash? God would have something to say, I know it. Our threesome of God's natural acts scrambles up my feelings of love for Clarice against my feelings of not-love for Ai, whose face I must wear over my own wrong-boned one. But this is part of the deal I accepted when Clarice became my girlfriend. And she is so full of beauty with the hair the color of mustard: who could possibly refuse that kind of offer?

No person, I think.

Not even God, if Clarice asked Him for the same arrangement.

I know Clarice's soul is clothed so well with light and color that nobody will ever understand how to put the beauty of her into words. In our high-up distance blowing *Shhhh* between us the smell this morning is wet in the air and the dawn is big and gold and Clarice's breasts are shiny and so much like orange Creamsicles that it makes my tongue begin to water and my mind to fill with thoughts of flavored ice cream.

And no one has to see us, just us three. Not even Mother P. Only myself and Clarice and the face of Ai's hard ghost.

*

Today the dawn sky over the mountains of Peru looks made from big gold. It is plugged full of spilled up ranch dressing, my favorite sky taste. Such beauty? What makes the tall light speak like this? I will have to ask God, when I meet him. *Stop that* says my girlfriend looking at my beak *I'm trying to be alone for a little while and just do some thinking. Can you just please stop that?*

*Oh... Okay.*

This is okay really it's totally okay by me yes everyone should be alone I back away through the sliding glass door and back into her apartment where the silence captures me and I let its capture start singing inside of my bones one by one my ribs my skull and spine I feel the silence singing and it's singing me.

*

We do not ever wash our hands. They get dirtier and dirtier. When they are barely touching the dirt touches, the dirt is like a magnet it sticks us together and then Clarice pulls away because there is something about the magnetism of dirt that is disgusting. Still she does not wash her hands and I do not wash my hands either. It seems impossible for us to leave the apartment. When we aren't in bed we stand up on the wood floor, or on the concrete balcony. Clarice broke all the chairs after Ai died. The splinters are still everywhere.

We try not to step on them but sometimes we do anyway and several have slid into the loose skin of my bare feet and toes. At least if they are in my feet they will keep the pain outside of Clarice who is my girlfriend.

I have learned piety, and also how to use God's natural action between my legs. Without both devotions, where would someone with such a wrong-boned face and a brain accident have ever gotten? Probably just another basement, somewhere else. Clarice drinks prescription codeine, but only a little bit at a time. She smokes Lnucky Strike cigarettes and fills the apartment with smoke. Sometimes I smoke too, but I don't like it. It is only when the smoke gets heavy that Ai's ghost can become potent and enter my form. When he possesses the emptiness inside me I get an erection.

The first time this happened it was quite surprising since I have not gotten an erection since I started my position 1.5 years ago as a professional subject. That job involves taking a lot of special pills. Mother P got me this job because she said there is no work for people like me with the wrong bones and the accidented brain and especially not in a place like Velton, deep in the squishy cornbelly of the US Americas. The company who I am a professional subject for made me move outside of the US because the special pills can sometimes be dangerous and I had to sign forms saying that I didn't mind if they were dangerous because they were special and eating them was going to be good for me in the end.

But when Ai died last week I quit being a professional subject and flushed all my special pills down the toilet, which felt great. Like a whole new flavorburst was being birthed from each of my fingernails. I have never felt this alive!

Ai possesses my body in the thickness of cigarette smoke and I put on my upside-down mask. I can really feel Ai's ghost hard inside my penis, but even so it feels good because Clarice is covered with the shapes of creatureliness belonging to so much of the world that even her sneer makes me swell!

For this and many things I scream out *Thanks! God!* And Clarice rolls her eyes and says *Shhhhh*.

*

This goes on for hours. I never come.

It is dawn when Clarice goes for a cigarette on the balcony. I stare past her belly at the crescent moon fading in the light of a brand-new mountain sun fresh from its packaging. Here in Peru we are much closer to the sun, I can feel. Perhaps one day with the technology of space flight we will all learn how to visit the sun. I know that if I visit the sun there is a chance I will meet God in person. Clarice can be there, too. These are the things I think about at daybreak, before she again becomes saddened with Ai's death and the bad laughter starts.

Hours turn to days.

There are weeks, suddenly.

I never come.

*

This evening as the sun sets onto the mountains I can feel Ai's ghost, which wisps around us with a great impatient. He is a very horny ghost, Clarice says. I can tell he won't come into my emptiness for another few hours. Not until the sun has left the sky dark and I have put on my scratchy upside-down mask of Ai's face. I pinch at the bony corners of my face where the tips poke out and think about those kids at school who used to say that my face looked like it had a dead bird trapped underneath it.

If they could only see me now!

Ha!

How jealous their own right-boned faces would become.

*

The biggest reason I don't like going to the bathroom in Clarice's apartment is that it contains something which is not good to think about. What it contains the body of Ai who died last week.

I must step over this body to use the toilet since it is lying across the floor. Clarice says we need to keep the body so Ai's ghost has a home when it's not possessing me and giving me an erection. This makes all good sense, I think.

But I do wish that my girlfriend will ask Erl to get rid of Ai's body soon.

I am now pretty sure that there is a small animal or insect making its home in Ai's head because I have begun to notice a big red shape gnawed into the skull. This hole is also making Ai's face look very sad.

Sometimes I think about all the colors of God's face on the distance above the horizon where I can sometimes rest my eyes at dawn.

Even God has the Holy Ghost, and I know that he wouldn't feel as whole without it, which is how I feel when Ai has given me an erection. It makes every inch of my skin shiver. But it is good to see God's face, and these dawn moments after I have put on the mask take me closer to my Creator.

I say a prayer hoping all of this natural action is OK with God, who is just trying to make us fill with His happiness. That's it, I think. What God wants – for us to be happy.

And we are, I think.

# Some People Are Just Like Itchy Bites

Outside on Secret Road the air was humid and the gnats rose up in clouds the shape of giant invisible hands, many-fingered, bandaged with the clouds. I burped. The electricity buzzed in the walls, a low murmur of something waiting to be left unsaid. On my belly. In my bed. In my still little-kid room. On the second story of a squat, flat-roofed house. Counting motes of dust as they hung in the air beneath a ventilation duct. I scratched hard at something on my ribs. Wet and pain. Ew. The house on Secret Road played home to my older sisters Clarice and Jody, Mom and Dad. The family Munn. *A big happy*, as Mikey D would say. With his grin that could make literally anything into a sexual innuendo, whether he was talking baseball stats or appraising dick-shaped frostycakes at Venus Treats. *A big happy.* Mikey D was my best friend. And even I knew he was kind of a shithead.

Clarice and Jody dyed their hair gruesome mauves without permission and spent most of their facial real estate on sullen, bored expressions. My sisters. I was a total brat to them, Clarice especially. Clarice called me Buttface. I called her Canker Sore. That was how we got along so well, us brother and sisters in the big happy, all together in that house on Secret Road.

I lay on my belly hating everyone I knew one at a time, looking out from the second story window. First, I hated my family one family member at a time. Then, I hated the kids at my school one kid at a time. I pictured the kid. Then I filled that image to the brim with jagged waves of contempt and loathing. I imagined terrible things happening to everyone I knew, one by one. Space debris hurtled earthward with smoking comet tails into the rooftops of my friends, enemies and loved ones. Semi-trucks filled inexplicably with ravenous wolves collided in fiery ka-booms, loosing their crazed lupine survivors upon the unsuspecting weak. Volcanoes conspired together beneath the linoleum of Ms. Unica Korn's science class, waiting for the appointed moment to erupt and encase us all in a grim, Vesuvian death.

I closed my eyes and thought about Marnie. Marnie with the brownblack hair and round, gold foil sunglasses legs of ripped denim. Marnie with the Absconder tshirts and the single streak of pale blue dyed down one side of her long bangs. Marnie with the fuckwords, with the Oberiu crimson hexagon stitched to her backpack. Marnie with the intricate, tangled-up doodles of lightning bolts and tentacles. Marniemarniemarnie. My thoughts curled into an endless loop of things that resembled her pale, heart-shaped face.

I wanted to be alone with her.

I wanted to lie in bed with her.

I wanted to tell her things I'd never told anyone, and to listen while she did the same.

I wanted her to understand how I felt like when I hated everything, when I hated myself for hating everything. I wanted her to absolve me of these feelings through every means possible, but

172

most of all through carnal acts.

What were these carnal acts, exactly?

*Marnie will know*, I thought.

*She would help me understand what exactly it was that I wanted from her.*

I rolled over on the colorful beefy-knotted elephants of my comforter to peer out the paned window onto Secret Road. An unathletic jogger lumbered by, knees bulging with each footfall. His name was maybe Vince? Or Frank? It could be Vince. I had seen him at a yard sale once.

Vince/Frank looked sweaty and out of breath.

I thought back to the previous evening when I had been hanging out with Marnie casually, along with Mikey D and Cynthia.

After Mikey called her a negative bitch Cynthia said she was done with him.

*Right*, Mikey said, rolling his eyes.

*No, I mean it!* Cynthia hissed back.

I liked Cynthia and Mikey together. And if not for Cynthia and Mikey being an item, how was I supposed to hang out with Marnie?

What I really wanted to do with Marnie was escape. Escape my stupid flat-roofed house, our stupid flat-faced town, the concentrated tedium named Secret Road, sweaty Frank/Vince, Mom and Clarice and Jody and Dad.

Get the hell out of here. Just go somewhere. Somewhere that didn't feel like waiting. Somewhere else.

In my head it was always with Marnie. We could escape together, go anywhere with just the two of us. But oh, Mikey. What Mikey likes to do is talk shit. What Mikey likes to do is sound like he's black.

Like last night:

*S'whatup, y'm'name is Mike Deez, like deez nuts, deez like the Mickey billions, talkin' Golden Arches Café n'shit, n'all dem biddies here know what's up wit Mike Deez, lookin' fine yasselves Marnie bae, what up girl: I see you peepin', damn lady you gettin' all growed up'n shit, ha ha yeah, everyone cool except dat Cynthetica she a negative bitch haha I'm playin', shit iz just Mikey from \*da block\*, yo.*

Mikey is not from the block. He's not from any block. Certainly not \*da\* block. He lives in a blockless housing development called Sagamore Glade. It's one of the most overwhelmingly nondescript places in all of Toulous. And Mikey is not black. In fact, he's about as white as they come around here. The guy literally wears Crocs *with* plaid shorts. Flip-flops. Shit. He's white even for most white people. Among (white) strangers Mikey tries to spin some story about growing up in a hood-ass suburb of St. Louis.

*Das why I got da ill flow, yo.* (Has Mikey ever even been to St. Louis? That is the real question.) Down in the hollow where the sassafras smell hung heavy in the twilight Mikey and Cynthia and Marnie and me had sat around on rotted logs and passed a flashlight around telling ghost stories. We passed around a jam jar of Mikey's dad's bourbon cut with some Hnawaiian Punch. Passed it and passed it around. Got a little tipsy. Fever-faced. We told the one about the half-faced girl. The toothless old woman with the haunted meth lab. The triple-bodied gods who walk around disguised as humans, just waiting to get one of us kids alone.

*Ooooooooh*, said Marnie. I smiled and tried to scoot my butt closer to hers on the rotted log. Mikey tried to put his arm around Cynthia, but she shrugged him off with a look of pure venom.

*Jeez*, said Mikey. *Watsamatta Cynth? You mad, bruh?*

*

People always ask me: *Secret Road? So what's the secret? Henh?*

They always ask me this. Like a kind of stupidity reflex. The same way that Carl, the master baker at Venus Treats erotic bakery always always *always* gets asked which hand he master bakes with. Always. People can't help themselves.

The master baker groans. I groan.

There is no Secret. People suck. That's the secret. And really, that's not really much of a secret at all.

So after getting tired of dealing with this highly repetitive Q & A two-step, I made up a story that Secret Road is actually named after a man named Ted Secret, unheralded inventor of the edible fez.

*The edible fez?* They invariably ask. Those people. Who suck.

*Sure*, I say. *Like a hat, typically maroon, with a black tassel. Ted makes them out of coiled licorice. Sometimes textured marzipan. I mean, after 9/11 they kind of lost popularity over here but over Algeria and Morocco, man, they go nuts for 'em!*

To me, this lie is an obvious lie.

Who the fuck would eat a fez?

But you'd be surprise how many people just nod and go: *Huh, an edible fez. How 'bout that?*

Downstairs I sidled into the kitchen, still thinking about what happened last night. About Marnie. I pulled up the itchy part of my shirt where my hand had been going to work. It came up sticky, three little red bites. Ew. Shit.

*

The night before, after Marnie and Cynthia had all gone home to bed, me and Mikey D had walked along the bald roots of the silvery birch and beech trees, walking and listening to the shish-shishing of the forest all around us.

In the distance an owl hooted. Just me and Mikey D. We scratched our sides. The scratchiness of our t- shirts clinging to our ribs. The Hnawaiian bourbon stink on our breaths.

*Wanna go sneak into Marnie's,* Mikey joked. *I bet she'd make with both of us.*

*Shut up*, I kicked Mikey in the shins.

*Phleh*, he spat. *Bet she would, though.*

The sky had gone through a chromatic swing into a pale green, luminous behind the birch and beech trees.

*Hoot-hoot!*

*Wanna go back?*

*Shut up*, I said again. Our footsteps stuck in the soft

marshmallow goo of mud.

*Can you hear him?*

*Shut up. There isn't any one there.*

*No, I hear him!*

*Who?*

*Him. Ted Secret. He's sprawled out down in the underbrush. He's counting out the number of our footsteps. Our breaths. Don't you hear him counting? He's counting us on his hands. And then he starts over again. One, a-two. One and two. One, a-two. One and two.*

*Oh,* I said. The forest night rustled close around us, dry leaves and tangled thornbushes. I shivered in my tshirt and my nape hairs pricked up.

*Each person only gets so many footsteps. So many breaths. Then once you spend 'em, it's *ploof*, that's it. Sayonara. You're dead.*

*Mikey, that's the dumbest dumbshit thing you've ever said! Seriously, man.*

*No, it's true. Swear! Scout's honor.*

I took a deep breath and felt a little bit better, secure in my knowledge that Mikey D had most certainly never been a Boy Scout. But then I started having to keep myself from thinking about counting my footsteps, counting my breaths. Damn. I wanted an exemption. I wanted to stop even considering the possible existence of such an actuarial, detail-oriented apparition. Down the long slope we went to the edge of Erliss Pond and stood standing there, breathing hard, each alone with the nightliness of our own dim thoughts.

I thought about the tiny submarine. I thought about drowning. I thought about the three-bodied goddess on Mom's gold coin. I wondered if I should say something, if we should talk about the lostness of that day so many drowsy months ago.

I swallowed, saying nothing.

*Ever slept in a tree?*

*Yup, for sure. But I know you haven't. And I bet you can't*, I told him. I said it again, sing-songy, taunting. Mikey is very susceptible to peer pressure. Even if there's only one peer.

Usually just me. Peering. Pressuring.

It wasn't long before we found a sturdy-looking hemlock and heaved up, first me on Mikey's stirrupped hands, then pulling him up after me onto the back of a thick branch maybe six or seven feet off the ground. The bark was rough and I worried about those little ants crawling up my nose.

*Mikey?*

*Yeah Elwood?*

*Do you... I mean, okay, just give me the first thing that comes to mind here, but... do you believe in God?*

*Dude, of course. I mean, I believe that God totally sucks. He's way too old and out-of-date. Like, why hasn't anyone come up with a better God? I feel like, if you look at history, like, back in the day it was many gods, then it got to be the one God, then like the twentieth century is like zero, zero gods and then finally, now, we might be approaching like the equivalent of some negative number gods. Those are gods I can believe in. Negative. Less-than-zero Gods.*

*Mikey, what are you even talking about? You know negative numbers are just theoretical, right? You can't have a negative number of nouns, like a negative number of apples or toes or whatever. It wouldn't make any sense.*

*Well yeah, but so is God right? Theoretical, I mean. Like negative numbers: they're both real, and theoretical. Like money. Or power. Real, but not physical. Theoretical, too, in a way. And since it's up to us I'm gonna say that we can basically number these things however we want. Irrationally. Imaginarily. Exponentially. You name it. But really, I'm thinking Negative Gods are probably the next wave in terms of the future of Godliness. Some kind way-larger-than-life antigods. Maybe like giant, evil cartoon characters?*

*Pssssssssh, Mikey you're full of it. No one's going to start kneeling down and praying to a bunch of evil cartoon characters. Organized religion's existed for how long? Thousands of years! And you think it's just going to roll over and give it up to the magic of computerized animation and slick motion graphics? Come on, dude.*

*Dude, that's what I'm sayin'. Thass why we need to be inventing da fresh gods. I mean it. I'm tired of this bullshit. Don't you feel like we could be doin' some better?*

*Mikey, Mikey, Mikey...*

*Yes?*

*Now don't take this the wrong way. But what on Earth could you possibly have in your life to be tired of? Huh?*

*Shee-et, Elwood. You don't know shit one about my life. Dis is Mikey D rememba? Mikey from da block?*

It was the best hours of sleep I got during junior high. When the sun's rays swam into the vermillion of my eyelids I was lying face down, hugging around the hemlock branch. On a branch a few feet below I thought I saw another body sleeping, coattails parted over a skinny ass.

It wasn't Mikey.

*Hello*, I whispered cautiously. *Is that you, Ted?*

The figure turned around, looking up.

*Yeah that's me*, he said. *Ted Secret, at your service. I'm a cautionary tale.*

*Oh*, I told him, still whispering. *That's too bad.*

*All those fezzes, man,* said Ted. *I was a millionaire. Parties, girls, booze. Just like on TV. I had it all. I guess I just couldn't handle it.*

*What went wrong?* I asked him.

*You know,* Ted murmured. *I guess deep down I always felt like it was some kind of scam. The fezzes. The marzipan. The whole thing. Like I was an imposter.*

*So what about the road?* I asked.

*Oh*, said Ted. *That's me all right. Nights I sleep on hemlock branches. Days I'm a road. People walk all over me. I love it. Free massages. Actually I really should have started out that way. As a road, I mean. Screw the fezzes. I was never meant to become an international sartorial-culinary superstar.*

*Really?*

*Well, yeah. And plus, if I'd started out as a road I'd be way further along by now, that's for sure. Few more houses at least. Oh well. You live and you learn.*

*Oh, is that how that all works?* I asked him. *With roads?*

*Yup. Well, pretty much.* Ted Secret shrugged the back of his tailcoat. We were having this whole exchange over his left shoulder and it looked like he was getting a stiff neck.

*Gotcha*, I said, feeling lost as I returned to the sweet vermillion of my eyelids.

*

It was just before noon when Mikey and I woke up and walked into downtown Toulous. Mikey said he needed to call his parents. To check in, or something.

*No charger*, he said. We went into the knickknacky little vase shop and loitered over to the register while pretending not to look like suspects in an upcoming crime.

*Ummm, do you possibly have a phone charger?*

The proprietor looked like he'd had sleep apnea for a decade. Wait, I knew him! Who was he? Vince? Frank? The sweaty guy! He looked at Mikey and me and said: *What?*

Mikey repeated the question. *For an iPhnone?*

*All we have is chargers.*

*What!?* Mikey looked confused.

*Just kidding. We have vases, too. We're really a vase store, not a phone charger store. But I'll charge your iPhnone. No charge. Ha. Get it? Give me your phone. But look around, why don't you? Maybe even buy a vase? It wouldn't hurt, you know. Support the local economy. Vases make great gifts. Flowers for your little lady. Quite affordable, too.*

The proprietor took Mikey's iPhnone and hooked it up to a bendy charging cable behind the register. When Mikey was handing it over I noticed next to the register a squat vase that contained one of the tiniest, rattiest dogs I'd ever seen.

*That's a dog*, I said.

*It is,* said Vince/Frank. *In a dog vase. Patent-pending. You have a dog?*

*Nope. No dog.*

*Shame. Well, you could always get a dog vase and then down the line if you get a dog you'll already be set up for it, vase-wise.*

*Can I still put flowers in it?*

*Um. Well, we really recommend not. You'll notice we sell flower vases aplenty. Keep the flowers with the flower vases. Dogs with the dog vases.*

*Hey,* said Mikey. *You remind me of my friend Ted Secret. Know Secret Road? The place that's named after him?*

*Yeah,* said Vince/Frank, snorting. *I live on Secret Road. And I know your friend here does too, although I don't know his name.*

*Elvin? Kelvin? Something like that?*

He pointed at me and continued. *You came to a yard sale at my house. I sold your dad Mark a half- used box of frilly toothpicks. I mean half-empty, not half-used. Jesus, why did I even say that? It's not like we used half of each toothpick and then put them back in the box. That would be an odd thing to do, wouldn't it? Secretly foisting used toothpicks on our neighbors? How bizarre! No one should ever do that. You think we would? We wouldn't! Scout's honor.*

Vince/Frank looked visibly uncomfortable. *But no,* he continued. *I didn't know the road was named after Ted Secret. What'd he do?*

*Inventor,* said Mikey before I could jump in. *Invented the edible fez. Edible hats of all kinds, actually. It kind of reminds me of your dog vase. With the patent, and all.*

*That was a joke*, said Vince/Frank. *You can't file a patent on a dog vase. Whoever heard of such a thing?*

*Says who?* asked Mikey, and from the slurring I thought he might still be a little boozy. *I'm Mikey D and I do what I want! Matter-a-fact, I'll patent \*your\* dog vase. Boom.* He grinned slyly to make the sentence sound like a sexual innuendo. I nearly burst into the kind of snorting laughter that clears allergy season sinuses. Vince/Frank scowled. Mikey yawned.

*Hey man*, said Mikey. *I think I need my phone back.*

*Fine*, said Vince/Frank. *Here's your damn phone. Friggin' freeloader. Just so you kids know, you can't just glide through life on the kindness of vasiers. There aren't even very many of us left, not since the crash. And I don't for a second believe that cockamamie about Ted Secret. Who'd wear a friggin' edible fez? That's ridiculous.*

*Sorry*, I said. (Why did I apologize? I wasn't even involved! Plus, I was not particularly sorry. And also, I felt like my feelings had been hurt. Particularly by Vince/Frank's use of the word *cockamamie*. Like, what even did that word... *even mean...?*)

We shuffled out in prickly silence.

Once we'd gotten some distance from the vase shop I gave Mikey a hard time for ripping off my Ted Secret bit. And for messing it up, on top of that.

*Get your own material*, I told him. *Stop sponging off of me! What, you want people to start calling you Mikey the Sponge?*

*Jeez*, said Mikey. *So-orry!*

It was already getting hot and I had some bites were puffing up red and juicy under my shirt. I scratched them which made them itch more. That's how bites work. They're like a one-step recipe for more unpleasant versions of themselves. You do what they tell you to do and then they screw you over. They're like tiny red sociopaths, those bug bites are.

*Mikey*, I asked. *D'you think you and Cynthia are broken up for real?*

*Nah*, he waved me off. *Biddies be cray-zee. Biddies be always-comin'-back. Me'n Lady C gonna be knockin' boots again before y'know it. I mean: I got them deez! Cuz I'm Mikey Deez! Ha-ha!*

And he leapt and clicked his sneaker heels twice in the air.

I'll admit those kind of antics still kept impressing me, regardless of how juvenile or idiotic the anticker might be.

*Look up there!*

*What?*

*That cloud... man, that cloud looks like a dick!*

Henh. So it did. Mikey stumbled on the bald of a beech root and almost careened full on into my collarbone. I caught his shoulder to keep from falling and turned to face him, drawing us both up.

*Mikey*, I asked. *Have you ever even been to St. Louis?*

# Snatur9

*Kssssssssh K-k-kshhhh!*

The heat won't go up any higher. Marnie plays with the knob. How can it still be so cold in here? Behind the goldfoil frames of her small round sunglasses Marnie feels her eyes close and stay closed. Listening to the sound of the Snaturn's heating system. *Snnffffffff.* She takes a big whiff, just to see if she can actually smell what she thinks she smells. Hair and dust and dead skin cells, motes roasting on orange-hot metal coils. Marnie can feel each speck of dust and hair and skin grow bright orange with heat before it expires in a wisp of traceless smoke. *Snfffffffff.* Shoot, when did she get this stuffy, this nosesick, this congested and jittery? *Stay closed, eyes. Inhale. There's nothing to see here. Snffffffffff. Ackhhhhhhh.* Marnie feels the rush of dry air melting away the phlegmy sealant from those cracks in her mind's obscure exoskeleton, filling her senses with a rush of sudden, liquid presence. *Ackhhhh.* Flooding. Gushing. Here, here beneath her face. Her face clogged with all the slimes of winter smoke, her face of closed eyes behind round sunglasses, slumped and resting, here, hundreds of miles away from home. Nearly further than she's even ever been from home. Right? Velton. The foot of the hillsloped Velton Cemetery. Stone angels. Black grass. Wintercrust. Everything's a prism, jagged. And the cold does not stutter. It does not relent. *Brrrrrrrrrrr.* Marnie tries to feel as relentless as the cold, as the burning-scented cold of Snaturn's burning-frozen air. Tries.

*Relentless!* Bites her lower lip, bites until it nearly bleeds. Squeezes herself together. Wincing. *Relentlessness...*

It makes her fingernails hurt copper sparkleblossoms when she sucks on them, when she bites down on their nubbiny numbness one by one so hard between her teeth. *Ch-ch-ch-ch.* Teeth. Hers. Chattering. *Come on. Hold. Hold still. Please? Won't you? Can't you just? Hold. Me. Together?*

Ice crystals whip around the spikes of the cemetery's wrought iron fence at the crest of the hillslope's edge. Deep-sunk footprints frozen scars into the mud beneath. Footprints trampled by the distant gathering. Peering up she can see them, and... *Ch-ch-ch-ch.* Marnie clenches, gazing up at those mud scar footprints, following the line of that dark, shadowsoaked fence. Keeping one world out. One world in. Slats of ashmilk light between the black fence poles, kissing the icecaps of each halberd finial with a frayed asterisk of brightpale trembling gold.

Voices edge their way through the wind's keening and pool at the low spots of Marnie's clenched-up memory. Other murmurs. Other reals. She can see the figures of the crowd now, lining up. Tombstones in the dead of winter. Figures bound in black, bundled and shaking in shapes of wool. *Sobs?* Marnie swallows. Tailcoats and hats with dark brims. Veils. Shaking lumps of silhouetted bodiness beneath the icyblack skeledactyls of the cemetery's alder trees. Cold and cold. So very cold. Marnie's breath is vaporous enough to feel like a big white beard of knitted fishline, puffballing around the

187

corners of her face. *Pshhhhhh! Aaaaaaaah!* The beard elongates, undulates and then contracts with her inhale.

Silence. Breathless. Dead-time, an eternal interval before she chokes, coughs, snufflechatters *kkksssssshhhh-ch-ch-ch* yet again.

Ouch. Shoot.

Marnie hunkers down again above the pipe of colored glass, white lighter clasped in hand. Clenching. Wincing. It's too cold to even smell anything. Butane. Burning. Clicking. Lighting. Inhaling. Blowing out and up over the bloody cracks in her pale, dry lips, a plume of raveling-and-unravelng beardsmoke up towards the hairline nick in the Snaturn's windshield, up towards the graymelting shape of distant clouds hung low above the figures darkly shaking shades.

*

M: r u going to tell me?

K: ophelia. but with your smile

M: the one from your profile pic, the one that changed it to

M: ok go on

K: so she's tied up, right? with like a hostage-type situation? terrorists trying to steal the throne of denmark. but no one sees what's going on. they don't get that it's a fake suicide ploy. and there's no time left to spare.

M: wait, where's hamlet?

K: hamlet? oh yeah, that fool's off with horatio knee-deep in the bowels of castle kronberg's wastewater treatment system, both of them done up in ghostbuster gear and rubber waders and walking in circles with the hopes of re-locating hamlet sr.

K: hamlet sr.'s poltergeist to demand clarification w/r/t what the fuck is actually going on

K: with gertrude and claudius

M: ah ok

K: but little do they know that they've been basically conned by wily guildenstern into this whole ghosthunting boondoggle, guildenstern who is not only making an absolute killing on the referral bonus for two quite-pricey sets of boutique ghosthunting equipment (plus the branded ghosthunting waders) but

M: but?

K: but... (and here's the rub), who may or may not be *also* on the take from a certain shadowy int'l terrorist network

K: thereby giving the terrorists precisely the sort of distraction they so desperately need

K: to snatch ophelia, fake her murder at the hands of norway and

K: provoke a revanchist denmark into starting world war iii

K: pretty slick, huh?

M: wait

M: start wwiii?

M: by faking ophelia's death?

K: exactly. now what we don't know at the time is what's motivating the terrorists, whether it's pure damn-the-world nihilism or daesh/isis-style antisecularism or even if the group's funding might reach all the way back to a certain fortinbras

M: aha! i knew it!

K: haha yes, fortinbras the young king of norway, a man who's not only still p. salty from the battlefield asswhoopings his dad endured at the hands of hamlet sr.

K: but is also, coincidentally-or-not-so-coincidentally, an obsessive practical effects enthusiast and one-time prizewinning haunted house franchisee

M: i'm guessing that backstory's long on that one

K: um, well yeah

M: okay okay, i'm with you. so we're talking about a norwegian monarch with penchant for pyrotechnic hauntings, for hair-and-makeup corpsifications and, presumably, for generally faking peoples' deaths (e.g. ophelia's)

K: and even for simulating the occasional hyperrealistic poltergeist. so...

M: ooooooh ah ha, okay i see where this is going...

M: lol such a troll

M: and may i ask where we are this whole time?

M: as in, you and me? ok

K: well, as star specimens of hamlet jr.'s func. equiv. of seal team 6 it's basically all up to us to uncover the shadowy/fortinbras-sponsored terrorist connection, rescue ophelia and return to castle kronberg before hamlet/horatio get sucked into the escalating anti-norwegian war frenzy by persuading them that the whole thing's just an elaborate trap

M: damn

M: so you'd probably be re-classifying this remix of hamlet as action/adventure rather than the traditional, you know, *tragedy*

M: i'm guessing

M: does that sound about right to you?

K: well, i mean it could still end up being pretty tragic, right?

K: ok but yeah so you're not wrong haha

M: i know, dude. i know i'm not wrong

K: walk with me tho

M: ha ok

K: an isolated cabin out in the woods on a hillside

K: above a peaceful little pond

K: ducks are chilling

K: cattails stirring

M: a couple blackberry bushes?

K: full and ripe and waving their berries in the breeze

K: then: ka-blam! you

K: kick down the door. i circle in around you, uzi

K: drawn, let my back hug the wall as you fell terrorist hench ppl left and right with professionally deft karate chops. and then

M: but wait, why?

K: why what?

M: like why do we even care? i mean, we're talking about serial homicide here. let's not play games when innocent lives are at stake

K: serial homicide?

M: what!? don't you think those low-level terrorist body guards totally have kids and pet goldfish and shows to watch and stuff? that's what i can't ever stand with the action/adventure movies – like, you're working a shit job to begin with

M: henching for some egomaniacal dickbag and then bam, some other egomaniacal dickbag swoops in and twist-snaps your neck or whatever

M: bam, right there, dead as a doornail

M: and we're all just supposed to sit back and applaud? is that the idea?

K: k but what about ophelia? what about hamlet jr.? preventing wwiii?

M: yeah, okay why is that *our* responsibility? i mean, how did we even get involved in the first place? what dark episode in our backstory brought us to the point of going on a lethal rampage to protect the crown of denmark in the freaking first place?

K: i mean, well...

M: dude, didn't you even like think this through!? come on!! you could drive a freaking zamboni through that plot hole

M: !!!

K: so you're saying you aren't pro-ophelia? like, from a sympathy/empathy standpoint?

M: omg that's soooo beside the point. you're framing this whole metadrama around an absurd contortion of scandinavian geopolitics and

M: i mean

M: it's like we've been roped into defending what to me is so obviously a corrupt and illegit monarchy to begin with that i, like

M: i can't even

M: like why are we henching for hamlet jr in the first place? huh? why do we even want to save the day for this totally despotic wishy-washy danish manbaby?

M: idk dude, i just don't know

K: damn

K: ok ok

K: so you don't wanna save ophelia? from the terrorists? from a totally unpleasant form of assassination? we'll just sit back and let them drown her? just cross our camo-clad arms and shrug, like, *oh well, that's not really our problem*

*K: ...?*

M: well...

K: what if we saved her and then the three of us team up in act iv and in a surprise double-cross unite with the remaining terrorists to take down the despotic hamlet dynasty

K: and then

K: maybe ophelia emerges in the play's final climax to deliver hamlet jr.'s broadsword execution, disguised as a hirsute viking until

K: the final denouement, ripping off her shaggy black beard just before

K: delivering the poetic, fatal blow

M: haha ok

M: i like that one better

M: :D

M: but what's the thing about ophelia stealing my mouth? that part's random. too dreamlike

K: yeah. well tbh i'm not really sure about that one. i mean, i just kind of added it on at the end to see how you'd react

M: again, i question the motivation. like, why?

M: why do i want to get my mouth back? why couldn't i live a perfectly happy mouthless life?

K: jeez idk

K: sandwich-eating?? sky-kissing?? frantically yelling the word QUIET at ppl?

M: haha. but no. i say no. let ophelia keep my mouth. let her get kidnapped. let her get assassinated and start wwiii. why not let the terrorists win? why not let two monarchies duke it out for a few grim centuries? to get back a fucking mouth? please.

K: damn. you're stone cold haha

M: maybe my mouth will autonomously multiply and then ophelia's drowned corpse will become covered in my mouths, like her body'll be wearing a muumuu of big toothy-grinned polka dots. really i don't mind if her skin is pierced the panting of 20+ of my mouths. why would i mind that? really. i'd be fine with that...

    K: you're so fucking weird

    M: pot

    K: kettle

  ·  K: haha

    M: :D

*

The real face of Killem was a fact that Marnie could only guess at. But as far as faces go, what does *real* even mean, anyway? No, not in the dumb reality-might-not-exist way, but in the what-if-someone-has-two-faces-and-one's-made-of-pixels-and-one's-made-of-skin-which-one's-really-the-real-face? Because riiight? Kind of? Killem's chat avatar showed 50% of Willem Dafoe's headshot from his role in *Shadow of the Vampire*, melded with 50% of a red-eyed Lovecraftian cybercorpse. So creepy! Marnie wrinkled her nose the first time, the second time, the third time that it caught her eye. And the fourth time? Well, she thought, the face does have a sort of chthonic pizzazz to it, maybe the same way old gneocities websites plastered with clip-art of runic talismans or pixelated Masonic symbols end up having a sort of chthonic pizzazz. Cyber ruins. Crypts with static URLs. The echoes of ancient mouse clicks on the cerulean blue of underlined links, broken, all broken, leading outwards towards the empty tombs of last century's 404 Errors. What was old even, and what was young in this airless, timeless series of tubes?

195

Like Killem's face, such things make Marnie feel half-pleasantly uncertain.

*Ignition slits to other reals,* as Killem would say. *Find the right key, and a whole new kind of hum starts turning over.* Images. Sounds. Scenarios. Supercollisions. Marnie approved. Immensely. That feeling. Of playing a part in some lavish and ineffably complex dramaturgy, typing breadcrumbs off the floor of a swaying, jiggling moonbounce labyrinth, her bare arms held open to the LCD flicker of all far-off worlds. It got away from her. Not him or his creepy face or even the suggestion of his body but the density of her own unknowable intentions that she felt herself reacting, responding and then thickening against the texture of his keyboard voice. Tapping. Typing. Clicking. She held it close, this density, picked bright specks out from its fuzzy seedcoat, inspected and rearranged them within the collection of her own overextended longings. Biting her nails to copper sparkleblossoms beneath the sealant of her pressed-tight lips. Squeezing. Awakening. Peeling off the skins of nightliness and standing naked, steaming and dead-feeling beneath the spout of the upstairs shower. Even naked she'd feel a buzzing at her thigh where a pocket would be, a phantom buzzing from a phantom phone. Killem. Sitting, kneeling, crouched and hunched and slouched and cross-legged in front of her phone, her computer, her exit portals to another her, another future Marnie. Night after night. Day after day. Together, they exhausted one another. Talked about anything and everything, about distant places, about the future of language and about the fictional people that they felt some kind of way about in dregginess of tired light through all those hours close to dawn.

Click. Clicketty-click-click. With hours as heavy as this, who has time or need for anything else? Click. Blinka-blinka-blink. Blinking tab, blinking icon. Another message has arrived. And the ellipse, that painful ellipse, showing another message being written, being deleted, being re-written, waiting, arriving, being typed. How can the mere act of getting and receiving tiny lumps of text contain so much pleasure, so much torrid, gruesome energy? Click. And yet, didn't it? Feel? Just? So? Real?

Years afterwards Marnie would wonder half-seriously if it hadn't all just been some kind of dream or medically-recognizable delusion. Only reading back over the saved chat logs of their conversations would answer that question with both *yes and no*. Yes, because it was a delusion, a delusion in which two people lived via strings of vivid symbols and no, because it was real, just as all delusions must be real to someone in order to exist at all. And yet still, she'd wonder, doubting, unbelieving at the strange suddenness of it all. Unslept night after unslept night of typing, chatting, imprecating and intricating will begin to warp the human mind. Marnie felt this, felt herself warping, peeling, fading into the shadowy edges of the hallways at school, the corners of her classrooms, the margins of her homework pages where her eyes would rest and often close in little bursts of sleep. In these short dreams she would become filled not with images but with the text itself, the typings, the sounds, the lusciousness of punctuation. Faces, faces made of keyboard symbols. His. Killem's. It wasn't long before every colon started to resemble a pair of tiny, beady eyes. Before every dash, a nose. Parentheses, mouths and Ps were mouths with tongues, stuck out and jeering. Os lips opened with a gratuitous, lambent wonder and Ds brought forth a mouthvision of utter, unequivocal delight, brimming over with a thousand furious joys.

*How will I know when I'm in love?* Marnie wondered this to herself as she clicked, as clean morning light fell through the attic window across her dusty keyboard and at last she allowed her tired lids to close. *Because it feels like... feels like...*

*

M: do you ever worry about being clingy?

K: haha am i supposed to read some kind of truly unsubtle hint into that question?

M: no...

M: well, i mean, read whatever you want into it. i'm not going to nannygoat your hint-reading on this one. but

M: i mean no i was just thinking. it is something girls worry about. clinginess. cynthia's always talking about how she has to like instill a sense of discipline in mike,

M: mike her bf mike, i'm saying

M: like to keep him wanting more, etc. etc.

K: that sounds like bullshit

M: no but i mean it works

198

M: ish

M: it works for her

M: not that i'm the biggest fan of her dating mike in the first place

M: obvi

K: well, this all sounds kinda creepily pavlovian

K: and to answer your question, yes

K: as a matter of fact

K: although with guys *clingy* is typically reworded as *creepy* and generally

K: suggests some darker pathology than a case of mere clumsy overaffection. no?

M: omg speaking of cynthia she totally sent me this amazing thing earlier today

M: you're gonna love this, it's this series of german stories about roy orbison getting wrapped in clingfilm

K: wut

M: http://michaelkelly.artofeurope.com/orb2.htm

K: ahahaaaahahahahahhaha

K: *The satisfaction is unparalleled by anything in my previous existence.*

K: haha marnie i didn't know you were into this kind of thing

M: ???

M: what kind of thing? you mean awesome literature?

K: no you know this is fetish stuff, right?

M: what are you talking about

M: no, killem, this is two people in love. ulli and roy

M: orbison

K: hahahahaha

M: haha

K: ok so you've clearly answered your own question here

K: the whole drama here is about a guy who's anxious that he's perceived to be clingy

K: literally

M: even though he totally is

M: and knows it

M: and writes so matter-of-factly about it. without irony

K: exactly

M: well then

M: it seems i have

M: answered. my own

K: question

K: ha

*

*Who is he, honey?*

Marnie's room is dark and messy, the floor covered with dirty tshirts and crumpled jeans with the knees worn out. Windowshades hang heavy across slats of a wintery scrimshaw afternoon. The silence strings black licorice between the doorway and Marnie's bed, thickening, drooping. Mom lets her arms go akimbo. She looks around the room, at the Pnokémon posters and the stack of Jhonen Vazquez comic books, at the flight of an albatross across a poster advertising *The Absconders' Truthbleed Antiworld Tour 2011*. On the little wooden end table a coven of paper witches are superglued around the rim of a pale blue lampshade.

*I don't know*, thinks Marnie.

*I'm fine, except I'm the opposite of fine*, thinks Marnie.

*No one. He's no one, Mom*. Not now. Not anymore.

Silence, hesitant. Sympathy and cautiousness wend together in the space between Mom's parted lips. What's really going on here?

*Marnie, you know you can't just shut yourself up like this without me worrying. I can't help it. I'm a Mom. Let me be a Mom for a second here. Okay?*

For a moment Marnie considers it. Opening up. Spilling it all out. It would feel better, wouldn't it? But at the same time wouldn't it ruin everything? Her. Killem. Other murmurs. Other reals. Love, or some adolescent parody of love? Wouldn't they wilt against the ugliness of awkward empathy, the tawdriness of the silence that comes after an admission that cancels any hope of fantasy? Her. Killem. Wouldn't it then become unbearable? And when Marnie feels unbearable it is not just an expression, as Mom would say, but rather it is literal: *she cannot bear it*. Squeezing. Pain in the red darkness of squinch-closed eyes. Wincing. Breathing fast. Thinking about the after-image of a fictitious 50-50 face, capillaries and circuitry, wondering about the way memory disintegrates and turns to rainbow curlicues and pain inside one's eyelids.

*As if this terrible pain wasn't even real*, she wonders. *As if I've made the whole thing up.*

*Marnie, don't you think you'd feel a little better if you told me about it?*

Nothing.

*Hey. I'm your Mom. Right? Remember?*

*There's nothing. Nothing really. Nothing worth talking about.*

Mom sucks in her breath, thinking about all of the things that nothing could or could not be. *Sssssssssss.* She exhales slowly through her nose, waiting, wondering, waiting for a sense of what comes next.

*

*Killem Dafoe wants to chat. Push Yes to Accept.*

Boredom, gray upon its stations across the milk-colored Kentucky sky, the kind of sky that portends uncertain rain. Outside could not have been more catatonically suburban if it was an ancient boredom-themed screensaver instead of an actual town in actual Kentucky. Lazy, unoriginal neighborhood choreography. Loser lawns and white khaki-clad dads with station wagons and minivans parked beneath the shadow of garage door basketball nets. Vom. Quadruple-vom.

This was back when Marnie was still fourteen, still coming out of her deep Japanophile phase, finding Nietzsche through Mishima instead of vice versa (Mishima through Tezuka, Tezuka through

202

Miyazaki, Miyazaki through Dianna Wynne Jones). Daily life involved a lot of jagged pencil drawings of Super Saiyans and a data-stick full of pirated Neon Evangelion Genesis and Cowboy Bebop. Her role models. Jaunty outlaws with the swagger of interstellar love affairs and faces eternally youthed by the future-miracle of deep space cryonics. *What does innocence really mean?* Marnie wondered. To feel that one is transgressive for reading fantasy books, for thinking unspeakable thoughts, for staying up late to watch exotically spikey-haired cartoons? Marnie still avoided anything that was actually 18+ with a compulsive diligence, completed homework a safe number of days in advance and made her bed neatly before rushing off to catch the first bus to school. She read the classics and never skipped a footnote. Other than Cynthia she had few friends and when her hand shot up to answer a question in English class her fingers quivered with real fervor. She even began saying aloud that she was a morning person, knowing it wasn't true but hoping that, through saying enough, she might change. Those days. Days of school and home. Days of trying. Days of boredom. Days that didn't even feel like days, and nights that passed in fitful, sharp-edged drowsings that awoke to sweating, clenched-tight palms.

*Killem Dafoe wants to chat. Push Yes to Accept.*

Marnie had already clicked through Rneddit, finding a few of her guilty pleasures in r/WTF, r/yesyesyesno, cryptozoology, polari, kiki/bouba, Blodeuwedd. Click, scroll. Marnie had already felt frictionless. Ingesting the text of symptoms belonging to strange

203

delusions. Capgras, Fregoli, Jerusalem. Exhausting her daily fact-ache. The knee-jiggling pentupness of abstract-yet-connected information. Her painfully unsatisfied desire to feel, to feel real feeling, to feel alive and excited and exciting. About the future. About anything. When would Cynthia be off from Snubway? They would go to the Toulous-Sheffield Shopping Centre and stroll around together, like they always did on Saturdays. Amble here and there, talk about school or the politics of the track team or the tyrannical conductor of the classical music ensemble in which they both played the violin. Why not? Why wouldn't they do just what they always did? Why wouldn't life itself turn out to be an endless repetition of the same?

*Killem Dafoe wants to chat.*

Hmmmmmmm... Much later Marnie reflected that the appeal of Killem's out-of-the-blue chat request lay only in the indelible perfection of its timing. Because any other day, any other Marnie might have ignored it. Pushed *No* to *Decline*. But any other Marnie wasn't around, leaving this sterling decisionmaker (her) in charge. And his handle, Killem Dafoe. Something odd about that kind name. Right? *Sure,* thought Marnie. Well, he could have been a bot. Or a predator. Or any kind of sleazeball, really. That would be okay. On a day of devastating boredom, even a sleazeball can provide at least a minimal distraction.

*Push Yes to Accept.*

Click. Marnie did.

*

M: so riddle me this

K: your wish

K: is my command

M: sure

M: haha

M: okay so w/r/t ophelia

K: yeah?

M: the terrorists are trying to spoof her murder by a foreign enemy (norway) in order to provoke denmark into an unwinnable war, yes?

K: that's about the size of it, yeah

M: okay so 2 things

M: 1) ophelia's death is ruled a suicide-by-drowning by castle kronberg's medical examiner in the actual play. so unless that changes in your version i don't get how the storyline flows, and

M: 2) why would fortinbras want hamlet jr. to make the first move in a war, like, why go to the trouble of having ophelia whacked when it seems like he could just as easily invade?

K: ok so

K: both good questions, and idk if my answers will satisfy but

K: here goes

K: so 1) the suicide ruling would be indicative of our commando squad's success e.g. the fact that she doesn't end up becoming a franz ferdinand-style wwiii spark means that fortinbras effectively fails and so voila: happy ending

K: and 2)

K: there's presumably a slew of peace treaties in place between fortinbras and numerous other sovereigns, treaties that deliver stiff penalties for wars of aggression and that would furthermore cast fortinbras' whole regime-change foreign policy in a negative light.

K: hence

M: hence this whackage of ophelia =

M: pref over a sudden surprise attack

K: exactly. fortinbras can't afford even the appearance of backstabbing, particularly

K: since it would also then cast doubt on his role in hamlet sr.'s death/poltergeist, which could be a whole stinking can of worms as far as claudius is concerned

M: so we're talking a woodrow wilson/gulf of tonkin-style scenario

K: you got it. fortinbras wants to play the victim, act reluctant, force hamlet jr. to make the first move

K: that way he gets to say that he tried for peace but, well, military action just

K: *became unavoidable*

K: not to mention that he then gets to fight hamlet jr.'s troops on norwegian soil and wear them down in fjordy skirmishes before reversing the invasion's tide with devastating force

M: damn ok ok

M: i mean, that all makes sense

M: well at least 2) does

M: but, and i'm just thinking out loud here

M: for 1) if we, you and i, in the for-some-reason-deeply-invested-in-preserving-the-corrupt-hamlet-dynasty hench squad are so slick, then why does ophelia have to drown at all? i mean, if we're saving the day then why don't we arrive in time to stop the terrorists from killing her in the first place?

K: unless...

M: unless what?

K: unless the suicide itself is faked, a metareversal of the original provocation

K: bc ophelia, in a moment of tragic courage comes to the realization that as long as they think she's alive the terrorists will come after her to get at hamlet jr., that it'll never stop, that she'll have to live her life always looking over her shoulder, a forever-object of weird power plays, a pawn in other assholes' games

M: aaah, yes! so ophelia escapes!

K: yeah or makes the ultimate sacrifice, however you want to look at it

K: and we, you and me, the danish seal team 6

K: we help her do it

K: we fake her drowning by dressing a slain terrorist up in a wig and petticoats and then arranging for her to get a new passport and a plane ticket

K: with the idea that she'll start a new life as one deena thompson, notary public and clairvoyant radio personality living in new rochelle, ny. deena

K: thompson whose radio hour gains a small but fiercely loyal following of listeners drawn into the husky lilt of her late-night voice and the notorious viciousness of her call-in astrology readings

M: haha jesus

M: what sequel are we on at this point?

M: i'm thinking 2 or 3 minimum

M: and do people, like, fake their own suicides?

M: is that even a thing?

K: well

K: i mean if you're saying: has it ever been done? i'm sure the answer is yes. although sussing the answer here is gonna be a bit difficult, since by definition if you do it right then no one would know that you'd done it at all. faking suicide, i mean

M: oh oh right yeah

M: do you ever think

M: about...

K: what?

M: nevermind. no.

*

The Snaturn blasts down through what may well once have been a hidden valley southwest of Chicagoland, flattening the little stands of snowbound cypress trees into a spidery motion-blur. *Jesus Is The Truth, Real \*Live\* XXX Girls, Injured? Call Koumana Jayrouz Today, Next Exit Real \*Live\* Tigers, Don't Wait! Koumana Jayrouz, Not Tomorrow But Today...*

Marnie's body feels pressed down, squirming with the weight of waiting, a sense of rushing to arrive too late. The feels. All the feels. Her body now aflicker with an incomprehensible urgency. Because what's far worse than the worst panic of anticipation is the feeling that comes with having *already* waited much too long. Flipping the radio through Biblejabbering static Marnie recalls discussing Poe with Killem, an essay preluding one of Poe's odd tales entitled *The Imp of the Perverse*, which offered a clutch meditation on the emotional intensity of dawdling, of procrastination, of heading towards a place that one anticipates arriving much too late and being judged, intensely and intimately, for that lateness. The feeling is strange, the way you're reading it here, the weight of overwaiting is what turns to little lumps of ice in her throat. Pale dry lips exhaling the burnt-frozen air of the Snaturn's heating system. Ice lumps melt morsel by morsel down the back of Marnie's throat. Swallow. Start over. Then again.

*Faster*, says her heart, pounding. *Floor it!* Marnie puts her foot down and hurls the Snaturn past eighty, ninety, swerving into the deserted turnpike's fast lane. She's never even been to a real funeral before. Not in person. Not in her body. She's not even dressed accurately. Shoot. And what would it feel like anyway? To walk up to the black-clad figure of Madame Pommeranz? And say what? Marnie would say nothing and then Madame Pommeranz would say something like *So nice you could come, dearie. Now please, won't you tell me who you are?*

A logical and unanswerable questions.

Marnie wrinkles her nose. And the question echoes still.

*Who am I even being right now?*

And why am I driving nine fucking hours to attend the funeral of a boy I have never met?

About her on every side the snowy landscape streaks with sun and looks somehow runny, like a skillet of bad eggs. Marnie's cheeks feel hot and beestung. *Kzzzzzzzzsssssshs!* The Snaturn's old heating system kicks into full blast and suddenly without warning or compromise Marnie desperately needs to pee.

*

The heels on limestone make tiny echoes run along the dull corridor of the Toulous-Sheffield Shopping Centre. It is a solemn corridor. The light falls through clean slanted windows and makes clean slants of light hold fast upon the floor. For a moment it catches fire on the thin shoulders of a white Christian youth group, all wearing matching red tshirts. Marnie and Cynthia stroll by the Christian youth, both lost in thought, eyes swimmy and vaguely sullen-looking. Cynthia's swinging her arms a little, trying to

210

remember something. Over the loud speakers a kind of slow, hypnotic snake charmer muzak plays. The white Christian youth group gaggles about in pony-tails, bowl cuts and French braids, squirming happily as they wait in line to procure crucifix-shaped pretzels from the Shopping Centre's lone Christian-themed pretzel vendor, pepperoni Jesus optional. Marnie watches as the first youth get their pretzels and begin licking, sucking, savoring each stigmata of salt. Some of the rowdier boys start brandishing their pretzels, opening their mouths wide, gesturing obscenely. Supervising adults in red shirts see the mischief and point fingers, saying *Stop that! Billy, you stop that right now! That's not how we eat in public!*

*In public?* Marnie wonders dreamily, imagining a stone tablet inscribed *THOU SHALT FELLATE THY PRETZELS PRIVATELY!*

*This is how,* says Cynthia, gesturing at a pious trio of pretzel munchers. *This is how the terrorists win. Right, Marina?*

Marnie looks over at them, smiles a little. *What?*

*This. We'll think back on this day and think: this is the moment, the moment it all went to shit. And we were there. We saw it go down. Decadence. Empire's twilight. Pretzels. Who'd have guessed?*

Marnie grins, glancing over a red-shirted Christian boy who has placed the pepperoni Jesus flat against his tongue, sticking it in and out, in and out from between his pulled-apart lips. Two pony-tailed girls stand by scowling, hands on hips, clearly at a loss.

*Are you saying that the terrorists don't eat pretzels or something?*

Cynthia makes her mouth into a skeptical asterisk at the center of her left cheek. *What?*

Marnie keeps grinning. *No one's immune here. You mean to tell me that there aren't pro-ISIS pretzel vendors out there right now, hawking their own iconoclastic snacks in the mall rotundas of Raqqa or wherever?*

Cynthia stops swinging her arms. Both her and Marnie's face become way too bright all of a sudden, like the sun's rushed out from behind a cloud. *Henh, um, no. Mall rotundas in Raqqa? Somehow I... That's... just, just no...*

*Ooooh, what about pretzels depicting Muhammed? What about that? I bet that could get someone in lots of trouble!*

*Marnie, shhhhhh!*

*What!?*

*That's not a good thing to just go around saying, you know? I mean, people get shot for stuff like that...*

*What, are you going to shoot me? Come on Cynth, lighten up. Psssssshhhh.*

Cynthia sighs, shaking her head at her friend, at the Christian youth group, at the world's general lack of common sense.

*Well, well, look who it is.*

Marnie spins around to face the voice. It's a tall girl with enviable cheekbones and dark, greenstreaked hair gone wild around the pinched corners of her face. She's wearing an unzipped leather jacket and skinny jeans with one of those cool Venus Treats staff shirts that no one's Mom lets them wear because erotic bakeries are too risqué.

*Heyyy...* A chord of recognition clangs about the alcoves in Marnie's slazzerweak memory. *You're... you're Elwood's sister. Clarice, right?*

*Yeah Marnie, that's right. And how, may I ask, did you come to know our dear friend Elias?*

Marnie's face freezes as Cynthia turned to look at her, eyebrows raised. *Who!?*

*Who?* Clarice breaks into a cruel, v-shaped smile. *Well, well. You know, as long as you're not playing on my baby bro it's no thing how you kill your alone time. Please, go on and live your life. None of my business. But you know your Fnacebook friends are public, right? I mean, you did know that, right?*

*Elias...?*

*Ha. Okay girl. Okay.* Clarice strides past them both, tossing her head a little so that a strand of greenstreaked hair moves from one side of her face to the other and flows out behind her as Cynthia and Marnie stand, perplexed, watching her go. Cynthia snorts loudly, pulling the kind of face that makes them both *shhhhkpffftttttthhhhhhhhttttt* into laughter and then reel back, putting their hands down on their bent knees, just letting it all splutter out. Marnie glances over at Cynthia's tshirt, getting an eyeful of her friend's skeptical-looking zebra. Too much! This is what friends are for, aren't they?

Cynthia's just one of those people who can make absolutely anything seem totally ludicrous. Together they stroll off down the limestone echoes of the Toulous-Sheffield Shopping Centre mezzanine, gulping down the nectared air of a passing perfume shop until finally Cynthia says. *Well so.*

*So?*

*What was that all about?*

*I,* begins Marnie, the crazed smile still playing about the edges of her lips. *I have no. Freaking. Clue. Shhhhkpffftttttthhhhhhhhtttt*

And again, she and Cynthia both burst into an uncontrollable duet of uproarious laughter.

*

Marnie makes the Snaturn shudder before sliding the front wheels to a hard stop by the rusty titanium-white flagpole. The lone restaurant, prosaically christened *The Rockin' Chair.* American. Flagged. Flapping. Grommets tinkle against the metal pole. The frayed flagcloth is here half-mast above the hand-painted sign to show overcoming. *These Colors Don't Run.*

Killem would have something snarky to say about that, maybe via taking a .jpeg of that sign into Phnotoshop and applying a couple filters so it looked as if the colors actually were running. Dripping. Flowing. Another big wooden board has the POW/MIA symbol stenciled on. Marnie gets out. Shivers. Stretches. The parking lot's rubbed with sheets of ice and snow. In the distance an echoless cawing sound, the sky empty as far as her eye can see. That cawing doesn't sound real, Marnie thinks. What that cawing sounds like is one of those symbolic devices used in movies to indicate a sense of profound, spiritual desolation. It cues the audience to the fact that the protagonist will soon encounter a situation in which intensive, even painful introspection becomes utterly unavoidable. *At least in movies*, thinks Marnie, *isn't that what the cawing usually means?*

*

M: can you even fake a suicide?

K: my understanding is that people do it all the time

M: really!?

K: yeah

K: i mean what do you want

K: life sucks

K: lots of people wish that they could snap their fingers and magically become someone else, or at least stop being themselves

K: don't think with my face-thing i haven't thought about it

M: ugh stop with that

K: no i mean faking

K: well doing and faking-doing

K: those nights before i knew you when i was stuck in my basement in velton full of mom's junk, full of old receipts and take-out menus and a whole wall hung with cloth masks

K: from back when i used to go outside

K: ugh

K: now when i close my eyes i see you

215

K: i see you in text form, faces made of text

K: and when i open them again it's just the dust of my basement room lit with the eerie glow of the computer screen

K: dust making more dust

K: loneliness making more loneliness

M: awwwwww

M: poor killem

M: are we ever going to be together?

K: i

K: i don't

K: [     ]

M: ...

K: what i'd do if i did it

K: i'd take something to make me forget

K: i'd clean out my memory and i'd go away

K: maybe south america, somewhere

K: i'd live away from basements and computer screens

K: i'd hurt my brain and i'd forget i even had a face

M: :( :( :(

M: stop

M: don't say things like that

K: why? why would that even be a sad thing?

K: you know what a sad thing is?

K: that you're the person i know the most and we've never even met

K: that we probably never will

K: that our bodies will probably never even share the same room or taste the same breath of wind

K: that's what's sad

K: not death or pseudodeath

K: death's not even close to being sad

\*

*Who was this Killem, anyway? Some creepy old man? Some acne-scarred perv? Some phantom? Some bot?*

Marnie signed off after the suicide discussion, after he'd tried to send her some weird little novella he'd been working on, some sequel in their thread of Hamlet fanfiction. But even as she tried to put Killem out of her mind, even as she tried to return things to the innocence of excruciating normalcy, even as she tried to forget all about him, she found that she simply couldn't. His not-a-face had a hold on her idle moments, and when her mind wandered it wandered back to him.

Days passed and passed. But he was always, always online, almost always, and when he wasn't she missed him and wished he was. As digital illustrators go Killem was a decent hack, gaudy Warholian dripscapes, cats and spaceships and rainbows and cats and unicorns and planets and cats and penguins and many, many, many more cats. Zombies and brand logos, Samuel L. Jackson's stern gaze knitted into the sand-colored peak of Mt. Rushmore.

*because i can,* typed Killem.

217

*because why not it looks funny, doesn't it?*

*because this is something people have always wanted to see without realizing it and now they can see it, now everyone can see exactly the kinds of strangeness that they want and there's no excuse not to anymore.*

They chatted phone pics of the clouds in the sky outside their windows, each morning as the sky grew light. Marnie went to the girls' bathroom and sent him gigapixel shots of the scratchings on the metal stall walls, heart-encrusted boy names, anonymous confessions of the mundane and inexpressible. Killem made her gifs of her favorite sitcom characters. He sent her photographs of handwritten poems copied out of big collections. He sent her sound files of him reading these poems in that nasal, scratchy voice of his. Sylvia Plath. Frank O'Hara. Audre Lorde. William Carlos Williams. Dickinson. Hass. Ashbury. Whitman. Ginsburg. Mayakovsky. At night they torrented and watched old TV shows together at a distance of two hundred and fortysome miles. Marnie began to have the same maddening thought that always snagged in her mind just before falling asleep: *Am I... am I in love? And how would I know? If I were? If I were in love and you only get one shot and this is it, this is my shot and I'm just waiting, I'm just waiting for something to happen, I'm just waiting for him to show me his real face? Is that what's happening here?*

Once begun, the task of trying to picture Killem's body had no fixed endpoint. Marnie's imagination was pitiless. Early results were grotesque and even clownish — a putty nose bulging upturned and piggish between two bloated, spongy cheeks. For skin she gave him a mix of acne and leprosy. His forehead became a sloping phrenology model of nineteenth century moronism. Eyes crusty and purple-lidded. Teeth the orange of traffic cones and poorly imitated cheese.

*What does the word hideous even mean?*

Marnie lay in bed realizing her breath had quickened at these thoughts, listening to the house settle, her younger brothers' cottony snuffles, the heavy silence of their parents' bedroom. The wind chimes outside the back door by the trashcans clangored lightly in the wind. This face she had designed made no sense when all the separate features were put together. It was not only monstrous but implausible, goofy. His face in her mind. Why was she even doing this? Marnie thought about her laptop's keyboard, about all of those parenthetical smiles and hyphen noses and winking semicolon eyes. It seemed ghastly somehow, as if her keyboard were an ossuary. To chat she must pluck out the facial features bone by bone, arranging them into a correspondence with her own inner sense. Her face, her symbol-faces, her keyboard, the skeletons of her emotions. Because aren't colors and shapes, aren't words even somewhat arbitrary? Isn't the way that we see the world mostly a matter of luck, and beauty too might just as well attach to its opposite? What would that feel like? To be turned on by the ugly, the hideous, the grotesque?

To make ugliness into a fetish? Wouldn't that make it, by definition, *no longer ugly?*

Marnie turned the pillow over, feeling its other side cool against her flushed cheeks. Thinking of her keyboard speckled with the bones of unmade faces, not-yet faces, faces that could be Killem's forever. She couldn't manage to fall asleep that night and til dawn there were such storms across her body.

*

M: do you ever think about like, what computers even are

K: you mean, like do they have souls and shit like that?

M: no, i mean like what are they? are they tools? are they pets? are they friends? are they just like big, glowing telephones?

K: or small, chocolate bar-sized telephones?

M: well, right

K: no, i guess i haven't

K: you mean as a trope?

M: sure

M: or a setting

M: or a character

M: i mean, you have to admit that they could qualify for nearly every element of literary composition

M: setting, character, language, style

M: (not that i'm saying they should, god no)

M: but what if, i mean what

K: if?

M: like what if the computer is actually death

M: the image of death as the reduction to vibrant particles of pure information

K: an apostrophe, a present absence

M: yeah, like a skull!

M: and the person hunched over their laptop is really hunched over the future image of their own sterile voidbrain, clicking away through the rotting cavity of their own future corpse

M: then, the person hunched over the phone is...

K: hamlet!

K: i mean, eulogizing poor yorick

K: no?

M: haha you got it

M: you totally have a weird obsession with that play

K: well, i mean

K: shouldn't everyone

K: shouldn't they

K: what's wrong with that

K: huh?

K: ...?

*

Daily it was hard to hide, but far harder still was the idea that anyone other than Marnie could ever know what she was feeling. Of course, Cynthia noticed something, an awkward buoyancy under their usual duo routine of teasing and acid moodiness. Marnie didn't want to say anything. She was on her phone more, sure. Tapping. Texting. Who could raise an eyebrow at that? The two friends had gotten comfortable sharing silence anyway. But of course Cynthia did notice something. She didn't want to bring it up. But shouldn't she? Their separation had started by degrees. First, they stopped hanging out after school every day. Then Marnie stopped sleeping over. Slowly, the surface of their togetherness halted and grew tense. *Should I say something?* Cynthia wondered. *What exactly should I say?*

There was a feeling, a slow joy of dim exhaustion that hung suspended inside Marnie like a cord of red silk, humming and pulling and deeply fragile. She could barely contain it. It cozied up behind her cheeks and made Marnie blush when she least expected.

Cynthia thought it might be something she'd said?

Cynthia though it might be something too secret to talk about, a family thing, an arrival of grim and distant news?

*We're both growing up*, she thought. *Maybe this is natural. Maybe we are destined to grow apart, bit by bit, until we both go away to college and then we'll hardly even be friends. Is that how things are supposed to work?* The detailed montage of this estrangement played out through Cynthia's daydreams made her ache with sharp-edged sadness. She was ashamed, even, ashamed of how much she ached, how much she already missed her best friend. *Where are you?* She wanted to scream. *What have you done with Marnie?*

Marnie's eyes hazed over with a glassy accumulation of sleepless hours. And week by week, the fragile red-string hum grew dense and denser inside the most guarded chambers of her mind. It slipped under her tongue at school and made all her afternoon words come out sluggish and disordered. It lay behind her sunken eyes through the endlessness of AP Chemistry while she struggled to not-remember the molar numbers for the lab they were supposed to all be doing. It hovered in her pauses, the humming did, hovered in the moments when Marnie straight-up forgot what she was talking about and discovered that no longer could she even pretend to care. Red. Silk. Humming. And behind her eyes new plans and dreams were busy taking root. Even during those rare moments of thoughtful focus e.g. staring hypnotized by the colorful derangement of her sock drawer, well, the red hum lingered on, pulling deep across the blurry folds of distance.

*

Lunch time Marnie spent in a bathroom stall. Lost in fantasies of running away, of living like an outlaw with Killem forever. Traveling to Paris, hitchhiking to Berlin, crossing Russia by train, living out doors, living with a troupe of charismatic strangers, however it might happen, well, they'd manage, wouldn't they? Because the whole world was out there, just waiting, waiting to be seen, heard, smelled and licked up by the two of them and together, well, nothing would get in their way. Marnie imagined her and Killem crossing a mountain range, traversing a desert, entering a glittering city upon the mirror-embroidered saddleback of a massive, miraculous mastodon. They would climb the tallest towers, weather the wildest seas, feel the spray of foreign winds dense and cool upon their faces. At the day's end they'd lie on the edge of a chalky cliff, staring up at the night sky and inventing new constellations with overclever handles and crass epithets from the stars, the inverted keyboard of the sky. Marnie frolicked upon this delirium daily and even hourly, her sky filled with tender emoticons fashioned from twinkling semicolon-stars, flashing emdash-comets, spinning nebulae of clustered asterisks. It gave her succor to sit still, still and almost normal-looking until the next class bell rang and it was time for a different varietal of droning that would cue her mind to begin the fantasy over again, slumped down at her desk in a radiant flush-cheeked reverie.

Finally Cynthia had no choice but to ask who it was and what the fuck was going on. You can't just give best friends free passes on such obvious wholesale moodshifts, can you? You can't be best friends and not at least ask. Right? Marnie didn't know what to say. How do you say something when the mere act of saying might destroy it? Cynthia didn't care. Cynthia grabbed Marnie in one of those classic you-have-to-tell-me best friend embraces while they were walking by the mall's second story fudge shop. She gave Marnie a stern and not unhard full-body shake.

*Hey!*

Up close Cynthia saw how Marnie looked so happy in her lopsided, half-awake way and for a moment she nearly flinched with buried jealousy. *You have to. You have to tell me. What's. Going. On.*

Marnie's breath caught in her throat for a second, and after only a tiny hesitation she arms around Cynthia's zebraprint shoulders and said that she would but that there was honestly nothing real to tell because she hadn't even met him, not in real life, not yet, at least. *He's just some guy from the Internet*, said Marnie, shrugging. *We've been talking about poetry.* And then she turned and asked Cynthia, *Now, have you ever really sat down and read Rimbaud? I mean really read him? What about Larkin or Rilke or Stevens? What about Jericho Brown? What about Kim Hyesoon?*

*No. Not yet. I. I haven't... Not yet.* Cynthia shook her head again and kissed her best friend lightly beneath the ear, rolling her eyes a little without meaning to and thinking how what she loved about Marnie was her oddness, her nerdiness, her sudden and effusive gushes of passion but that God, the girl could really make up drama out of nothing, couldn't she?

*

*Is this... is this someone that you met online?*

Mom's voice has gone nighthusky, the way it does when she's asking her most worriedover questions. Questions that she has been coached to ask by newspapers, by the television experts and the book on *Parenting Your Digital Native* that she bought last week on a desperate impulse.

Silence. Stillness.

*Mom, can we just talk about this later. I don't feel very well. Really, I don't.*

*Marnie, I'm worried. Your father's worried. You've been down in the dumps like this for days. Just throw me a bone here. Okay?*

It's such a silly phrase that Marnie almost starts laughing and then catches herself. A bone? She imagines two people playing catch with a bone. Marnie and her Mom, Mom saying throw me a bone and then catching it, and then throwing it back. In Marnie's head the bone is a femur. And maybe because of this incomprehensible femur-throwing-and-catching image Marnie bursts out laughing despite herself and laughs so hard that Mom chimes in weakly with a few giggles and now they're both laughing, just laughing and laughing out these big, crazed, gutbusting guffaws. Marnie body's doubled-over beneath the covers and she feels herself begin to hurt from laughing, feels herself wondering if this is how regular people know that they've finally gone insane.

Marnie pictures Ophelia in her hostage situation, the terrorists demanding Denmark's ransom. Ophelia with her arms and legs and torso poxed with tiny, screaming mouths. Ophelia in an Absconders tshirt, the one with the coffee stain on the back and a pink albatross biting the nipple. Ophelia bound and tied to a heavy rock as the terrorist drag her over to the blackberry-rimmed pond. Ophelia yelling for Hamlet, yelling for Horatio, yelling for anyone who might be able to hear. But it's no good, thinks Marnie, and Ophelia struggles, flopping against the rock she's bound to, looking like

226

someone trying to do a somersault with one hand nailed to the floor. Ophelia going hard, spasming in panic, twisting around in the classic pose of a hostage that Marnie and Killem could have saved if, you know, if certain realworld things had worked out differently. Suddenly Marnie's stopped laughing, all at once, her eyes gone bright and wet and full. Mom keeps going, just out of momentum. Laughing. Laughing. Stopping. Not-laughing. Shoot. Everywhere inside herself Marnie's tasting blackberries, the overripe juiciness of some sweet and impossible despair.

*

K: do u think that u r cute

M: what kind of question is that???

M: are you like vetting my self-confidence bc that is totally condescending

M: bull

M: i call bull, man

K: no not at all

K: like, it either confirms or disconfirms an image of yourself you've already privately validated, positive means acceptance, negative means rejection

K: right?

M: that's a weird question

M: i mean, guess i think i'm pretty cute

M: :D

M: but like i said

M: i don't really think that your question makes very much sense

M: you want an honest self-impression? that's an oxymoron. what i think about myself is necessarily private, necessarily before words. i think in colors, smells, viscera. words are like models, inexact and lackluster in comparison to what my senses do to me, even when i'm shut off, asleep, wrapped away. like, you

M: you can never see what my body looks like the way i see it when i look in the mirror. never. no matter how many words

K: maybe it's stupid but even if there are paradoxes the question is important. bc people with negative self-images feel differently about getting affection. they mistrust it, like *any expression of affection feels unfamiliar-hence-suspect-hence-probably-dishonest*

M: how clinical of you. this seems like what dr. freud would describe as a very very clearcut case of psychological projection

K:...

M: e.g. i assume you are the type who believe all physical-beauty compliments are secretly disingenous?

K: in my case, how could they not be? i have, ahem, a somewhat irregular visage

M: ...don't be like that, um

M: what's regular, anyway?

K: (insert self-answering feelgood q & a)

M: ugh fine

M: i mean i would like to SEE YOU some day. like we've talked about

M: killem...

K: i go back and forth. it would be terrible to ruin this thing we have. to me it means more than you know. but then sometimes it's like my whole body just aches for you and i think we should meet up. but it would have to be like eros and psyche. with the lights off

M: lol are you saying you want someone to spill hot oil on you? bc that's kinda kinky haha

M: no clingfilm but still

K: haha lol

K: who knows maybe

K: maybe that's what i really want i mean

K: i've never tried that

M: and no one likes what they see in the mirror, not at our age. faces are really just a matter of taste, don't you think?

K: so is poetry. but you can't escape taste just because you disagree with it. there's still bad poetry. and then there's a tiny bit of the good stuff

M: isn't there a beholder? an eye on that beholder?

K: you're equivocating. and you have to understand that i can't plausibly deny my self-loathing. when i look at

K: at my scars, my beak, my twisted-up bones i can't help but see myself through other people's eyes. i know what i look like

M: you still sound like you're fishing for consolation. stop thinking about your own body for just a second. it's so

M: so shallow to hear you go on and on this way. don't you realize there are people who have it way way way worse

K: i know i know

M: way worse

K: i know

M: you're overthinking this. you know what your formula is: self-pity and wait for praise. like,

M: no

K: you're right

K: i do that

M: ...

K: don't you think we should maybe stop

K: i don't know

K: not talking but maybe just talking like this

K: this way, i feel like you're

K: well

K: nothing about this seems healthy

M: ha

M: and when exactly did you become a health nut?

M: you wanna stop talking to me?

M: huh?

K: no...

K: :)

M: ugh what an unoriginal emoticon

M: ÷°Θ

K: haha, what's that?

M: it's an angry girl with a lip stud and a tongue ring. (::-:) and you can guess what that is. damn, im like Pablo freaking Picasso of the emoticon over here haha

*

Stepping through the solid oak door of The Rockin' Chair Marnie inhales the dry air and the plank floor and waits for her eyes to adjust to the gloom. The restaurant looks empty and she really just needs to pee and get the heck out of here. She inches forward, leg over leg to maintain her bladder's equilibrium. Shapes dissolve in the air around her and each footstep echoes twice, the way footsteps tend to echo around the edge of an indoor swimming pool.

*Hello...?*

Beneath the weak glow of The Rockin' Chair's wall lamps Marnie notices that there's a knobby-looking waiter, balding, his back turned to her and pate tilted down with severe intention. He wears an apron and stands by a hunting trophy of a buck deer, polishing its antlers with a little acid green squirt bottle and a rag.

*Help you, ma'am?* The waiter doesn't even look up from his polishing but shuffles around to the left, as if to give her a better view of his work on the dead-eyed deer.

*Really I'm just looking to use the bathroom, if that's alright?*

Right away the waiter tightens up, all his knobs thrown into furtive motion. *I'm sorry, ma'am, but like the sign does say. Bathroom's for Customers Only.*

He waves his hand at a runny underlayer of the restaurant's many shadows. Perhaps there's really such a sign hanging up in there, up in somewhere. Marnie scrunches up her face, hoping for sympathy.

*But I really need to go. Pleeeeeeeeeeez?*

Shoot. She's going to miss the whole funeral by the time she makes it all the way to Velton. She'll get there and won't even be able to find where the ceremony had taken place. Won't even be able to find the grave. All that trouble for nothing. Or else she'd burst a kidney right here and die on the cedar planks of The Rockin' Chair's floor, stuffing a little note down into her waistband saying *Next to Killem, Please.* Ugh. How totally cringing. No one except maybe Cynthia would know what that note could mean, but even Cynthia probably wouldn't say, shaking her head in exasperation at the spilled urine and the banal juvenilia of it all.

*Fine*, snaps the waiter, unprompted. *Free pass this time. But you gotta learn to carry cash with you. This ain't no Russia over here. G'wan then.*

Sitting on the edge of the toilet after she's done peeing, Marnie sucks in a few dry breaths and thinks deep into the present moment, into the rust-tinged pipework of The Rockin' Chair's *Women's Room.* Feels the emptiness of death and boundless winter highways aching, stretching, curling around themselves in the hollow of her voided perineum. She sucks in air, hard, fast and holds it, breathless, waiting.

232

*

The blood smells of mothballs and linseed oil. Marnie never dreamt there would be so much or that it would leave a shape that so greatly resembled a squid on the old grey horseblanket, a squid with irate-looking tentacles raised high and poised to strike. The attic around her laptop screen feels suddenly emptied of air and her eyelids do a little flutter dance of surprise and panic. Dawn. Dawnish. Finally her breath escapes her all at once, a sharp squeak, the sound of a glasscutter. The egg-shaped webcam peers down from the palm of her hand, down to gaze upon the irate squid unfurled between her legs. The joystick's smeared with fluids that pull her face and finally make her look away. On the screen, the outline of an avatar that half resembles Willem Dafoe.

The voice in her ear says, *Are you... are you okay?*

*

M: killem?

M: hey i know it says you're not online

M: but if you were online you'd answer me

M: right?

M: you'd answer me

M: i know you would

*

Marnie had been alone for hours and hours, emblanketed, a mess of sheets and pillowcases. Hours that seemed like days, days which seemed like weeks. Not even responding to Cynthia's text

233

messages, her face wrapped up in a greasy chrysalis of sobbing, greasy brown hair.

Sobbing and sobbing, just. Feeling inconsolable yet strangely craving consolation. Hoping that Mom would come back, just once more and ask what's wrong. Even if Marnie said nothing, even if she turned on her stomach and repeated the word *nothing* again and again. Because, right? What was wrong *was* nothing, a big disembodied, person-shaped feeling of *nothing.* Marnie ached desperately to be asked what was wrong, to feel the presence of Mom's deep and probing concern. Marnie felt cold again, teeth chattering, hands trembling with a palsied quiver. Wincing. Squeezing. Biting her fingertips. Copper sparkleblossoms, blooming silent, ephemeral, fading.

She thought about Killem and it was like staring at the sun too bright. Look, look away. Killem's face, a face half-drawn on a ghostly Etch-A-Sketch, floating in the shallow of a certain pond by Ophelia, floating face down, her Absconders tshirt ripped and swollen. *Schhhhhhhhhchaaaaaa.* Marnie exhaled, feeling ghostly, reaching back towards the words, towards the dark pixels behind her and Killem. The little pieces of machine-glow that encrusted something real and beating, the whir of her heart's flickering wireless router as its signal stretched back across the the two hundred and fortyish miles of wintering Midwestern cropland. Outside her bedroom window it began to pour down sleet as if the clouds were vomiting with milkdrunk grief and for the tenth time that day Marnie began to shake with wettish, manic sobs. Because *unbearableness*. Because the idea that she would have to live the rest of her life with this piece missing was bleeding from a wound too deep for her to ever possibly heal. Because WWOD, right? *What would Ophelia do?*

*

Time in The Rockin' Chair nibbles its own edges. Corrodes. Marnie blinks the minute hand, ten minutes, twenty. The soup turns stone cold, the surface thickens with a viscous milkskin. Why did I even order soup? I ordered soup to not-eat soup. I ordered soup to wait while it got cold.

*Something wrong? You didn't hardly touch it, now.*

The knobby-looking waiter's standing way too close and Marnie can smell the medicinal quality of his pores and breathing, Vap-O-Rub and black soap, skin as rough and intricate as the bark of a sycamore tree. Marnie lets the question sit between them for a moment, becoming cold, becoming inedible.

*To tell you the truth, I'm not quite feeling myself today. I think I might be coming down with something.*

*Well, that's too bad*, says the knobby-looking waiter, cracking his face into a wavy, lipless grin. *With the weather cold like it is, you gotta be careful. Now sit tight and I'll get you something you can take it home with you.*

Now Marnie's alone. She's all, all, all alone.

And then she's not.

Because suddenly there he is. Sitting right across from her in an old rocking chair. Two dimensional .jpeg body illuminated, the way Christian saints get haloed with little cranium-canopies of concentric gold leaf. Him, unmistakeable. Not Willem, but Killem. Here. Across from her. Sitting. A body. A face. He has thin, slumping shoulders. His features a pixelated chiascuro beneath its thincurled scalp, pair of dim, haunted eyes and Dafoeish blurs.

Marnie swallows. *Hello...?*

With her hands she silently offers him some cold chicken soup. The apparition accepts, lifting a metal spoon from the table, eating a bite and swallowing. Nodding in appreciation. Killem wrinkles up his 50%-nose, dark eyes lustrous, cheeks taut and smiling. There's some kind of joke at play. Killem here, thinks Marnie. Killem here and so alive.

*

*Turn off the lights.*

The voice comes through her headphones. Each consonant sounds like a dead twig snapped in half.

*Okay.*

Marnie gets up and goes to the wall switch, leaving her headphones by the keyboard. Then sits down on the chair which she has covered an old mothballed horseblanket of no consequence.

*Point the webcam down. Take off your pants.*

The voice is sharp and nasal. The voice sounds older, crueler, more business-like. Marnie's scared shitless. She swallows hard and

236

asks herself for the billionth time if she's actually going to go through with this. There's something dissociated about her standing there, alone in her attic, the audio cord still connected to the jack on her laptop.

Outside the tall window a barn owl hoots. *Hoot! Hoot-hoot-hoot!*

*Are you going to show me?*

Her voice speaking now, sounding pretty hoarse.

*Yes.*

It was part of their deal. She had sent him pictures. He gave her information, but only pictures of his extremities. Once, his hands. Once, in a gesture to Dalí/Buñuel, a picture of his eye close-up with a zombie wound Phnotoshopped in a slash across it. She sent him more intimate things. Her ear. Her lips. Her left nipple, pinched slowly to a painful red erection. It was a sort of David Hockney game, assembling each other's bodies from all the little bits of digital photography. Now he's looking at her panties, horizontal stripes of deep purple down her crotch with a thick frilly waistband of black lace. And she still hasn't seen his face.

*Do you have the joystick?*

She nods. It's what they had said. She had said. Why had she said things? Underneath her dollopy buttocks the mothballed gray horseblanket covers her office chair's cushion with a dense scratchiness. It prickles her with a dense tingle of anticipation. The handgrip of hollow plastic in her hand. The joystick. As good as any of Killem's incarnations, but this one here, so close, so close to something finally happening.

Marnie nods again, then remembers that he can't see her head and says, simply.

*I have it. Yes.*

*

File sits. Still. Written. E. Pommeranz's external hard drive written. Its name is *excellent fancy*.

*

Marnie pays, pees again. Leaves. Leaves her rocking chair. Leaves The Rockin' Chair. Leaves the parking lot. Leaves the universe where Killem's pixel-ghost fades to a colorless nothing-space without ever speaking, without ever saying a word. Exits to other murmurs, other reals, the long intestinal tract of turnpike huddling beneath the frosted, imperious gaze of Koumana Jayrouz. Marnie exits when the GPS tells her to and then sees a sign floodlit from below *The Ugly — where Happy Hour lasts all day!* The route takes her onto a small, ice-rimed road so unpatched with potholes that it's barely, *barely* drivable. Marnie looks up and brings the Snaturn finally to rest, idling by a decapitated parking meter at the hillfoot of Velton Cemetery. Here the sky is the color of boiled milk and cinders. Marnie pulls out her bowl again and pushes the seat way back. Torches the hell out of it. Tries not to burn her thumb. Then burns her thumb. The Styrofoam container of Chicken Bone soup sits on the Snaturn's rubber floorpads, trembling slightly whenever she turns the engine back on to warm her feet and fingers up.

Like an urn, she thinks. Like a Styrofoam urn of Killem's ashes, and here before her, a communion for her cannabis prayer. The sloshy mournfulness of leftover soup in wintertime, an over-obvious missive. Well, at least it could be her totem to whatever was meant by his enigmatic presence in her life, a presence left in trace, caches of saved chat dialogues, photos and abbreviation, megabytes of memory, all and only hers. *My memory is where you'll live now*, thinks Marnie, addressing herself to the Styrofoam soup bowl, to the long shadow of a granite cross.

*

The webcam goes black, a disruption in the optical signal.

*Where are you?*

The voice in her ear. *Keep talking*, she whispers. *I can hold your voice between my teeth.*

*It surrounds me*, says Killem. *I don't need your body. It's a bit that cuts me and drives me closer.*

*Tell me what you're doing to me.*

*My arms around your collarbone, like I'm hanging from your neck. Pulling you down. Your hair spilling out in a tangle, I can feel all of you at once.*

*You're scratching me, fingernails leave red marks across my chest, my shoulders. The pain drives me crazy, making me go faster.*

*Omigod Omigod Omigod.*

239

*You're standing at the edge of a great precipice and behind you can feel me, feel my flesh in yours*

*Omigod, I'm*

*I'm*

*Ah!*

For a second, the electrical buzz of the signal over their headsets overswarms and then collapses, hanging itself up within a frizz of mute applause. An exultation of tremors. The distance stretches into reams of painful silence out between them, out between two mouths and sets of blackpadded headphones, out between what empty dazedness Marnie feels they have both too fast become.

*

Deep in her lungs Marnie holds the sourness of marijuana smoke, forcing herself to open the promised doorway of transubstantiation; bone soup to bones, then bones to reborn flesh. Coughing her freezing mucus, wheezy, no longer even high. She can already feel that she'll be sick for weeks. Feverish. No longer high in the slightest. Coughing, coughing forever. Killem spinning everything off-kilter, the funeral flinging off black crepe and Kleenex, flinging off the out-of-season daffodils into the fog-shrouded welter of the tombstones. Too cold, too cold to even think. Marnie shudders, torches the hell out of it. Sucks butane and ash, coughs, coughs. Lights a cigarette. Coughs again and puts the cigarette out, unsmoked.

This happens again and again.

When all the figures are gone away in their little cars and the graves of Velton have succumbed to engulfment by nightfall Marnie drives away and gets back on the Interstate and even drives all the way back to Toulous, back through the night, back to home where Dad yells at her for not saying where she's been and Mom says nothing and then Marnie breaks a window and locks herself in the bathroom and takes a long, hot shower, sobbing as outside the gray dawn rises much too quickly. And yet still, when she clenches up her body and closes her senses off to the world she can sometimes hear it, just barely, the knocking of a stranger's voice, tapping, touching, typing. So that deep in her night this voice reaches out, again and again, across an infinite ellipse of frozen sadness to ping her, to place its bony keyboards symbols out upon the surface of her world.

Squeezed up this way, Marnie can feel it, just barely, the voice of a faceless shape belonging to the only face she's ever truly known, a face that holds an echo, an echo of a love worth mourning.

# The Eternal

*Come on,* says Marnie.

I look down and Ms. Unica Korn's lips are right there beneath the silver-foiled surface of the pond. I can smell the medicinal fragrance of her chapstick.

*Come on,* says Erliss Pond's mouth. *Get in me.*

I take my bare foot and place it in the mouth, feeling around in the darkness for the rung of a ladder.

The heel of my shoe makes contact. Then another rung. I'm in!

*Come on,* I say. *You guys...!*

Mike shakes his head.

*Come on,* says Marnie.

*Cunh ahh,* Erliss is saying with that liquid-lipped mouth, as best he can with both my legs jammed inside. Erliss Pond wheedles. His eyes are bloomed with deep indigo rings, Neptunian and sparkle-edged. Beneath the duckweed surface of the pond I can feel the thickness of a tongue. It is gray. It is glowing.

The three of us crawl down inside the pond's mouth. Marnie, Mike and I. There's room enough for all three of us to sit comfortably without touching.

None of us touch.

None of us speak.

There are no words spoken and none of us touch. There are fishlines made from black hair and I see the little submarine, the little submarine that was lost long ago containing Mom's gold coin, the gold coin that had shown three identical bodies of the Roman goddess Trivia. So here it is! With us now for good. Shall we become identical? *Errrrrr. Lisss.*

*Nice,* I think. There is no hurry. *Everything is really nice.*

With a jolt I awaken and remember nothing other than the terror, other than a red, jagged hole, fleshy, stained with the breeding oozes of unspeakable insects, zizzy-zizz swarmfuck echoes, ah, I catch my breath in a heave up, onto my elbows in bed and fumble my phone off of the end table's corner, thumbing into Fnacebook as my heart races and slows, races and slows as evenly as two longdead horses might race each other in the scattered dreams of a retired, feverish jockey, my heart, jockeying, ka-buckabuck-bah, ka-buckabuck-bah and I don't even see what faces scramble past me in the dark, laughing, crying against the pukka-patter greenishness of a late spring rain.

The pick-up location for Whitetail Buslines is a bit of a hike from my apartment complex on Burlingham and I estimate it'll take me twenty or thirty minutes to head all the way up Klapp towards Gottlieb, following the crookedy sidewalk down the hill and along the curve of the Velt River. Twenty or thirty minutes give or take, if I don't stop and stare distractedly at my untied shoelaces or the polyped shadow of a crabapple tree. Familiarity means different things to different people — for me it's learning how to walk down the street without getting totally distracted by nature, by sidewalk cracks or the presence of real fluffly dogs. Shiny objects, my only weakness. I re-estimate that it'll take about forty-five minutes. Give or take five. Give or take ten. If Velton is a sleepy town then its sleeping position is distinctly fetal, with the head resting beneath the comforter that forms the rest of the hill above Houch Park. Its back is snugged up against the Velt River and the pick-up location for Whitetail Buslines rests roughly where the coccyx would be. Or possibly backboning the tip of a nubby, vestigial tail. That's nice, I think, my sleeping town. And of course my sleeping town would have a tail.

Down Gottlieb I follow the sleeper's spine until I finally pass the windswept intersection with Colling and the broad, redbrick hindquarters of the Magnus Building with its gray transformer boxes up on stilts and several blue metal dumpsters overstuffed with compostable Stempler's Roast cups and clamshells because even though Stempler's Roast makes sure all of its containers are compostable, well, the town of Velton is a bit behind the municipal waste game's eight ball and doesn't even have a fucking recycling plant, let alone anything approaching a public composting area. Ha! Haha! Despite the Stempler's Roast crew's best eco-intentions, into the dumpster it all goes, off to not-biodegrade in the methane traps of the Velton landfill along with all the Styrofoam and plastic bottles, each layer of garbage sealed away within the same sedimentary sarcophagi of eternal, wasted youth. *Good job Stempler's Roast,* I think to myself, rolling my eyes. *Good job Dion and Ariadne, good job Meagan. You twee fucking asshats.*

I sigh, slinging my gym bag over my other shoulder. Why am I so mad? Like it or not, I am a creature so thoroughly energized by jealously, loathing and wistful sentimentality that were I ever to kick the habit no doubt my life would fall apart completely. Oh well. At least it's a pretty nice spring day outside, the air thick with the smells of germinating grass seeds and the quack of toy-sized ducklings. The sun's out and beaming like it's making up for lost time and all the little houses up and down Gottlieb Street have families of small children outside, all digging in vegetable gardens or playing with little footballs and basketballs or roasting corn and tomatoes and spare ribs out on their smoky little barbecues. Isn't this nice? All in all an effusively wholesome scene. Across Gottlieb I spot Lucky Benny weaving his way up the sidewalk, his stained houndstooth shirt unbuttoned to reveal an ample mane of graying chest hair, long arms swinging at his sides.

Seeing Lucky Benny not in a bar and specifically not in the Ugly feels somehow wrong, like watching an aardvark merrily descending into a moon crater or an octopus levitating without the context of an aquarium. And, outside he's actually much taller than you'd think, walking down the street like this, even slumping he's still like six-three. I notice that Lucky Benny's toting a large wooden spoon in his left hand and when he looks up and we make eye contact I give him a kind of casual, slanting salute off the forehead and he almost thwacks himself in the face with his large spoon trying to reciprocate, which in turn nearly spasms me into a fit of laughter that I half-suppress by making it look like a sneeze.

*God bless ya, E-wood!* His response is immediate, enthusiastic, genuine. Lucky Benny is the kind of guy who, when you sneeze, really does want God to bless you.

*Thanks, Benny!* I call back. *You, too!*

*Anytime, E-wood! Anytime.*

The Whitetail Buslines ticket booth isn't so much its own ticket booth as the stamper vestibule at the exit of a poured concrete parking structures, where a marshmallow-headed tyrant named Dwayne discharges his station as a seller of bus tickets with a maximum of unpleasantness. His skull is pale and large and hairless, draped over on all sides with the marshmallow goo of his face; eyes glistening black and stuck as close together as eyes can get stuck before they start overlapping. His massive lungfish of nose hangs above a mouth as red and puckery as a sick dog's anus. That's Dwayne for you. For twenty-seven dollars and a visit to Dwayne you can get most places you need to from Velton; to Des Moines or the Quad Cities, to Sioux Falls or St. Louis or Chicago, and in my case, from Chicago to Cincinnati and from Cincinnati to Toulous. Kentucky. Home. Home for Memorial Day, home for a surprise visit, an unplanned return, home for fun and friends and nothing else. Home to see Mike, to see Cynthia, to see Jody and Mark and Mom. Marnie? I wondered, feeling my body tense involuntarily. What? What was I

246

even worried about? It would be fine. It would be fun. Why not let home be fun?

Today Dwayne's credit card machine is broken. Dwayne can't spare any singles. *We're not doing singles today. What do you think this is, some kind of charity? Now beat it. I'm serious, no hanging around. See?* Dwayne jiggles his marshmallowy face at a brand new metal sign tacked up outside his vestibule. It says, in plain block letters, *NO LOITERING*. No loitering? At a bus stop?

I walk around the block, turning off Gottlieb onto Page Street and hoping that there might at least be some good puddles or tags on the parking structures, but alas, there are none. The sun's already getting its slant on for the second act of mid-morning and the blueness of the air feels ripe and warm and so tingly-luscious as to be almost edible. I take out my phone and start thumbing through Fnacebook, liking some of the comments in a Real Jews discussion thread about why there are like, a zillion kung-fu movies but basically zero krav maga movies and whether or not that's how it should be. Who's gonna step the fuck up and start making some krav maga action flicks happen? Is this something we could potentially crowdfund? Ricardo has already commented that he would totally watch a krav maga movie and that, should it ever be made, he would support Quentin Tarantino as the director, even though Quentin Tarantino is not, as far as anyone knows, Jewish. This has sparked a nice little flame war about whether or not the directors of the original kung-fu movies ought to know kung-fu themselves, and if so how

247

much, and whether or not you had to be Asian to direct a kung-fu movie anyway. *clearly u do not,* Ricardo writes back, *exhibit A being Quentin fucking Tarantino.* Then more sniping. Nice, nice. Actually all in all the whole Real Jews thing has turned out to be a total Fnacebook goldmine.

*Hooooooonk!*

Shit, the bus's here. Aaaaaaa! I look up, feeling strangely pantsed by the honking noise and throw myself into a little jog towards the Whitetail's open door. Today it looks like I'm Velton's only fare, but the rest of the bus is packed pretty full already. This big, curly-haired guy in a maroon sweatshirt stands up so that I can squeeze in next to him and I say *thanks* before making myself as small as possible against the window next to him as the bus slowly pulls out and away.

Yesterday after work Ricardo and I had planned to eat some acid but then it got late and I lost interest. Sometimes it sucks to see the world in such like, enchantingly bullshit detail. I'd take an egg-smooth face over one with bark-vivid detail any day. (Pores are basically disgusting). That's why I prefer cartoons to oil paintings. Too much. Already much too much. And *our brains are cognitive misers*, at least so I read on some brainwork blog the other day. What we don't need we throw away, like insta-throw insta-away. When we look at a tree, you think we see every single leaf? The Velt River, every single eddy? Ha! Most days we don't even have time for all the clouds crisscrossing the sky right above our heads. Then, when we notice them, it's like their obviousness leaves us basically unimpressed, shrugging, asking why, asking who really cares?

Acid makes the trees seem boring. It makes the sun boring. I get filled up with how all the visuals stop knowing what to do with themselves, hoping that every little thing must really-really-really mean something. Because, see how the way the sunlight hitting the leaves of that oak tree looks exactly like your face? So cool, right? No, no. So cool, yeah once. Now it's not really all that cool. Sigh. Nostalgia for the acid trips of our youth. Now there's a thing we could all use a word for.

So Ricardo and I didn't end up eating any acid after all and I went to sleep early and now I'm here, on this bus, heading out to Kentucky, heading home. When I close my eyes I'm remembering walking down Klapp and through Clough Wilderness Area yesterday, watching the light hit the thornbushes and tufts of shadegreen moss, glancing off the quartz gravel lining the mudgummed trail, a trail that winds away through the ancient rows of chestnut and sycamore and willow all the way down to Paper Creek, Paper Creek with its artificial smells of lilacs and lilies and the fleshy whiff of dissolved Vitamin E and shea from the little soap factory upstream. When I close my eyes I can hear the rush of water and the voice of Ms. Unica Korn, saying *Today we have a special treat. We are going on a field trip to the Museum of Earth's Waterfalls. There will be many types of waterfalls on display, though none from other planets. You can even see how it is that they make the foam, the steam, the mist. Isn't this exciting class?*

I nod my fourth grade head hard, sucking hard on my bottom lip.

Ms. Unica Korn watches as we file onto the yellow school bus, sits at the front with her smoked glasses that she wears to imitate Anne Sullivan from the cinematic adaptation of *The Miracle Worker*, watches as we file off the yellow school bus towards her, through the plate glass doors of the Museum of Earth's Waterfalls.

*Here, look! This waterfall is just a baby. One day the ground will sink at the bottom and its spout will grow. There is headland enough for a wide cascade to form when the spring snowmelt comes down and swoles out the whole big river's run.*

*Yes, Ms. Korn.*

*Right now you're just looking at a misty trickle. We call this type of waterfall a* horsetail, *which implies that it was formed through cataracts or other alterations underlying bedrock. How many types of waterfalls can you name, Elwood?*

*I can't name any, Ms. Korn.*

*That's not very good, Elwood. Not good at all. Were you even paying attention during the lesson?*

*I'm sorry, Ms. Korn.*

*That's alright. I'll tell you again. The types of waterfalls I expect you to be familiar with are:* ledge, plunge, horsetail *and* staircase. *There. Do you think you have more appreciation for this specimen, now that you know the proper name for it?*

*Actually, Ms. Korn, I'd rather have preferred not to know. Aren't waterfalls supposed to stay a kind of namelessness? Now when I look at this waterfall all I can see in the rock is a horse's butt with the tail of water coming out. I don't even see the water, really. Just the butt. Of a horse. And the bright, crystal tail.*

*Oh dear.*

*Are you sad, Ms. Korn?*

*I am sad, Elwood. I have always been sad.*

*Don't worry Ms. Korn. I'm right here.*

# Popo & Ix

The semester after Cynthia Tsang and I split up I had what some people might call a nervous breakdown. Everything felt like it had gone underwater. My roommate Sam taped cardboard to the staircase. For falling foreheads, he said. I told Sam I knew he was stealing my spaghetti. He denied it with accusing eyes. Like: *we both know what happened to that spaghetti. Don't we?*

I slunk back to my half-lit corner by the window where I could watch a scrawny house spider spin the first draft of her web. Sam let out a ffffffffffffffft noise. He grabbed his raincoat and we didn't speak to each other until the next weekend, and then later, after it happened, well, he didn't really have much to say.

*Who cares?* I thought. My inner speech had become echoey and faraway as if it were piping up from a Delphic oracle chamber. The sink in the kitchen was full of last week's dirty dishes and the microwave's digital clock blinked the wrong time in an evil, keylime green. I inhaled the stale air common to all poorly kept kitchens. *I'll clean it after my exams are over. I'll clean it once I get the rest of my life together. And Sam can just go fuck himself. What do I need to be hanging around a low-life spaghetti thief, anyway? One plastic packet of $2.99 angel hair. Who does that?*

I sat at the kitchen table, studying for my French exam. Above me our upstairs neighbor was having very squealy sex. The other sex-person wasn't making any noise at all. I was learning the French past participles of different verbs relating to animals and cooking. *Moi, je suis delicieux!* exclaimed an aproned pig wielding a spatula.

(*I am delicious!*) Squeal. Squeeeeeeeal.

The pork-themed verbs weren't giving me much trouble. It's just a matter of learning the rules and memorizing the exceptions. Manger, to eat. You keep the e in the imperfect of manger so that the g stays banana-soft, je mangeait, I was eating. So I tried to concentrate, focusing my ears on the downbeat of some Feelz Goodman track, a downbeat that syncopated oddly with the squeals from above, bumpf, ba-bumpf-squeal, bumf, ba-bumpf-squeal, I was eating, je mangeait, I ate, j'ai mangé. Je buvais, j'ai bu (I was drinking, I drank). Bu.

It looked wrong. Bu. What makes a word look wrong?

I took a break from verbs and shuffled to a flashcard reminding me that verre means glass and not cup which is tasse as in *tasse de café* except when that cup is made of glass, in which case it can still be a verre, as in *à voir le verre à moitié vide plutôt qu'à moitié plein* (to see a glass half-empty, rather than half-full). That thought prompted a verre plein of my own in which I cut the sting of lukewarm vodka with a bottle of flattish tonic and then remembered apropos of half-emptying it into my mouth that the word cliché in French does not actually mean a US American *cliché* but instead means a picture, as in *cliché echogrammatique* (which is French for *ultrasound*). And then, also, to think of ultrasounds or fMRI images of beating hearts and jaundiced livers as clichés in the US American

253

sense (or at least in my own sense) felled my face faster than the early autumn light from Toulous's tree-lined sky, sex-squeals now pushing up against all my verbs: *boire, eee, avoir bu, eeeeep, buvair, eee, boîve, eeeeee-eeeep-eee...*

At which point I realized that the verre I was holding had cracked into three distinct and jagged pieces and begun slicing new and ominous lines of irrevocable misfortune into my already fractalized palmistry. I gushed forth a spatter of dark red and made a few of the verb flashcards bleed. Across the table I stared down an eyelash floating in the meniscus of yesterday's coffee, tasse. I peeled sliced skin and shards from the wound, verre, adding a visceral hue of pain to the operatic tremolo-gasms falling in flitters all the pump of Feelz Goodman around me, shrieking, bursting, yowling, screaming. There's nothing like re-learning the past tense to make one wax nostalgic, especially at this noisy time of night, completely alone in a shitty little apartment on a shitty little street in a shitty little section of the town you grew up in. I thought again of Cynthia Tsang, hoping that she might also be sitting at a kitchen table somewhere off in a better version of reality, thinking wistfully of me. But actually there is no reciprocity rule of wistfulness. One finds this out quite quickly. And when did Sam even go out? The past tense returned, to worry itself inside me: *Has everything already ended? Not life, perhaps, but the feeling of life, the feeling that life's still out there, somewhere, waiting?*

I imagined spending the rest of my life speaking in the French past tenses. *This might be the most important exam you ever study for*, said the echoey Delphic underground-voice in my forehead. *Study hard...*

Aimer, j'ai aimé (I loved), j'amais (I was loving) which sounds enough like *jamais* (never) for another thousand years of Francophone pop music choruses. *Here I am*, said the voice. The plaintive lines of black maroon went on streaking out over the tabletop. They left sanguine stains across the gills of cheap wood grain. *What will Sam say?* I sat and watched them reach the edge and spill over, dripping dots of alarm-liquid onto the floor.

Cynthia Tsang, her

- long silky-black hair, wire-framed glasses
- soft, round face dimpled with a permanently forced-looking smile
- charismatic tshirts, that frustrated-looking zebra waiting for its milkshake
- impossibly long fingers, fingers that would startle passersby as she gestured at the world
- breasts the shape and sweetness of bodega moonpies, XL brown nipples, black bras that hooked in the back
- Chnucks that she never tied or untied, shiny gold laces triple-knotted tight, flopping this and that way as she walked

The sounds of Toulous's night faded to zero in an abrupt decrescendo beneath my sliced-up hands. I began to look at the flashcards and instead of pieces of French grammar on blue-lined paper rectangles I saw the pieces of my life laid out in front of me, conjugated in a series of vacuous maintenance activities (eating, drinking, sleeping, bathing, using the toilet, staring out at a flurry of birds pecking around at dew-limned footprints), dozens of sunsets (each one clichéd in a different, terrible way; echogrammatiques of hearts beating inside small thrushes and frisky tree squirrels) red spotting the distant linoleum, a frosty pane of dull colors between myself and the world, standing at a suburban front door with a bouquet of fresh-cut flowers, wondering if I hadn't gotten the address wrong, the messiness and giddy laughter of young children at play, and then alone, waiting in the food court of a mall that might as well have been anywhere for an inevitable rendezvous that ended in a duffel bag of objects passed from one hand to another, a duffel bag that has since been in a musty cubbyhole beneath mine and Sam's rickety staircase ever since, latched up behind the two wicker doors. Those objects, and their adjuncts in a series of past tense verbs (to eat, to have eaten, to sleep, to have slept, to drink, to have drank, drunk, to have been sleeping... to kiss, to have been kissing, kissed, to leave, to have left, to have been left).

Along the lucid blue lines of my sentimental twilight's cardstock the face of Cynthia Tsang hovers between two fluorescentine bloodstains, her forehead and cheeks inscribed with tendrils of shiny ink-soaked angel hair, wan and bodiless above the telephone lines, calling with a chorus of dial tones that have become new intervals of silence, silence beneath a smooth and sharp-toothed nothing, the sizzle of answering machine lips whispering static before a shaky voice (mine) goes to leave its last saliva-purled trace: *Goodbye.*

(I was becoming a small place cut from fragrant wood, the latch re-closed, a blotted nothing, feeling with my hands for the cupboard door, the zipperlip ridges of a duffel bag —I was a collection of objects that had become unglued from the meaning of myself; paperback Kundera, old drawstring purse for marbles, a necklace made of spoiled Halloween candy, a pair of one-lensed sunglasses set in matte plastic frames, coins with Chinese symbols from one of her uncle's business trips —untangled from the whichwayuppedness of all past emotions I flew across the floor cracks breathing hard, inhaling the sweet air of lamentation and yes, I was floating, yes, I was bouncing, yes I was clattering, clanging, clamoring, a shopping cart of greased watermelons rolling hard down a flight of stairs.

And yes, I may have made a racket all the way back to where that face lies stiff beneath the ink-blackened hair of a fallen angel stroked into smooshy pasta clumps, aloft upon a woodgrain sky, where every gesture faded in and out through lumps of congealed morning. Plain air kissed at the bottoms of my feet with that char-hot breath scraped from the end-places where time and space ran out their wooden spools and this feeling of being superglued to 10,000,000 oblivia overwhelmed all comers and sprung my latch apart to open for that sweet release, a release from all the clichéd ugliness of TV-flavored feeling).

And but so then I kept moving my hands around the paper verbs and went on repeating out their past tenses in poorly accented French as if incanting some kind of dazed and murmurous spell. Inside of me that disconsolate underground voice went on echoing and echoing. I tried to blot it out with my sliced-up hands, hurrying the verbs faster and faster, imagining within each shuffle of flashcards another day-cycle, week-cycle, month-cycle and then year-year-year of life hurtling me off towards the banality of death. Isn't that life; a series of paper verbs, advancing consecutively rather than this circular motion upon the woodgrain of a blood-spattered kitchen table?

Sure, sure it is. So I maybe did become a little more frantic when the throaty sex squeals began again from the apartment above, louder this time, syncopated with the slap of a calloused hand on unknown asscheeks, slaps that then plinked down into the wormholes of my nervous ears, my gritted teeth, my splayed, burning fingers, my spine infused with agony, face gone wild in the reflection of a bathroom mirror that I had only just shattered, the floor covered with broken glass, my shirt soaked red and unrecognizable, the room covered in bits of bloody paper because of all the verbs I'd shredded with my heaving, spitbright mouth.

At the time, I didn't think-say-to-only-myself: *Oh, I'm just having un petit nervous breakdown.*

No.

What I thinkspoke-to-only-myself was: *This magic feeling is called love yes this is what love feels is this irresistible totality like yes I am in love I am really in love now I know what it feels like and I must not let go of this feeling no matter the consequences! Because love! Right!?* What I needed more than anything else was to figure out how I was going to undo the mistakes of the past and get Cynthia Tsang back in my life. Because, what I realized at that moment was that I missed her and needed her more than I needed anything else I had ever thought I had ever needed; without her there was nothing and nowhere and no point in even going on.

First things first: I swept the bits of French past participles into little piles on the linoleum of the kitchen floor. Second: I fetched a writing pad and a pen, sat down and took a deep breath. I resolved to write what was sure to be the most perfect love letter ever composed, an epistle so tender and expressive that it would breach all of her barriers, subdue all of her doubts and open a door for us to start talking and eventually get back together.

*Yes,* I muttered, feverishly. *This can really work! Isn't this what happens in the movies? Right?*

I started writing, curling my tongue out just above my upper lip and really cutting into my best tight cursive, flying through paragraphs until about three pages in I realized the whole thing was just leprous with clichés in the bad US American rather than charming Francophone sense and way, way, *way* too sentimental

259

and besides that, it sounded whiny and pedantic and pretty much complete shit.

So I ripped the pages out of the pad and tossed them to the ground where they curled up into little telescopes atop my sanguine verb-piles and I, unfazed, began again, working myself up into the same self-possessed lather as I'd done before.

This effort would be a draft, I decided, after a few cross-outs. But still, getting the flow and the overall gist of the letter down tonight was the really important part; otherwise this feeling of vital certitude might recede and never return. Ruled or unruled for the final version? Handwritten was a must. The key would be to send something heartfelt, something euphonious and clever, something capable of moving Cynthia to little, secretive smiles and (possibly) even to open-mouthed gasps of real feeling. Right? I eschewed adjectives and kept my sentences short. I muted the use of parentheticals and always used my Oxford commas as Cynthia Tsang, of all people, would insist upon. My hands flew and cramped up and then flew again. I ran my first pen out of ink, then my second. I went to the gas station a couple blocks down the street as soon as the sky turned light so I could re-up on my stock of black Bnic pens. The graveyard shift cashier looked at me like I was crazy, like I might be purchasing the pens in order to stab someone in the eye.

All I muttered back to him: *Have you ever? Been? In love? It really does make you crazy.*

It was daylight by the time I finished the letter and noon by the time I opened and then promptly choked down the rest of the lukewarm vodka. I wasn't even tired! Not a bit. I read and re-read the letter. It was perfect. It was addressed to Popo (Popocatépetl), from Ix (Iztaccihuatl) and drew from the repertoire of a long-standing argument that Cynthia and I had been having concerning themes from Malcolm Lowry's epic novel *Under the Volcano*. The letter contained several elements composed in blank verse, though most of the text was written as a kind of teleplay, a love story in dialogue between the two volcanoes above Lowry's fictitious Cuernavaca (Quanhuac). Two more pens shattered into their rubbish of sticky plastic, and I felt lost (perdre, equating a losing of otherness, subjective or objective, whereas to lose oneself is the reflexive *se* perdre) and now my eyes pulled wide and tumid as foxgrapes, my mouth opened, breathing labored and spilling with pungent fumes, cheeks blood-grimed with sweat in the lavender-colored glow of late Tuesday afternoon when, thick with a kind of hazy delirium, I finally gazed down at the floor (shredded flashcards, blood spatter, French verbs) and then up at the wall clock (6:45 PM) and realized that I had completely missed my French exam.

Along with my other Tuesday classes it had taken place hours ago, started and ended, a blot of encircled, star-studded, exclamatory ink in my spiral dayplanner — and given our French class's ironclad attendance/exam policy (*no misses, no retakes, any absence must be given advance notice and granted prior approval except in the case of severe unplanned medical emergency!*) there would be absolutely no possibility of me passing the class, the hard work of my scraped-by B- being no match for the GPA-imploder of a 0/100 exam score, which in turn would snip the final threads of my academic scholarship, thus forcing me into a loan situation that I doubted even the most charitable of financial institutions would qualify me for, on top of making me re-take this semester of French as a requirement for graduation which would make it impossible for me to graduate with the rest of my class, a situation I knew would sit poorly with the parental units even if I did manage to either keep or conceal the loss of my academic scholarship.

Shit!

And all of these realizations came blasting towards me with such torpedo force that I very quickly arrived at the conclusion that the only suitable course of action was to implement a real-deal severe medical emergency, whereupon I seized one of the broken shards of verre from the not-yet-previous evening and jammed it into my left hand's little finger, spurting blood everywhere. Encouraged by the rush of pain I stood and went to the cutlery drawer to finish off the poor digit with Sam's stainless steel meat cleaver. Not bad. But still I wasn't satisfied and went back for the ring. Finger. They looked ugly, severed, lying in my palm.

Chest heaving, the blood in full-spatter mode across the amber-lit desolation of mine and Sam's kitchen I scanned the room for my phone to look up directions to the University hospital. Honestly, it was more blood than I had expected and after toweling some of it up I began to feel a little woozy, seeing the kind of spots in my vision that appear on old films to signal to the projectionist to change over reels. Adrenaline kicked in and all of a sudden I began to wonder if something in my overall mental state might have gone seriously haywire.

Outside, the squealy sex neighbor was standing on the second story fire escape smoking cigarettes with last night's stallion, a scrawny whiteboy tattooed with a curly bib of cursive.

*Hey*, she waved.

Huh, I thought, waving back. So this is what it feels like to wave a hand with only two fingers, plus thumb. Not that different! Not that bad!

She grimaced.

The white boy gave a stoned-looking grin like: *Cool hand, man!*

I turned and tried to concentrate on concealing what I was doing. Why? Was I? This was the feeling, serrated and slippery. I stepped along in an unstraight line. It was feeling a little more loopy to actually walk and simultaneously maintain my composure than I could have anticipated. Growing desperate, I kind of half-jogged-half-skipped the eight blocks to the University's hospital emergency room.

The intake nurse was appalled at my condition and didn't hesitate when I asked her to indicate that my injury happened early this morning around 9:00 am while I was on the way to my French exam and that the fingers had then fallen into a difficult-to-reach storm grate, forcing me to spend much of the rest of the day fishing them out with an apparatus made from several coat hangers knotted together.

*Do you have that right?* I said. *The timing of everything? Do you have it in your notes?*

The next afternoon I took my French exam with my Gabonaise TA bringing her two small children to help proctor because she had already used up some quota of proctoring-related daycare dollars on the day of the actual exam and she looked very mordant and reproachful and scared even, to look at my bandaged and sewn-back-together left hand. Later I wrote her an apology note, but then didn't feel sincere enough about the apology to actually send it. I got a B+ on the exam and a B in the class which was better than the average and way better than I expected, all things considered.

The thirty-seven page handwritten missive draft (Dear Popo... With all my love, Ix) got folded up and jammed in the index of a very used copy of the DSM-IV on my bookshelf, a tome which I opened years later in a trial-and-error effort to self-diagnose pseudomania. Which is to say that I never even considered mailing it. The thing about that letter was that it stayed with me as a certain kind of proof, proof of what can happen when the need to make myself understood achieves a certain psychical velocity, a velocity that I once thought was love and now consider more closely related to some kind of extreme, episodic personality disorder. But what is a passionate love anyway, if not some kind of madness? And even though some years have passed since this episode, I'd still say that the lines between those notions, between desire and insanity, between sacrifice and stupidity, between reality and fiction, well even now they may still run a little thin.

# The Beforehand

> 'I want the beforehand of a book.' I just wrote this sentence, but before this
> sentence, I wrote a hundred others, which I've suppressed, because the moment for
> cutting short had arrived. It's not me, it's necessity which has cut the text we were on
> the way to writing. Because the text and I, we would continue on our way.
> - Hélène Cixous, *Without End, No, State of Drawingness, No, Rather: The Executioner's
> Taking Off*

So what was I talking about again? Oh yeah, writing. Writing and
the affect of distraction in writing, writing that is either distracted
from itself or distracting from its otherselves, that draws attention to
its lack of attention-drawing capacity in such a manner that the
engaged reader feels compelled to literally look up from the book
and notice all the microscopic suckbots clinging to the inside of their
own over-optimized mind's eye. Sorry, what?

So I guess that writing this book has felt at times like the
turduckening (stuffing a duck inside of a chicken, then stuffing that
chicken inside of a turkey) of at least three extraterrestrial
amphibians who are not only still very much alive during said
turduckening process but are desperately trying to harmonize an a
capella version of a commercial for an eccentric insurance company
that indemnifies business owners against attacks by cyborg
mirrorpeople and, as these 3+ extraterrestrial amphibians (stuffed,
one inside the other's highly elastic anuses) reach some kind of
frantic crescendo, I get inexorably interrupted and off-kiltered by the
insectile buzzing of a phone, the Internet wanting my mind back,

saying *Hello little prisoner, wherever did you scamper off to? Time to come baa-aaaack!*

Maybe once upon a time it really was all about who owned the means of production, but today where some high % of economic activity is dictated by frictionless, virtual clicks it's become all about who owns *the means of seduction*, a category that both includes and subsumes the category of writing and perhaps even art within the interactive metasymbol of Content. But what was I looking for again? Oh that's right: a contradiction, I wanted to contradict myself. Because really, it's not so much about turduckening but its opposite, a kind of head-extracted-from-anus act of writerly anti-turduckening. Why? Well, because how else can one think about something while simultaneously being entirely inside of it? Otherwise, there's no vantage point. No place to stand to gain a meaningful sense of one's own near-total lack of perspective.

If, like goddess Trivia, it is still possible to live life triple-bodied (and, possibly, as the aforementioned three extraterrestrial amphibians) then what's eventually called for is a total removal of the scaffolding surrounding the writing machine so that the words can go about their best business with an absolute minimum of disturbance.

\*

I was 24 when Aziz showed me the ropes, 15 when I met Ted Secret, 23 when Cynthia split up with me, and 20 when I saw Curmudgeon live on a smoky Memorial Day. Or was it all backwards, upside-down and inside-out? Names, like words, are just bad habits. And by then, they were all becoming me, becoming us, becoming Elizeya and thickening into blackbright drupes so juicily that I'd yearn each night to take in the whole world beneath my sunken eyes, into my Rorschach cloud shadows and my grim, askance wrong-wordedness. One surely loses track of time, reflected selves and even friends in all those shallow, dirt-scarred puddles!

We seem to move around a lot. A year here, a year there. We take what jobs are left before they too decide to leave. We are strangers to ourselves as much as any other. The fact that we are anyone at all becomes a source of endless mystery. It's all so very overwhelming! And even a single word leaves our underfaces in the squiggly lapis scars of a single cup of river water regarding its Venusian delta from up in outer space. As Kim Hyesoon writes in *Sorrowtoothpaste Mirrorcream*'s Influenza; *When I pronounce "bird" / only the wind remains in me.* Indeed! And what shall remain in us, when we have pronounced so many new words, so many new ideas for words, what new shapes shall take root within the overflowing cup of our sublime and contradictory indescribablenesses? Surely, there many taxa of this wind. As the inimitable Maggie May says: *New words we like: why do we like them? Maybe what we like in new words is a kind of aha, that now we have more things with which to Google ourselves even harder! Because these words are us, or rather, they're what we'd maybe like ourselves to become.* I like this idea, that new words that resonate with us are simply a way of

268

whiffing the future, of looking ourselves up in some kind of Borgesian Thesaurus and gasping at all of our implausible synonyms. Because really, *what are we* if not the words that contain us, that say us in our moments, in the moments when we most feel we mean?

In her excellent meditation on digital everydayness and the future of literature entitled *In the Corporeal Age, We Will Know The Names of Trees*, Sonya Chung writes: *Art, commerce, and technology are colliding like so many boiling point particles. All the players are scrambling to survive, to thrive, to stay ahead of the (hairpin) curve. As a writer, it would be easy to fall into all that arranging and projecting and twisting about; it could also be fatal.* Mega-snaps to that! I wonder if the fatality of writing lies precisely in subsuming one's style via a badly overboiling medium, a medium perhaps constituted through its own disruption (or stylistic indecisions, even) and therefore a medium without any discernible repertoire, without a viable literary refrain. Possibly? The point here is not that we can't have great books or fun books or even delightful books made from the Internet, or that we can't have writers savvy in the use of platform-driven composition. Rather, the point is that *the social function of the book has been put out to wander the Internet in search of itself,* and what it has found is a readership so hooked into their own respective platforms and self-curated networks of social content that it (the book) no longer knows what the fuck is going on. Are books meant to imitate, absorb, intervene or completely ignore the omnipresence of digital communication?

Short answer: no one really knows and everyone's writing on eggshells, at least with respect to the Internet as a trope within all metafiction After Wallace (A.W.). There have been some pretty neat fizzles but nothing's really caught on, and now we're left wondering what shape the next move could possibly take now that reality no longer resembles itself with any meaningful or durable consistency. This is maybe why in self-proclaimed *literary* novels you don't see text messages, social media statuses, or even very many phones. This is maybe why first person narrators rarely *feel* terribly realistic Because there truly is something distinctly un-literary feeling about slick tech motifs cropping up all over the place, getting in the way of character, scene and voice. But, then again, for many of us millennial types, a world without them isn't exactly realism qua realism, either. Our moment is heteromorphous, metaechomaniacal, autosimulacraphageous — *The Dysmaginarium of Dr. Ursula Buckminster Kafkapynchon*, the world where Oedipa's kids have to grow up dealing with the gnawing suspicion that they were only ever created as the MacGuffin of an overclever language game, a game that got so far out of hand as to become entirely banal. Conclusions replaces premises, the axiom coding our worldpicturebuilding machine zooms out another order of magnitude, sculpts a new Russian doll to hide the violence of the past within. Our moment is infantile. Our moment is forgetting itself. Our moment is deeply hallucinatory. Our moment is creepily unafraid to announce that if almost certainly means nothing.

Books today are (rightfully) totally terrified of the future because they (books) not only have everything to lose but have already lost quite a great deal already. Whether you look at the mess of the publishing industry or the state of contemporary libraries or simply the number of times that one hears books brought up in casual/professional conversation, well, *something massive has changed,* even from five and ten years ago. People can both/and about digital humanities all they want, but the reality is that there are very real trade-offs in how people spend their time and cognitive energy and books have been on the losing end of nearly all of these trade-offs. With so much more so-called *disruption* planned for the attention economy, it hardly seems insane to imagine that current trends (away from bookreading) might *dramatically intensify* among the generation of people who've been coddled, nursed and raised on Internet phones (more than, say, TV). Which is to say that yes, seismic shifts are indeed afoot. And no one likes to worry that their guiding passion, indeed the animating force behind their entire existence is in real danger of being rendered backwards, curious and quaint. *Wait, so tell me again. What exactly do you do?*

Let's get specific. What the distributed Internet really does is to redefines the notion of *relevance* as a quantitative relationship between a reader's *location* and *identity.* This relationship predicates *proximity* and *homophily* as the core drivers of *engagement.* Things that are closer to us matter more. Things that are more like us matter more. This is affect. What we're interested in here is the role that belief plays in perception, how machines of narrative coherence knit together the symbolic fabric of meaningful reality. Time goes in, events come out. Space goes in, cartographies come out. Both ribbons interlace to form the background against which *place* emerges, against which *scene* emerges. Relevance is what's near and dear to us. Engagement is how we respond to that nearness and dearness. And it pertains, primarily, to the real. Real things. They take up all of our time. Practically speaking, this mean that as more and more time-sensitive, geography-sensitive, demography-sensitive media platforms launch themselves into cut-throat competition for larger and larger ownership stakes of our distracted, interrupted, harried-feeling eyeballs, well, books will just plain *feel* less relevant. They will lose their time. They will lose their place. They will look out-of-place within our daily scenes.

Because the word *relevant* no longer means what it used to mean and instead what it's started to mean is here-now-pay-attention-aaaaaaaaa-because-you-could-be-missing-out!

Over time, the effect of this megatrend will likely be that an ever-growing % of us, the readership, simply *no longer has the bandwidth* (spare time or cognitive energy-surpluses) to read the kind of writing that doesn't insta-hook us, that doesn't bodyslam us into uproarious flabbergastedness or at least gets us going with a jag of nice, primal terror!

Crux: writing beholden to the evolutionary selection pressures of a scarcity-driven eyeball economy must be *always written to grab, and never written to last*. Full stop.

Whether or not this writing is very good, well, it has its moment and then it's gone: obsolescence planned, disposability guaranteed. Who knows if the words or the brands or the platforms will even survive? And after the moment is over and all the newest hashtags have trended off to die, well, are you even *supposed to want to read it*? Now that it's no longer *relevant to the crowd*? And what about re-reading!? Ha!? Surely you jest! Writing today, well, it's not exactly optimized to last, is it? Nor really are its words. And perhaps, then, neither are we.

*

If we think of last century's writing as characterized by an ever-more-fraught relationship between writers and readers, today's writing is broadly characterized by the figure of *the user* in relation to *the developer*, with both writers and readers now haunting the technology platform as ghostly apparitions. Writing (now relegated to a subset of metasymbolic Content) is now only one of several layers of textualism that a reader experiences in apprehending any (virtual) publication. *Reading*, once the prime currency of influencing people, has now in many precincts been replaced by the metricized social performance of *clicking* — related, but markedly different. And writing, once viewed as evidence of a person's passionate intellectualism or earnest spiritual striving, is today simply equated with what many of us sit and do all day on our email boxes and wish more and more that we could please *just please* get away from.

Because, in the so-called knowledge economy of perpetual connectedness, all reading can begin to feel like work and sometimes *even thinking itself* starts to feel like putting in unpaid overtime. I know I'm not alone in knowing many totally-real-and-totally-functional people *who no longer even read books*, or do so only very rarely. And (as they'll endlessly claim) *it's not because they don't want to read! Don't for a second imagine that they haven't spent long, formative periods of their life as lovers of reading!* No, the reason that they don't read books anymore is because *there simply isn't any time or energy left for reading-for-fun after a long, drudgy day of reading-for-work or reading-for-distraction-from-work.* There simply isn't any time left at all.

As a so-called knowledge worker (or whatever you want to call it), I can totally relate to this never-having-enough-time feeling. It gets frantic and always leaves me deeply perplexed about what exactly the endgame of all our shiny, new-fangled technology is supposed to be, given that we end up working longer and longer hours while feeling more and more psychosomatically unwell. And I completely accept that there is a great deal about the Internet, other people's brains, other people's machines and the world at large that I shall simply never comprehend. Maybe this is simply one of those things: I don't get it. But that doesn't make me any less suspicious about the growing normalization of cognitive overwork, about the fact that people often refer to turning off their devices or exiting from the world of 4G signal service using the language of *detoxing*. Shivers.

These days the magisterium of smooth, glowing space never really leaves the background radiation of my imagination entirely alone. This is why, as a reader, I have often delighted in things being broken.

In collisions.

In pandemonia.

In frantic paradoxes.

In vignettes of tragicomical eroticism.

I like it when things are unhappy and tangled and Boschian.

I like it when *people other than me* maybe feel a bit muddled and mocked and bewildered, too.

And what I really like is to feel lost in the remote company of others, a crowd of lost strangers who are nevertheless lost together, lost in a book, a distributed clump of tilted heads with whom I shall likely never share anything more than the experience of reading, thinking, *re-reading, re-thinking*.

Getting stuck. As Lauren Berlant has argued, *Most of the writing we do is actually a performance of stuckness. It is a record of where we got stuck on a question for long enough to do some research and write out the whole knot...*

Getting *un*stuck isn't really the point, Berlant reminds us, and actually the *real point* is to figure out why exactly we got stuck somewhere in the first place.

To the extent that the smoothness of ubiquitous social Internet fucks with us badly, I'd suggest that it interferes precisely with our ability to perform extended acts of stuckness.

That it overthins the viscosity of our thinking to the point that we can too easily move on, too easily extricate ourselves from the stuckness of our most exacting quandaries.

Rather than sticking there.

Rather than forcing ourselves to dwell upon frustration.

Which is really too bad. Because frustrations are how we grow. Because quandaries are where the action is.

That's where we get our real work done.

Scrolling away has become too easy. And so we can too often forget, distributing ourselves to the service many small tasks rather than meditating upon a single emptiness, rather than thinking and rethinking, reading and re-reading, folding and refolding our sense of contradictoriness without precisely knowing why. Wandering towards an unknown destination. You only know you've arrived once you've arrived. That's, fortunately or unfortunately, how the most worthwhile achievements tend to work.

Perhaps then, the truest calling of contemporary writing is furnish an unexpected grounding, to catch us around the ankles, to slow us down in movements of recollected flesh. Writing poses to the reader the challenge of deliberateness, mindfulness and slowness always figured as the body. What Bataille called *acephalic*; thinking without a head. Writing is sometimes capable of furnishing such a body via a density of feeling, an intricacy of movement, a claustral intensity of language. This, I'd suggest, is the kind of writing that's vital for really excellent thinking. And by *body* I do not mean some hypothetical, abstract body but the real, specific tangible body made of eye goop and crotch sweat and elbow skin and abdominal rumblings. A body made for getting stuck.

- Elizeya Quate, San Francisco, 2016

# Acknowledgements

Several of these stories miraculously tumbled into prior publication as follows: "Not Anything. This." as "Slowly Fading Out" in *Joyland's Michigan Writers Series* (2014), "The Lone Inhabitant of Gratiot's South Leg Traffic-Control Island" in *Sleepingfish* (2015), "Peru, Illinois" in *Axolotl* (2015), "Mescaline" as "7/Mescaline" in *3Elements* (2015), "Popo & Ix" in *Maudlin House* (2015) and a very small section of "The Face of Our Town" as "Overextended" in *Voiceworks* (2013). Peter Markus, Kelly Luce and Olga Zilberbourg saw this collection when it was still protozoa squirming in the petri dish and were kind enough bestow several stimulating zaps. Fred Amrine was the first professor I had in college who encouraged me to stop fucking around and actually write something. Anne Carson and Bob Currie said something about doing stuff in basements and having fewer, *much fewer* words that most likely changed my everything. Becca Rothfeld drew me towards elements of her impeccable style, as well as teaching me certain needful feels regarding contemporary poetry. Joe Ponepinto was an early mentor who imparted many shards of his frank and worthy pessimism. Alexandra Pasquinelli, aside from being a total cyclone of vivacious intellectual intensity, gave me the perfect place to live and write when I started working on this book some years ago in Oak Park, Michigan. Dr. Dave Hingstman offered his uniquely canny support for writethinking at a time when it was most desperately needed. Ralph

Paone has always made time for literary pep talks and attaboy Zarathustra sessions during this manuscript's extensive revision process. Josh Raab and Aaron Foley both offered their editorial ears and some very wise words during moments of profound overwhelm. Bob Leiken has been a longtime mentor and pushed me to research many more parts of the book than I otherwise would have. Poet Andrea Passwater gave her ultrasharp edge to the twentyfifth hour of proofing. In no order: Kellen Braddock, Maia Asshaq, Jim & Mike & Will & John Gentile, Jesús Castillo, Pablo Balbontin, Giuseppe Caputo, Kyle Vint, Brian Dehinden, Cassie Lucy, Jessica Krcmarik, Dylan Box, Jacob Mendel, Rachel & Parker Cronin, Peter Trout, Taffy Davenport, Sirus Fountain, Ketan Hazari, Laura Maddox, Megan Touhey, Nicole Wanzer-Serrano, Laura Foote Clark and Rebecca Power are also deserving of tremendous thanks, as are Project MK-Ultra, Alia Volz & The Leporines. Y'all are the bestest.

My mother Mary assisted extensively and heroically with manuscript revisions and proofing. My father Adam dispatched several early versions of "The Beforehand" with thorough and relentless critique. My brother Oliver offered strong words of encouragement throughout and has always been there to help me pick apart the knots of life. My aunts Lea & Ashley furnished some solid materternal sagacity. Thanks, family! Three utterly marvelous humans volunteered to give feedback on the final version of this manuscript and I'm much obliged for their efforts: Andrew Akhlaghi, Benjamin Friedman and Brooke Kimbrough. Outside of my parents the person to whom I am undoubtedly the most indebted is Lucia Moore, who not only provided yearsworth of earnest incitement to bookwriting but also offered a crucial room/writing desk during this manuscript's final, brutal heat.

Obrigados to the 18 De Liceiras Temporary Arts Community for the opportunity to polish the hemifinal version of this text during a writer's residency in early 2015, and for the help of fellow residents Ana Peñas, Anaïs Florin and Bianca Tschaikner for listening to literally hundreds of this book's pages read aloud over the course of several weeks. Ditto to Monument in San Francisco for allowing me to take up a room of scarce living space and for providing me access to a writer's studio in the early months of 2016. There are a number of crucial caffeine venues that surely had more businessworthy priorities than letting me camp out typitty-typing away for hours on end: Detroit One Coney Island (MI), 1515 Broadway (MI), Java House (IA), High Grounds (IA), Terrace - Arts Café (PT), and Sweet Inspirations (CA). Mega-snaps also to the Deadwood in Iowa City and, separately, to the night staff of the Willard Airport in Champaign, IL who once went far out of their way to rescue a crucial notebook.

As with a lot of writing there are a ton of other people's voices mixed around in here, and I'd like to acknowledge a few (perhaps obvious) influences. One cannot spend as many years as I did imbibing David Foster Wallace, Brad Neely or David Sedaris without starting to feel one's own head resembling their voices. Maggie

Nelson, Bob Kaufman, Fred Moten, Barry Yourgrau, Saul Williams, Eileen Myles and Beth Lisick's words have also taken up quite a lot of my mind's square footage, and I consider myself quite lucky for each and every inch. As for the classics, Clarice, Sherwood and Friedrich are the obvious ones, Franz and Hunter perhaps less so, and of course, ever the wily Vladimir. And while I'm over here just rattling off writers' first names as if we're all best buds or something, well, why not just go whole hog? Donna, Elena, Karl Ove, Etgar, Junot, R., Daniil & Alexander, W.G., Bruno, P.G., Rivka, Haruki, Ramona, 2 Victors, Italo, Richard, Brady, Irvine, Jhonen, Fernando, Daniel (C.), Roberto, Rainer, Joan, James and Jorge – much ❤ for how you word.

The book *Weaponized Adorable Negotiation Tactics* by Rachel Law and McKenzie Wark served as inspiration for some of the book's philosophical underface, as did a lecture by Quinn Norton given at Monument on Erving Goffman's concept of *civil inattention* in our age of the so-called *attention economy*. The description of narrative mechanics in "The Beforehand" owes an intellectual debt to Mikhail Bakhtin and also to the Afropessimist work of Frank B. Wilderson III and Jared Sexton, with some material directly informed by a Q & A with Professor Wilderson following his appearance in UC Berkeley's Holloway Reading Series. For more reflections of reflections, simulacra of simulacra and representations of representations see also: Joy Williams, George Saunders and Jean Baudrillard. What else? Quate's description of *lingua optima* and *lingua ultima* is rather shamelessly pilfered from a proposal for diplomatic geoengineering entitled *Pangea Optima* that was delivered by artist Jonathon Keats at Modernism Gallery in 2015. Doug Bock Clark's excellent 2015 photo essay *The Bot Bubble*, which appeared in The New Republic, was a terrific resource while researching the proliferation of fake identities online. Then there's Cervantes and Kraftwerk and Stoppard and Feelz Goodman and Shakespeare, a zillion Wikipedia contributors and subredditers, a Hugh Sykes Davies poem concerning a stump with the heart rotted out, &c.

See what I mean? Accumulations. Mutations. More anythings than are possibly rememberable.

10,000 plaudits are due to Mike Kelly for permission to include a quotation from his classic "Roy in Clingfilm Story 2". Ditto to Laurent Berlant, for granting permission to reproduce a sliver of her incisive stuckness. Snaps to Joyelle McSweeney and Johannes Göransson at Action Books for graciously allowing me to excerpt Don Mee Choi's translation of Kim Hyesoon's poem "Influenza" from *Sorrowtoothpaste Mirrorcream* (2014). The Electronic Literature Organization deserves heaps of praise for making Alan Sondheim's "Blood" available on an ongoing basis, as does Sonya Chung for allowing readers to access the Corporeal Age via her personal website. Kelly Rogers at Johns Hopkins University Press provided expedient counsel on quoting Cixous, as did Quinn Davis at JSTOR. I'd be remiss here for not also directing interested readers to the original Cixous citation for further inquiry, as well as to view her title with its proper enjambment in New Literary History, Volume 24, No.

1 (Winter, 1993) pp. 91-103. I may be nearly alone in wanting to read the Federal Highway Administration's 1961 Manual on Uniform Traffic Control Devices (MUTCD) as a work of poetry, but whatever you make of it Richard C. Moeur deserves a resounding ovation for the work he undertakes to keep this gorgeous archival material maximally accessible on his website trafficsign.us. The website 1 Line Art provided one of the ASCII motif for "The Lone Inhabitant," as did several other ASCII photo-to-text generators. While it was not possible to obtain permission for the use of a previously published English translation of either Lispector or Pessoa, the generous Lusophone Maria Correa agreed to perform an original (and in my view, much improved) translation for this book. To enable Maria's work it was first necessary to locate the Portuguese passages in the original text using keywords translated back from the (unusable) English versions. For orchestrating this daunting task with headspinning rapidity, (and for many other small acts of care and loveliness) I remain forever grateful to the singularly amazing Shaina Hyder.

Last but certainly not least, my most resounding thankwords must go to Jesi Buell and the team at KERNPUNKT who decided to take a big chance on a new author and, without whom, this book would surely not exist.

Photo Credit: Lucia Moore

Elizeya Quate is the nom of Edmund Zagorin, writer & absentminded charlatan of ovbious typos, vivacious orality and Stories By Mail. Inspired by Clarice Lispector and OBERIU, Elizeya Quate is an invitation to dance and/or denounce the equals sign as a self-negating sham. @elizeyaquate